HOT COPS

HOT COPS

GAY EROTIC TALES

Edited by

Shane Allison

Published in the United States.
Cleis Press Inc., P.O. Box 14697, San Francisco, California 94114

Printed in the United States.
Cover design: Scott Idleman
Cover photograph: Paul Burns/Getty
Text design: Frank Wiedemann
Cleis logo art: Juana Alicia
First Edition.
10 9 8 7 6 5 4 3 2

Contents

EMERGENCY ROOM

C. B. Potts

"We've got a code!" a nurse in royal blue scrubs bellowed, her harsh tones half deafening me. I scrunched against the wall as hospital staff converged from everywhere, rushing in, hoping to snatch someone from the jaws of death.

"Whas goin' on in there, boss?" Shackled to the gurney next to me was my companion for the evening, a drunk and disorderly that had mistaken my sergeant's front yard for a urinal. Somewhere along the way, the prisoner had fallen, and was now complaining of back and neck pain. I'd lost the toss and got the singular privilege of bringing him to the emergency room to be checked out.

"Don't know. Sounds like someone's having a hell of a time."

"Poor bastard." My inmate shook his head sorrowfully, and then looked up at me with big, brown eyes. "You think I could go have a cigarette?"

"Fat chance. If you're good, maybe I'll let you have one once we're done here."

No response, just a sullen stare. It was a look I got used to over the next few hours, as we watched two more trauma cases wheel through the metal swinging doors, a heavily panting woman get whisked up to labor and delivery, and the triage staff coo over a surprise delivery of flowers to a newly engaged nurse.

"Jesus Christ, man! This is taking for fuckin' ever."

"It does," I agreed. "They've got to deal with all the emergency cases first, y'know."

"Well, I'm an emergency! You dirty cop bastards hit me upside the head, I got bleedin' on the brain, I just know it!" Rattling shackles as drunk and disorderly tried to sit up on the gurney. "If you don't let me go have a cigarette, I'm a gonna' sue!"

"Are you?" I laughed. "Make sure you get my name right. It's Donovan, Mark Donovan."

"Mark Donovan, you are a son of a bitch!" A wet glob of spit hit the floor near my feet. "And I gotta take a piss! Get me to the bathroom!"

"What do you say we get Mr. Wonderful here to an exam room?" I turned and found myself face to face with the most brilliant pair of blue eyes I'd ever seen—especially on the face of an ER nurse badly in need of a shave.

"That would be great," I said, helping him turn the gurney.

"I gotta go to the bathroom!"

"You've got to hold on a minute," the nurse said, winking at me. "So don't go running off."

"Fuck you too!" More thrashing around on the stretcher. "I'm gonna sue every one of you bastards!"

"Looks like I'm in good company." The nurse extended his hand over the stretcher to me. "I'm Bob Jacobsen, pleased to meet you."

I laughed, took the proffered hand. There was a moment

there, a spark, and our eyes met. "Mark Donovan, fellow defendant."

Then it was all business, Bob grabbing a green binder from the wall. "And Mr. Wonderful is Steve Wilt, correct?"

"You fucking tell me!"

"So, Mr. Wilt, says here you've had a little too much to drink."

"No shit, Sherlock! Yeah, I've had too much to drink and now I gotta use the goddamn bathroom. Let me off of this bed."

Bob shook his head. " 'Fraid I can't do that, at least not until you go to X-ray." He grabbed a urinal and handed it over. "Why don't you use that?"

"I'm not using that fucking thing." Steve was fully enraged by now. "Let me go to the goddamn bathroom like a man!"

"Listen, Mr. Wilt," Bob said, straightening up a full four inches taller. "You can use the urinal, or I can get an order for a Foley and run a line up your penis right into your bladder, or you can piss your pants, but you will stop this nonsense and you will stop it right now."

And completely inappropriately, especially given the time and the situation, my cock gave a little jump inside my pants. It knows authority when it hears it.

So did Steve Wilt, apparently. He deflated like a pricked balloon and took the urinal.

Bob and I shared a quick glance of triumph, interrupted when Steve threw the urinal at us. Hot yellow piss sloshed everywhere, splattering across my uniform and Bob's scrubs.

"That's it," I barked, falling automatically into cop mode. Putting both hands on Wilt's shoulders, I pushed him back down onto the gurney while Bob fastened restraining straps around his torso. "No more crap out of you."

"Aarggh! My back! You hurt my fucking back! I think it's

broken!" Wilt was screaming at the top of his lungs.

"Mr. Wilt, if your back was truly broken, you wouldn't be able to scream that loud," Bob said. "We need to get some vitals from you, but that can wait until you're a little calmer. In fact, I think everything can wait until you're a little calmer." He gave me the nod, and I followed him to the front of the room. "Maybe a little nap will help."

He switched off the lights.

"You son of a bitch!" Wilt screamed.

Bob laughed. "He's charming, isn't he?"

"First prize." I nodded at his scrubs. "Sorry 'bout that."

"It's all right. I've got another set in my locker. Want me to grab you a towel?"

"Yeah."

He disappeared for a few, returning freshly dressed and carrying two small towels.

"This will have to do for now. Wish I could offer you a shower."

"You can," I replied, startled at my own boldness. "But it'd have to wait until seven o'clock."

He glanced at his watch. "Cool. I'm on a seven-seven too. Hold on another couple hours, and we'll see what we can do."

Then he was gone, flitting from one room to the next, joining in the throngs when the ambulance brought yet another code through the doors.

I stood and watched, drinking in his long, lithe form while my prisoner worked his way through an entire litany of profanities and threats. Had he taken my comment in the spirit intended, or was I merely going to be offered use of the hospital shower room at the end of my shift?

The cursing had turned to deep, ragged snores and the sun was slowly crawling up the horizon when Bob came my way again. He tossed a thick packet of papers into my lap. "You'll want to give that to your relief when he comes in. It's all the orders and blood work that Mr. Wonderful has to have." He paused, looked me up and down. "That top sheet's for you. Bring some clean clothes with you, although the uniform's nice. Very nice."

On the top sheet, a street address, written in a bold hand. Very nice indeed.

I tell you, I've never been so happy to see my relief before. I filled him in on what kind of fun day he could expect with Mr. Wilt, down to the lovely pee-slinging, and handed over the paperwork.

A quick stop by the station house, largely to grab my duffel bag of civilian clothes from my locker, and I was back in my car, ready to do a little patrolling of my own.

"You came," Bob smiled, pushing open the door. "I wasn't sure if you would."

"Why wouldn't I?"

"Maybe Mr. Wonderful wore you out," he laughed. "Maybe I read you wrong." His eyes dropped to my crotch, where my cock was already stiffening. "Although all signs indicate that I was right."

"Oh, you were right," I said, dropping my duffel to the floor. "But first I think you said something about a shower?"

"You don't like wearing that fancy cologne? Then right this way, Officer." He led me down a narrow hallway to a tiled bathroom. "You understand we have some security measures?" he asked, one eyebrow arched. "Assume the position."

Arms splayed, I leaned against the cool tile wall.

"I've always wanted to do this," Bob said, lips inches from my ears. He gave me a fairly professional pat-down, although it must be admitted that he devoted far too much attention to my groin.

"What's this?" he purred. "You packing?"

"Maybe," I replied, grinding my hips back against him. "Maybe."

Uniform met scrubs, thick fabric brushing against thin, desire straining for desire.

"Shower," he growled. "Shower first."

He turned on the water while I shucked my clothes. One garment after another hit the floor with a noisy clatter while his scrubs floated down in a silken slump.

"Don't know how you guys ever sneak up on anybody," he joked, after my belt thudded against the tiles.

"Me either," I replied, turning toward him. My cock was so hard it was nearly slapping my stomach. "I'm not very stealthy."

He laughed. "I can see that." A jerk of the head. That authoritative voice returned. "Into the shower."

Is there anything better than a steaming hot shower after a rotten shift? Well, yes, there is and he stepped right into the tub with me.

"Arms up." I complied, closing my eyes and surrendering to the sensation. I could feel the sponge working over my shoulders, down my pecs, creating a swath of bubbles over my torso.

"Turn."

Now my back, from the very base of my neck to the base of my spine. It was a struggle to hold still as he moved lower.

"You have," Bob announced, "a magnificent ass. I'm going to enjoy having that later." His hands cupped my cheeks confidently, as if weighing each one.

I couldn't help but moan. It had been so long since someone had stepped in, taken charge. Usually it was all up to me.

"Oh, you're going to be fun," Bob said. "I can tell. Turn back around, and keep those arms up."

He sank to his knees in front of me. "Now, no shooting till I give the signal."

And then I was in the mouth of a master. His tongue swirled over and around the tip of my cock, slurp-sliding its way down to the very base, kissing my stomach with every stroke. Every now and then, he'd flick out and lick my balls, dancing across the bumpy surface before snaking back around my shaft.

"Jesus Christ..."

"Are you close?" he hissed.

"Yes," I moaned.

"Remember, not until I say so."

And back down, turning and twisting, sucking and tugging, working my meat in every possible direction. One wet hand clung to my thigh while the other, clad in a cloud of bubbles, worked between my asscheeks.

"Gaarrhh!" I said, my balls knotting up when his fingertip brushed against my pucker. "You've got to stop if you don't want me to..."

He responded by sucking harder and twisting one finger past the tight muscled ring.

"Oh no!" I cried, more than half frantic, feeling the load bubble up. "I can't stop now!"

Bob pulled his head back and watched almost clinically as my cum splattered all over the shower wall. Gob after gob of white fell, coming from some endless reserve I didn't even know I possessed.

I stood shuddering afterward, surprised by the force of it. The water had gone cold, sending icy rivulets down my spine. My arms were still overhead.

Bob looked up at me and smiled, reaching around my legs to

shut off the water. “I can see we’ve got some work to do. Been a long time since anyone took you in hand?”

“Or in mouth.”

“Sir.”

I swallowed, gulping down hot, moist air. “Sir.”

He pulled the curtain back. “Out. On all fours, please.”

Bath mats are thin, not providing much cushion for novice knees on tiled floors. But Bob didn’t seem too worried about that. He kept me in place for a long time, drying himself first while staring at me, and then toweling me like a freshly washed dog. All the time he was silent, contemplative, watching me while I kept my head down.

And got harder. And harder. And harder.

Finally he slipped into a pair of shorts and headed for the door. I listened to his footsteps, nearly trembling with need. When he reached the doorway, he stopped and snapped his fingers.

“Come.”

I started up, but he stopped me.

“Hup, hup, hup, my boy. On your knees.”

My damn cock lurched so hard I thought I was going to shoot again. Biting my lip, I crawled behind Bob, keeping my eyes fixed on the back of his ankle. We traversed an incredibly long hallway, coming into a living room at the end. Bob sank onto the couch, positioning me in front of him.

“Look at you,” he said, one hand confidently on my hip. “You need this almost as much as I do.”

“Yes, Sir,” I said.

“But you don’t take direction very well.”

“No, Sir.” Need choked my words. “I am sorry, Sir.”

Bob smiled. “I’m sure you are. But that doesn’t eliminate your need for punishment, does it?”

“N…nn…no.” I was trembling at this point, professional

adrenaline telling me to get the hell out of there, longtime need forcing me to stay.

"I've got a cane in the closet." His hand was on my ass now. "Long and thick. Makes a lovely welt, 'bout that big." I could feel his fingertips pressing in, an inch apart from each other. "Nice bright red stripes."

It was very hard to breathe. The room was spinning. My stomach was near to scorching from coming into contact with my flaming hot prick.

"But you weren't quite that bad, this time."

All the air whooshed out of my lungs.

"Nope, not that bad. Maybe just a spanking this time."

A pause, and I realized he was waiting on me.

"Yes, Sir." Another gulp of air. "Please, Sir."

The first swat was nothing, just a tap on the butt to let me know he was about to start. Then his other hand twined through the short hairs covering the back of my neck, and he lit into me.

Crash! Crash! Crash! His hand fell again and again, flat and hard on my ass.

I forced myself to hold still, locking my elbows to keep from trembling.

"You think you can hold out on me, boy?" A vicious smack, just where my ass turned to thigh. "I don't think so."

Every hit burned, every hit had my cock trembling. I was biting my lip to keep silent.

Then, on the next stroke, his fingertips brushed my balls.

"Aargh..." I cried, collapsing onto my forearms. My ass was still held high, beaming (I imagined) like a bright red beacon. It certainly felt hot enough to be fire red.

Bob pulled his fingers out of my hair, stilled his hand.

"Good boy. Good boy." He caressed now, running gentle fingers over tender skin. "You took a lot. You did so well."

Panting, I managed, “Thank you.”

“Don’t thank me yet.” His leg swept along my side, turning me on the carpet. I was facing the coffee table, my raised ass squarely between his hands. “There’s nothing I like better than fucking a freshly spanked ass.” I could feel cool air between my cheeks. “Are you going to let me do that?”

“Hell, I’ll beg you for it if need be.”

“No need.” Bob chuckled. “Let me get you ready.” His hands were warm, even with the cool slick of lube. “There are advantages to having this done by someone who performs digital exams on a regular basis.”

“I see that,” I murmured, as he slid inside. A few greasy strokes, widening my hole, and then he made right for my prostate.

“Knock, knock,” he laughed, drumming his fingertips while I kissed the carpet. “Can I come in?”

I can’t even describe the noise I made, but Bob took it as assent. Some quick fumbling behind me—I was too far in subspace to even turn my head and look, contrary to every instinct seven years on the force had given me—and then I felt the broad, flat tip of his prick nosing between my cheeks.

“God, you’re so hot,” Bob moaned, pressing in. I could feel my sphincter ballooning open to accept him, taut muscles collapsing out of the way. “And so tight!”

“You feel so good,” I replied, ratcheting my hips backward a fraction of an inch, filling myself slowly. “So big.”

And he gave more, and I took more, sliding and pushing, groaning and grunting.

“Almost there,” he announced, both hands on my lower back. Gentle pressure pushed me down, splayed my legs wide. “Yeah, that’s it.”

His furry balls bumped softly into mine.

“What a nice ass you have,” Bob moaned. “What a nice ass I

have, actually. Cause this is my ass, isn't it?" One hand squeezed a tender cheek.

"Yeah," I panted. "Yes, Sir."

"Next time, I'm gonna plug your ass," he continued, slowly sliding his hips back and forth. "With a big, fat butt plug. And then I'm gonna sit on your cock."

The mental image was amazing. I could feel my bowels convulsing around him.

"You like that idea. Maybe I'll tie you up to do that, tie up your hot spanked slut ass...."

We were moving faster now, quicker than caution, skin slapping skin.

"Yes, Sir, yes, Sir, please."

Iron hands on both hips, pulling me hard to him. It was his turn to be incoherent, arching his back as the condom balloon filled inside me.

Then we collapsed, him still in me, on me, around me. His hand circled my cock, confident strokes pulling me the last few inches to exploding again.

"My pretty boy."

"Garrh..." I replied, ever brilliant.

"I think I need another shower," I said, once we'd untangled limbs and gotten ourselves out of the narrow space between Bob's couch and coffee table.

He smiled. "Suit yourself, although you're on your own this time." He shrugged. "I don't think I could do all that again."

"Now," I asked, willing my voice not to break, "or ever?"

"Now, you dork." He nodded his head down the hallway. "Go get cleaned up, and I'll get the bed ready." One eyebrow arched. "Unless you had other plans?"

"Nope," I replied, gingerly working my way down the hallway. "No other plans."

One thing was for sure, though, I thought. The next time we had to take a wet-brain to the hospital, we wouldn't have to draw straws. I'd fucking volunteer.

BAD BOYS

William Holden

"We have a report of a ten-sixteen, please respond." The radio crackled and hissed while the dispatcher waited.

"Four-eighty-two here," I answered. "I'll check it out. Location?"

"Thanks, Lieutenant. Thirty-eight seventy-six Eighteenth Street."

"Here we go again," I mumbled to myself as I turned my car around and headed down the crowded streets of the Castro. It was New Year's night, and the energy of New Year's Eve was still running rampant.

I've been a cop now for ten years. I joined the police academy right out of high school and was assigned the Castro district as my first beat. I've been here ever since. I work the night shift, and let me tell you, every night is filled with some of the strangest and most unusual characters you could imagine. Don't get me wrong, I love my job. It's just that my line of work doesn't help when it comes to relationships. Most of the men I've dated just don't like being alone at night; I say most because I think I may have found the one. We've been together now for eight months—a record in my dating experience. His name is Steve and he doesn't seem to mind me working the night shift. In fact, he says that my job is a big turn-on for him. Our sex is amazing, that is when we can work it into our schedule. He says he loves for me to dress up in my uniform and use the tools of my trade to make him feel like a bad boy. It had been a few days since my last encounter with my bad boy, and I could feel my cock thickening inside my pants at the thought of him.

I made a left hand turn off of Eighteenth down Noe, and parked alongside the 7-11. My stomach turned as I walked by the open door and got a whiff of the overdone hot dogs sitting under the warming lights. As I walked further down the street, I began to hear the voices of two men yelling at each other from within one of the buildings. I looked up and recognized the address the dispatcher had given me. I never like going into a situation completely blind, so I stood outside the front window and listened to what was being said. I peered in the window but couldn't see anyone. Even through the windows and from another room, I could hear their conversation.

"Michael, I don't understand why you're doing this to me."

"I'm not doing anything to you. Last night was great. I had a good time, but that's all it was, a good time."

"A good time." The voice grew louder. "That's all I was to you? We made love last night. I gave myself to you completely and you returned that love. How can you say it was just a good time? I was there. I saw and felt the passion you had for me."

"Damn it, Stephen. It wasn't love we made last night. We had sex. We fucked. Yeah it was hot, but it wasn't love."

I saw movement from the other room as the guy I assumed was Michael came into view.

"Stephen, I want you out of here. It was obviously a mistake to let you in here tonight, but you were making such an ass of yourself at my front door, I didn't have a choice. Now get out of my bedroom and go home to your boyfriend and leave me alone!"

"I'm not going anywhere till we work this out."

It had begun to rain again, and I decided it was time to make my presence known. Just then, I saw the other man come into view. My heartbeat grew heavier, my palms began to sweat. Stephen was not just any guy, he was my Steve; my bad boy. I could feel the dampness of sweat building up against my skin. I became anxious. Nerves raced through my body as I saw him standing in the room. I took a couple of deep breaths to steady my nerves. I knew I had to stay calm; after all, I was a cop and a damn good one. I couldn't let my emotions get the better of me. I walked up to the front door and knocked. I heard footsteps coming closer, then the door opened.

"Good evening—Michael, is it?"

"Yes." His eyes were wide with surprise at seeing a cop at his front door. "Can I help you officer?"

"I received a call about some possible trouble here." His eyes never left mine. I could see fear and frustration in their dark brown depths. "Is everything okay?" Before he could answer, a voice in the background spoke up.

"Who is it Michael, another one of your good times?"

"Stephen, shut up!"

"Perhaps I can be of assistance. May I come in?" I waited for a response.

"I can't believe this is happening. Officer, really, I can handle this."

"I'm not so sure about that. I've heard some of the conversation here tonight and it seems as if you've made quite a mess of things. Why don't you let me take care of this?" He stepped aside and let me enter.

Steve was sitting in a chair. His face was red,, which only happens when he's nervous. He looked up and saw me standing in the small living room next to Michael. I could almost hear his heart beating in his chest. He stood up, his body trembling.

"Greg, what are you..." he paused. "This isn't what you think." He walked over to where Michael and I were standing.

"It's exactly what I think." I could feel the tension building inside of me. I took another deep breath and turned away from Steve to face Michael. He looked confused.

"You two know each other?"

"You might say that." I shot Steve a quick glance to see if he was going to say anything.

"Michael, this is my boyfriend." Steve stood still and looked at the two of us. Silence fell between us. Michael looked at me, then to Steve and then back to me.

"I can't fucking believe this." His hands covered his face and then ran over his thick, black hair.

"Well that makes two of us," I replied as I shut the door behind me. I slowly walked over to Steve. "So would you care to fill me in on what happened here?" He looked at me with his lips trembling, but he didn't say a word. "Well then, let me try a different approach." I reached behind my back and brought out my handcuffs. If Steve wanted to be a bad boy he was going to have to be treated like one. He looked up at me and then at the handcuffs. I turned him around and slapped the cuffs on his wrists. The sound of the metal clicking tightly around his wrists sent a charge through my body that I felt running through every vein in my cock.

"Oh, come on. Is that really necessary?" Michael walked toward us. "Listen, this has gotten way out of control."

"Back off Michael, unless you want to be arrested for obstruction; and don't think I won't do it." I glanced at him, and then turned my attention back to Steve. Sweat had beaded up on his forehead. His short, brown hair stuck to his face.

"So Steve, let's start over. Do you want to explain what's been going on?" I waited for his answer, but it never came. I pushed him down into the chair. He fell back against his cuffed wrists. Dark circles of sweat soaked his blue T-shirt under his arms. I could smell his nervousness creeping out of his pores. I could sense Michael walking up behind me and quickly turned around to face him.

"Do you have something to say, Michael?"

"Yeah—this is too much." He walked up and faced me head-on. "Let him go. This isn't the way to handle this."

"What, now you're going to tell me how to do my job?" I paused. "Especially after fucking my boyfriend." I pushed him slightly to make my point. "You don't want to get in my face again." I could smell the beer on his breath as it came out in short nervous puffs. His chest rose and fell with his breathing. The muscles in his torso filled his tight shirt. I noticed his nipples pushing against the thin material; they appeared large and erect.

"Perhaps you both need to learn your lessons." I reached behind me again and pulled out my spare cuffs. Michael backed away quickly, but not quickly enough. I moved around him and wrapped my arm around his chest. I held him tight as I placed the cuffs on his wrists. I could feel his heart racing inside of him. His body felt good against mine. My cock stiffened behind the dark blue material of my pants. Then I noticed a slight change in Michael's behavior. His body seemed to relax against my hold. I moved my hand over his chest, grazing his nipples and feeling the firmness of his pecs. My fingers slowly moved across his body, feeling a thick layer of hair beneath his shirt. He appeared to resist my touch, but I could tell he liked the attention I was giving him. I grabbed his arm and moved him over to a chair facing Steve and pushed him down into it. I stood back and looked at the two of them sitting there.

"Which one of you wants to go first?" I slid the billy club out of my holster and stood there tapping it against the palm of my hand. "Steve—or is it *Stephen* now?" He looked up at me. "Why don't we start with you?"

I walked over and squatted down next to his chair. "Why don't you tell me exactly what happened last night that started all this trouble? Was it the way he looked at you? He does have beautiful eyes. Or was it his deep voice that turned you on?" I paused to collect my thoughts. "No, that wasn't it. Was it the way he touched you?" I took my hand and ran it up the inside of his leg. I could feel his body responding to my touch. "Did he touch you here?" I moved my fingers up his leg and cupped his crotch. I could feel his large balls tightening behind the jeans as his cock expanded. I slid the billy club between his legs and ran it underneath him, sliding it across the crack of his ass. "I know how much you like having your ass played with. Did he touch you back there? Michael, did you touch him like this?" He sat there with disbelief in his eyes. My eyes wandered down to his crotch. I could see the enormous bulge behind his gym shorts. I knew I was getting his attention.

I removed my hand from Steve's crotch as I began to undo his pants. The sound of the zipper coming down seemed to echo through the air.

"Paul, please don't do this. I'm sorry about all of this. It won't happen again." His voice pleaded with me, but his eyes told me something else.

"Damn right you'll never do this again." I pulled his pants

and underwear down to his ankles. His cock fell against the chair cushion. I moved around to the back of the chair so I could face his accomplice.

"So, Michael, is this the way it was?" I gripped Steve's shirt and ripped it down the center, exposing his beautiful hairless body. Steve jumped at my sudden movement. The smell of Steve's sweat-dampened body rushed more blood into the veins of my cock. My hands ran down the length of his body until I reached his crotch. I began stroking him with one hand, while caressing his stomach with my other. Our faces were side by side staring straight ahead at Michael.

"Did you touch him like this Michael?" I watched him squirm in his seat. "Oh yeah, he likes it when you do this, doesn't he?" I could feel Steve's wetness covering my hand. I stroked harder. "Did he come right away? Or did he last a long time?" I could feel Steve's body shake as I continued to stroke him off. I kissed his neck. A moan escaped his throat. "Did he moan like this for you?" I winked at Michael. "I'm sure he did; he's quite a moaner in bed, isn't he?"

I could see a mixture of emotions on Michael's face: fear, frustration and desire burning within him. He tried to keep his legs together, but he squirmed from the ever growing bulge in his crotch and soon his legs slowly began to part. The dark hair that trailed out from the edge of his shorts covered his legs all the way down to his ankles. Sweat ran down the side of his face. Dark stains appeared in his shirt and ran down the length of his chest.

Steve's body began to quiver. His breath came in short, hot bursts. "Oh, Steve, you're getting close aren't you?"

I looked back at Michael. "I sure hope he lasted longer than this for you last night."

I covered Steve's mouth with my hand to stifle his loud moans as the skin of his cock tightened and became red with pressure.

His body began to jerk. His breath beat against the palm of my hand as he reached his limit. His body tightened and stretched. The hot, white come exploded across his chest and ran down his sweaty body. I continued to pump until another jet shot through the air. It splattered both our faces. Steve's body became limp and he fell back into the chair.

"So was that how it was, Michael? Is that how you satisfied him?" I walked around and stood between them and then turned to face Michael. I walked over to him and grabbed the edge of his shirt to wipe Steve's come off my hands. The heat poured from his body as I moved my hand inside his shirt. The hair on his stomach was drenched in sweat.

"Well, since Steve was of no help in sorting out this mess, I guess I'll have to rely on you to fill in the gaps." I stood back and took in all of Michael's body as I began to unzip my pants.

"So, Michael, what's your side of the story? Did he let you suck his cock? I bet he did. He loves a hot pair of lips running up and down his shaft. Let's see just how hot your lips are." I leaned down and kissed him. He hesitated, then relaxed and opened his mouth to me. I felt his tongue slip down my throat. I pulled away quickly.

"Yeah, he would have loved that hot mouth of yours on his cock. Did you like the taste of his pre-come? He has a lot of it, as I'm sure you know by now." Michael's eyes glanced down at my opened zipper. "Would you like to show me how you sucked my boyfriend off? I'd really like to know what it is *you* can do, that *I* can't."

I looked over at Steve. He sat there, trying not to stare at us. The come covering his body had dried to a crusty film against his skin. "You just sit there, Steve, and watch. You had your turn to tell your side of things; now its Michael's turn."

"Go ahead, Michael, show me how you did it." I moved

my body closer to him. I grabbed the base of my cock and held it firmly as his mouth opened up. I slid it in. His full, wet lips closed around my shaft. He shuffled in his seat to get closer to me and took another inch into his mouth.

"Damn, you're a good cocksucker. I'm sure my boyfriend loved this." I moved closer, allowing Michael to take another two inches of my cock down his throat. I grabbed the back of his head and pushed the rest of my cock into him. He gagged briefly but quickly recovered. His spit and my pre-come leaked out around the edges of his mouth, staining the blue material around the edge of my zipper. "Yeah, that's a good boy. Show me how you took my boyfriend's cock last night."

I looked over at Steve. His cock was still erect.

"Paul. You've proved your point." His voice was softer than before. "Enough is enough. Can't we just go home and work this out between the two of us?"

"Steve, I'm not trying to prove anything," I said as I continued to pump my cock into Michael's mouth. "I'm just trying to get the facts—oh yeah—straight." I pulled my cock out of Michael's mouth. He gasped as the pressure was released.

I knelt down and positioned myself between Michael's legs. "Steve's not used to hairy men. Did he enjoy running his hands over your body?" I moved my hands underneath Michael's shirt. His body twitched as my hands caressed his hot, sweaty skin. I raised Michael's shirt up and ran my tongue over his left nipple, then moved over to the right side. His nipple became erect and I sucked it into my mouth, tasting the salty flavors of his shaking body. "Nope, he wouldn't have done that to you. He hates getting hair stuck in his mouth. Don't you Steve?"

I moved my hands down to the waistband of his shorts. "Lift up." He obeyed. "Well, I can tell you are a law-abiding citizen the way you didn't even hesitate to obey me. I like that. It's people like you who make my job a little easier." I pulled his shorts and underwear off with one quick yank. His cock was unbelievable. The base was covered in the thickest patch of dark pubic hair I had ever seen. His cock lengthened as I watched it. The large, pink head poked out of the thick layer of foreskin that was covering it. "Well, well. This is an interesting turn of events." I turned to look at Steve.

"As the bottom boy of the family, I suppose you let Michael fuck you with this?" I grabbed Michael's cock in my hand and shook it briefly. "Were you able to take all of this? Because if you did you have more explaining to do." I looked back at Michael. "He's always been a little tight in that region. He has a difficult time taking me and I'm not nearly as big as you are." I stroked Michael's cock watching with enjoyment as the foreskin pulled over the head and then back down the shaft. I released his cock and stood up.

"We should probably move on with the interrogation, don't you think?" I kicked off my shoes, and then pulled my pants and underwear off. They fell to the floor in a wadded-up pile. I walked over and sat on the armrest next to Michael. "Now just a few more questions and I think we can wrap this up."

"So, Steve, how'd you do it? Did you just bend over and take it? Or were you flat on your back? Because I just can't imagine you taking a cock this big. I mean really, I'm not even sure if I could take it." I moved over between Michael's legs and lowered myself onto his crotch so I could face Steve. I knew the weight of my body would be heavy against Michael's smaller frame, but he didn't resist.

I could feel his cock pressing against the crack of my ass; lubing it up with more pre-come. I wiggled my ass in his lap. I raised myself up and reached behind me. Michael's cock was hot to the touch. I raised up a bit more and ran the head of his cock in small circles to loosen my hot, hairy hole. I moved downward letting the thick head of Michael's cock enter me. I watched Steve's expression as I further impaled myself on Michael's cock. It was a slight grimace, as if he could feel Michael's cock going inside of him again. I pushed further down, sliding another few inches of Michael's cock inside of me. The pressure was starting to build as his cock continued to thicken inside of me.

"So Steve," I grunted, "tell me, is this how you were fucked?" He didn't respond. "Did you ride him like this?" I pushed further down. "Come on now, help me understand this. Was it like this or not!" I yelled at him.

"No. I was on my back in his bed. Is that what you wanted to hear?"

"Now we're getting somewhere." I could feel Michael thrusting his hips trying to get more of his cock inside of me. "So you were in his bedroom were you? Did you take his entire cock?" I grunted as I felt more of Michael's cock enter me. "Did you?"

"Yes. Okay. Yes. I took his entire cock." His voice was trembling again.

"Really, because from my own experience at the moment, the facts as you've given them to me just don't add up." Michael's thrusts were getting more pronounced. "Yeah, Michael, give me that entire cock. Let me see just how deep you were inside my boyfriend." I pushed myself down as Michael pushed his hips upward. My ass met his body in a wet, sticky slap.

"Fuck, Steve," I groaned as the realization of just how large Michael was washed over me, "I just can't imagine you taking this." I sat still for a moment letting my muscles relax as I looked at Steve. It was time for the final question.

"So, did you let him shoot his load inside of you?" I began to pump Michael's cock with the muscles in my ass, raising and lowering myself onto him. "Come on, Steve. Did you or did you not let Michael come inside of you?" Sweat seeped from every pore of my body. I glanced down at my cock, and watched as a thick stream of pre-come shot out, soaking the fabric of the chair.

"Come on, Michael. Fuck that ass. Fuck it hard, just like you did to my boyfriend last night." Our bodies bounced against each other. I could feel Michael's body tightening, getting ready to shoot.

"Steve, answer me. Did he come inside of you?"

"No, Damn it. He didn't. He pulled out just before he came." He paused to catch his breath.

"Oh, fuck, Michael. Yeah, keep that up." The springs in the chair started to creak as our bodies pounded into one another. I could feel Michael's cock swelling. His breath came in short, heavy bursts against my back. Then he groaned as his come released inside of me. I fell back against him as come shot from my cock. We rocked back and forth as come shot out of our cocks. I took a deep breath to steady myself. "That's too bad, Steve." I said, panting. "You should have let Michael come inside you. You missed an amazing experience." I pulled myself off of Michael's cock and stood up.

"Well, I think I have enough information to go on here." I pulled on my underwear and pants and slipped back into my shoes. Steve and Michael sat quietly, their half-naked bodies still aroused from the interrogation. I walked over to Steve and pulled him off the chair and pulled his pants back up and fastened them. "You stay right there while I take care of Michael.... Okay, I'm going to undo the handcuffs. Can I trust you to stay put and not get up till we're gone?"

"Yeah, sure, whatever you say." Michael rubbed his wrists where the cuffs had been.

"I don't think you'll have to worry about Steve anymore.

He won't be back to bother you. But you may want to consider being a bit more careful the next time you bring someone home with you. You never know what you may be getting yourself into."

I grabbed Steve by the arm and led him out of the house and down the street to my squad car. Once inside, I started the engine and looked over at him.

"Do you mind taking the handcuffs off me now? We're out of Michael's sight."

"Oh. Sorry about that." I leaned over and removed the handcuffs. We kissed briefly before I put the car in DRIVE and pulled away. "I'll drop you off at home before finishing up my shift. Will you be awake when I get home?"

"Yeah, I'm too excited to sleep. That was really hot. I guess tomorrow morning over breakfast we should start planning our next night out."

"You bet. You were so amazing tonight, that was one of your best performances." We both began to giggle as we talked about our big evening out. Yeah, the bad boy scenario was a sure thing, one we'll take advantage of again in the near future.

ICE STORM ON FLAT TOP MOUNTAIN

Jeff Mann

Such heaps of broken glass to sweep away
You'd think the inner dome of heaven had fallen.
—Robert Frost, "Birches"

I don't know why Keith confessed when he did—just before he let me tie him one last time. It's foolish to madden a man and then let him render you completely helpless.

Sounds like the rain's turning to sleet. As high as we are up here on Flat Top Mountain, that's no news in February. There's a tiny, haphazard ticking against the cabin windows, as if the dusk were hurling handfuls of grit. I can't help but think of the sweeping gestures my grandmother used to scatter chicken feed.

I've got Keith just where he wants to be. He's met me up here for a couple of years now, just for this kind of rough and loving treatment, as often as his park security job has allowed. The fact that he and his wife are separated has helped things along considerably. Or it has till now.

I unsheathe the hunting knife, the one my lover Mike gave me twenty years ago when we went on our first deer-hunting foray. Normally I keep it in my pickup, just in case I need to defend myself on some back road. But tonight it glitters in bedroom candlelight. Keith likes submitting to it almost as much as he does to his own park-issue cuffs and gun.

Keith sighs when I press the flat of the knife to his forehead. He closes his eyes and starts to shiver. I kiss his taped mouth, let the blade warm up against his hot skin—he feels feverish, as if he's coming down with the flu—then run the blunt side of the knife across his neck. I press the pommel into the furry pit where his clavicles meet. I wrap my other hand around his throat and feel his carotid's rapid pulse.

If he felt any reason to resist, he isn't in a position to do so. Thus the bond between us, if you'll forgive the pun. Keith loves me because I tie him and I hurt him. Sometimes I think he hates me for the same reasons. He claims that submitting to me, more than anything else, makes him feel like a man. I think he says that not only because it's true, but because it isn't. He says it to whittle down shame.

I've fought his shame and failed. Well, at least I'll make sure he feels like one hell of a man tonight, this last time together. How he'll feel manly without me, how he'll bury memory and all it brings, none of that will be my concern. Maybe he'll father a few more kids.

I've got Keith tied in one of his favorite positions. He's naked, of course. I'll be jacking off to memories of his big shoulders, thick chest, beer belly, and hard thighs for the rest of my life. And the brown hair that spreads like spruce boughs across his pecs and belly—that would be a fine image to clutch on my deathbed. Sometimes, cuddling with him in our sticky aftermaths, I've drowsily decided that Keith is the finest specimen of a man I've ever found, as close to God's body as I've ever been privileged to touch. What I want is my own version of Veronica's veil, with Keith's goateed grin, torso, cock, and furry butt imprinted on the holy fabric instead of Christ's face.

I guess the religious references make some sense here, since right now it looks like Keith is crucified. I've tied his wrists to opposite sides of the bed frame, layered black PVC tape over his mouth, crossed his ankles, roped them together, then secured them to the footboard. He's stretched out tight in a Golgotha sort of *T*. He's in paradise.

I'd like, he'd like me, to keep him this way for hours, as I have before, but neither of us expected the sleet. Both our trucks are 4x4, but that won't help much on ice. I want him here in bed beside me all night, mouth taped up, hands comfortably cuffed in front of him, his fuzzy butt pressed against my crotch, just as we've spent many nights—not enough, never enough—but after he said what he said, mere minutes, the fucking fool, before the tape went over his mouth, well, he can't get stuck and have to spend the night. I won't want him here.

I want him here always. I ought to never let him loose. What I need's a cage in the basement. The bastard. He never has come to terms with what he hankers for, with what a sweet trussed pig he's meant to be. I always have to blindfold him when I fuck him. He can't bear to look me in the eyes.

The knife slides down his breastbone. I put the point—very sharp, I've seen to that, even got a whetstone in the truck—against his left nipple. How many inches of skin and flesh between keen steel and the surface of his heart? Behind the tape, Keith moans. I love the sounds he makes against his gags, and he loves to make that muffled music. We cherish so many of the same things. I bend down, lick his hardening tit, lick the knife blade, and press the point down till the silky flesh goes concave.

Why did he tell me when he did? Not when he arrived. Not afterward, when, untied, half-dressed, he'll sit on bed's edge pulling on his boots. No. Standing there naked in candlelight, eager to be taped and tied. I can't believe, after all their time apart, he's going back to her. Does he want me to really hurt him? Because right now I want to make this fur-edged nipple bleed.

"You fucker," I grunt, laying the blade down before real damage begins. It balances easy in his brown belly-fur. "Don't go anywhere." Standard joke no bondage Top can resist. Got to take a break, or I'm going to really hurt him. I leave him there—if it weren't for the tape, I think he'd be panting—and head for the kitchen.

It's full-ahead ice now. I can hear it on the tin roof. I should let him loose right now so he can get out of here. Instead, I pour myself a glass of George Dickel and sit at the table. It's nearly dark. Outside the window, white pine boughs are going gray with freeze, beginning to sag a bit with winter's weight.

"MmmmMMMmmm!" Keith doesn't like to be left alone, especially with a sharp knife riding the hairy ridgepole of his belly, but right now I don't care. "Shut up and keep still!" I shout toward the bedroom. I just want to sit here, listen to the ice storm, and sip awhile.

It was a deer that introduced us. Rainy June morning, fog filling up Bluestone Gorge like whipped cream, spilling over the rim into the roads. I'd only been a naturalist at the park for a couple weeks when the stag leapt in front of me as I drove to the lodge for breakfast. Swerving in the fog, I ended up in a ditch, used my cell phone to call park security. Keith showed up to give me a hand.

I'd noticed him two weeks before, the first day I started work at Pipestem Park, big guy in a khaki security uniform, holstered gun on his hip, sipping iced tea and munching a hot dog in the Black Bear snack bar. I ordered a grilled cheese and studied him through the screen of my sunglasses. Midthirties, about my age. Widow's peak, dark brown hair, hairy forearms, muscular torso suggesting a devotion to free weights, easy belly bespeaking a love of beer, doughnuts, and couch-lounging. Dark goatee glazed with gray along the chin.

I sat at a table where I had a good view of him. Cocked my baseball cap over my eyes and soaked him in some more. By the time my cheese sandwich was done, my boxer briefs were getting uncomfortably tight and I was fascinated big-time. Casually asked around that afternoon, found out his name, Keith McGraw, and his position, head of security.

Standing by my ditched truck a few weeks later, I was sure hoping it would be Keith to show up, not one of his minions. He must have gotten the message off-duty, because he showed up out of uniform, in a rusty Ford truck instead of a park security car. Now, I like a handsome man in uniform, especially khaki, but I like a casual good ole boy better, and that's what I got, Keith swinging out from behind the wheel in jeans torn at the knees, black cowboy boots, WVU Mountaineers T-shirt, and black cowboy hat. We shook hands; he called the park garage for a tow. I made note of chest hair pluming over his collar, big pecs and nipple-stipple and moderate belly curving under his too-tight T, and invited him to breakfast at the Black Bear, my treat, as thanks for his help.

He put away some biscuits and sausage gravy that morning, that's for sure. Really cocked a bushy eyebrow with interest when I told him I could make a mean biscuit, courtesy of my daddy's recipe. We warmed up to one another fast, shooting the shit about four-wheel-drives, local barbeque joints, football, and weight lifting, the sort of superficial enthusiasms that ostensibly straight guys don't mind sharing. I'd heard enough park gossip to know he was still torn up over his wife, who'd left him for another man and taken their daughter with her. Maybe that explained his tentative manner, a sweet shyness I found endearing. I just assumed he was lonely, wanted a buddy. Well, despite several years in college, I'm enough of a mountain redneck to enjoy the company of another mountain redneck, and the major letch I was feeling I figured I'd better shelve if I knew what was good for me. As hard as it was to keep my hands off him, I didn't want to ruin our friendship or lose my job.

I guess it was the weekend after that stag kindly introduced us that Keith had me over to his place, the little cabin where Pipestem puts up its head of security, to knock back some bourbon and watch some Braves on his little TV. It took some effort to appear calm, to focus on the game. Keith was couch-sprawled in the torn-up jeans he was wearing when I met him, big holes in the knees I kept trying not to stare at—hair on his legs thick, thick as the woods back of his house. And that damned wife-beater, too tight like his T-shirts, chest hair sticking out the top and sides, fans of fur in his pits when he stretched out and yawned, big arms flexing above his head during commercials. Hell, even the patches of fur atop his bare feet tugged at my attention. The details were like water rising behind a dam. I knew I'd better keep semisober, despite the good bourbon he was pouring. The tiny gap between his front teeth, his high little laugh...you know you're in trouble when the tiny, insignificant, not particularly erotic details start to seize on you.

That was the first night she called. Keith sat out on the porch, whispering, then swearing into the cell phone. Sound of shattering—he must have thrown his glass against a rock. Then he staggered in, teary-eyed.

I asked if he wanted me to leave. "Naw, need the company,"

he muttered as he fetched a new glass, poured more bourbon. Before the game was over, he'd passed out on the couch. I wanted to stroke his brow, fluff the fur in the pit of his neck. Instead I spread an afghan over him, drove the hour to my Flat Top cabin. Not entirely sober myself, I almost hit a possum. Home, I jacked off, thinking about how sweet he'd looked sprawled asleep, how much I wanted him, how I'd made a fucking career of wanting the impossible, surest way to stay single forever.

I told him to keep still, and Keith has obeyed: the knife's still riding the crest of his belly. He likes to obey, just another thing about him that I love and he hates. I put the blade on the bedside table, then slide onto the quilt beside him. He looks up at me, mumbles something I can't make out, tape-muted as it is. *I love you. I'm sorry. Hurt me.* I smooth the hair on his chest, grip his half-hard dick, curl up against him, my face in his left armpit. I love how he smells when he goes a few days without a shower. I wish some great hand would pull the tin roof off this cabin, let the ice fall over us, around us, freeze this blessed here-and-now, like those bodies found curled together in the charred ruins of Pompeii.

"The roads are getting bad. You got to go," I say into his pit's forest-scent, resting my arm across his torso.

Keith grunts and nods.

"I got to fuck you first. You want me to fuck you, right?"

Keith nods emphatically. He's so eager to feel me inside him.

In a minute, I'll get out the lube. Right now, I just want to lie here, feel his chest rise and fall. If I keep very still, the world is entirely his breathing, my breathing, the scent and warmth of him, and outside the click of ice.

The week after that Braves game, we met after work at Pipestem's pool. No one else around, pool closed at day's end, but of course head of security had a key. I'd never seen water of such vivid hue: the indigo that edges horizons just after midsummer sunset. Me, I just dog-paddled here and there, but Keith swam lap after lap. I cooled off in the water, watched last light ricochet around the pool, nets of restless red-gold; then stretched out in the grass. Keith joined me, panting, laughing his high little laugh. Side by side, we watched constellations swim to the surface of southern West Virginia's summer sky. We didn't say much. It's good when friends can share such easy silence.

Later, in the locker room, the first time I saw him naked. Smell of chlorine, Keith standing in the shower's steam, pulling off his baggy swim trunks and rinsing them, water running down his back, into the mossy crack of his ass. Just the kind of physique I'd imagined, having for weeks furtively studied the curves beneath his clothes. Body of a weight lifter going to seed, my favorite of Plato's Ideal Forms. Keith caught me watching him, and surely he couldn't help but notice the stiffening between my legs. He just gave his shy grin, tossed me soap—"That's quite a Jim Boco you got there, Dirk," he said—then lathered up his chest hair. I kept my back to him as best I could, trying to imagine fat women naked in a desperate attempt to deflate. His cock was half-hard too, but I couldn't believe that reality's draconian laws would allow that fact to mean what I most wanted it to mean. The wildest hopes are the first ones shattered. I knew that from experience.

The second time she called he cried in earnest. Late July, humid as hell. We both had the weekend off, and Keith had finally agreed to visit my high, lonesome Flat Top place. The possibility of biscuits and gravy had lured him in, he claimed. Another

Braves game, more bourbon, some chips with sour-cream-and-onion dip. And he'd brought his fucking cell phone, and she called again. This time he went into the bathroom for some privacy. He was too polite to break anything of mine, but after the phone-talk he left the cabin, sat on the front steps, paced around the property with his drink in his hand, finally disappeared into the rhododendron thicket out back.

I watched the Braves, worried, wished I could beat his wife to death, and watched the game some more. Then gave it up and turned it off, fried up ground beef and grated cheese for tacos. Bourbon bottle in hand, went out to fetch him in for dinner. Found him sitting on a boulder in the laurels, handsome as hell in another wife-beater, his stained pair of camo shorts, bare toes digging into black earth, a big beefy macho guy sucking down booze, cursing softly, and wiping fat tears off his face. Guess it was then I knew I loved him.

I sat beside him—"Ah, buddy"—put one arm around him.

"Shit, Dirk, I'm sorry," he gasped, shoulders stiffening beneath my touch. "Man, I miss her. Miss my kid." Then relaxing a little, letting me hold him.

Keith cried for a right good while, very quiet except for a little sob every now and then when he caught his breath. I refilled his glass, then mine, and he kept at the silent tears and the steady drinking till fireflies started to rise from the grass and gather like restless stars in the boughs of my ratty ailanthus tree.

I guess I should be thankful for her cruelty and for how deeply he loved her, since all that sorrow ended him up too drunk to drive home. He spent some time passed out on the couch—I was trying to be polite, trying to keep my hands off a man so wrecked and vulnerable—and he spent some time in the bathroom getting rid of dinner and drinks. But when I woke at four a.m. to piss and found him sitting in his underwear, still crying in the dark, I dragged his ass into the bedroom.

I had to hold him, he was hurting so much. And then one touch led to another, and pretty soon I'd peeled his briefs off. You know how it is with men. Sex is a handy, if temporary, way to numb pain. I gave Keith a damned fine blow job, though I think he was most grateful just to have someone strong hold him hard. We woke that first morning spooning, his broad back against my chest. I sucked him off again, and then, yes, I made him biscuits and gravy.

I figured he'd bolt after that, disgusted that he'd let me touch him that way, sick with fear after showing another man his weakness, the depths of his grief. But he didn't bolt. He spent the weekend. He told me about the infrequent liaisons he'd had with men during his marriage, how guilty they made him feel, how empty. He helped me pick beetles off the potato plants, sucker the tomatoes, pick a few hot peppers. We drove down to Ghent for some beer and some fried apple pies and a rental movie. That night I dragged the TV set into the bedroom and we watched the film in bed, curled up together naked. Halfway through, I heated up the pies in a skillet, topped them with ice cream, and we ate them in bed. I dribbled melted ice cream on his nipples and licked it off, then did the same with his ass. Never seen a man so sweetly take to a tongue up his hole. He bucked so hard I had to hold him down.

The middle of that second night, I woke to find him crying again, but that ended right quick when I reached across the sugar-sticky sheets and pulled him against me, wrapped my arms around him, pinning his big arms to his sides, and started working his nipples hard. When he really set into moaning, I clamped a hand over his goateed lips. That only het him up more. When he began to put up some fight, I pulled my briefs off the headboard, stuffed them in his mouth, and held him harder. When I dug my fingernails into his nipple, he whimpered, grabbed his cock, and shot within five thrusts.

He was the answer I'd been waiting for. We were each other's answer.

In summer, poppies, red and pink, line the road up here, where I-64 crests Flat Top Mountain, where I turn off the Ghent exit and head out to my cabin. Poppies start out looking like fuzzy testicles. Then, in answer to summer's heat, they split open. Their little hearts are black char, like ridged clumps of coal, the black that builds up in woodstoves. Around that smudgy dark, the fiery petals unfurl, delicate as blood-stained tissue paper. Next spring they'll burn again, I know, but tonight it's hard to believe that, with ice the dominant chord. The click of ice sounds like impatient bones, like finality.

I'm sitting on Keith's chest tugging on his goatee hard. Wet edges his eyes. I know how to hurt him without harming him. We've learned that together over the last few years. When he closes his eyes, I slap his cheek gently with one hand—"Look at me!"—and he does. I keep tugging, till tears run down his stubbly cheeks. I wipe the wet off his face and taste it. Don't know why, but I love him most when he breaks down.

Now I'm untying his feet, reaching for the lube and the knife, ready to give him the edgy play he needs. I know he wants blindfolding now—he's so ashamed of his eager ache to be fucked, he's mumbling and nodding toward the bandana on the bedside table—but I ignore this garbled request. This time, he's going to have to look me in the eyes, face what he wants and what he's giving up.

I prop Keith's calves on my shoulders, tug tenderly on the dark clumps of hair in the crack of his ass. I slip a lubed finger inside him and feel his flesh clamp down, relax, clamp down, relax. Amazing how rough and strong a man can be, yet still have a hole so sweet and soft, fragile and pink as poppy petals. I grease up the smooth handle of the knife and carefully push it up inside him, the steel pommel and then the black hilt. How will either one of us learn to live without this?

Denied the cloth lie of the blindfold, he's closed his eyes again. I whisper, "Keith, buddy, I want you to look at me and keep looking. Else I'll use this knife's other end. God knows you've given me cause."

Keith stares at me, and the fright in his eyes is fucking exquisite. I pull the hilt out, and he crosses his ankles behind my neck. I slide the knife in again, and he nods his head, murmurs into tape, stares up at me. Black eyes in candlelight, in daylight the jade of oak-tree shade mixed with brown of turned-over earth. I rock the knife slowly in and out, opening him up. I listen to his mumbled pleas and prayers.

The first time I fucked Keith was the first time I tied him. By that point, we'd wrestled around enough in bed—despite his bigger build, he'd always let me win—and I'd stuffed briefs in his mouth often enough to suspect that he wanted it as rough as I could give it. Gags and restraints sure seemed like the next step. I'd always had a taste for kink, both as Top and bottom. My lover Mike used to rope me out spread-eagle before he fucked me, and I used to do the same to him. So, about four months after Keith and I started sleeping together, I got out the ropes, bandanas, and PVC tape. They were spread across the bed when he came up one cold-rain September evening for venison chili. When he saw them, without a word he strode out to his truck, fetched in cuffs and pistol, and laid them beside my stash.

As much as he wanted it, still he got especially soused that night. Liquid courage, I call it. He was nervous as hell, I could tell, so I let the fire die down to midnight embers, let him get good and wasted, before I led him into the bedroom and ordered him to strip.

I hadn't imagined that things could get any hotter between us—how many times in a guy's life is he lucky enough to find a body he learns to cherish more than all the world, a body whose absence sets up in him a yearning damn near religious? But once I had Keith restrained, a whole new heat flared up. When I cuffed his hands before him and tied one bandana between his teeth and one over his eyes, whatever last resistance he might have owned was gone. I could tell by the way his body tensed and slumped, the way he groaned when I tied his cuffed hands to the headboard and pushed him down onto his elbows and his knees, the way he sobbed as I gently ate his ass. For a while there, I'm certain, he was set right in the cosmos' core, the black heart of the poppy in a circle of fire, chewing his gag sodden while I eased inside him for the first time and then fucked him slow, kissing the nape of his neck, cupping the thick, furry flesh of his pecs in my hands. When two men share a night like that, how can either ever leave?

We've both come. I've licked our mingled semen off his belly, methodically untied him, then begged and cursed for half an hour, wished him and her straight to hell. He's huddled under the quilts, silent, curled around a pillow, stared at the ice-spotted window.

Now I'm done, throat sore with shouting, and Keith is dressing by the remains of the fire, his nakedness disappearing piecemeal. It's as if he's evaporating before my eyes one beloved inch at a time. First his crotch vanishes in underwear. Then his goose-pimpled thighs in jeans. Now his chest, inside thermal undershirt and flannel shirt. I can't believe I'll never see the beauty of his bare chest again. Then his feet, inside socks and then those pig-slouch cowboy boots I bought him last spring in Wytheville. Too smooth-soled for this season: tonight he'll be slipping and sliding all over the ice. Fool should have worn work boots with heavy tread.

My hot-cop lover got everything he wanted for a farewell fuck. The rope, the tape, the teeth on his tits. The slow, hot slide of the hunting-knife handle. His gun held under his chin, then the greased barrel taking the place of the knife up his ass. Then my cock replacing the gun, riding him till he whimpered with pain and then pounding him for a good while after. I want him very sore tomorrow.

All that, and now he's standing here untied, unharmed, ready to risk icy roads and resume his life with others. Despite what he told me, I didn't cut him; I didn't slit his throat and bury him in the basement. Instead of hitting him upside the head with this poker, I'm squatting here naked, stoking low embers on the hearth. This fire needs lots more wood if I'm going to keep warm tonight.

"I wanted us both to know it was the last time," Keith mutters, slipping on his rawhide jacket.

I look up at him, then rise. I pull on my sweatshirt and jeans. We stand face-to-face.

He steps forward, as if about to hug me. I step back, lift his cowboy hat from the back of the sofa, and hold it between us.

Keith takes it from me, moves toward the door. He turns, says, "Don't think I'll be seeing you much 'round the park. Katie's got a job out Cincinnati way. I'm moving pretty soon."

He's saved this for last. I don't know what to say. Instead of speaking, I study his face, as if the sheer focus of my attention might make him reconsider, make him stay. Then I smile, cock an eyebrow, and pat my own cheek.

"What?" he says, confused.

"Tape," I say. He lifts his hand to his face, finds sticky residue the gag's left on the edge of his goatee and in a streak across his cheek. Keith rubs at it irritably.

"Still there," I say. "Might want to take a shower later."

"Dirk," he says, and then he's out the door.

I fall to my knees. Outside, his engine starts up, heads off. I stretch out on the floor before the fire and listen to the embers' simmer. Sure hope he makes it home safe. The hearth heat feels good on my bare feet.

Tomorrow, when the sun rises, Flat Top Mountain will be brilliant with ice. Maybe I'll lie down inside the white pine grove and watch boughs glitter like frozen fingers, feel sun-weakened ice split and shatter, fall over me like broken glass. Hell, if I were younger, maybe I'd walk out into this night stark naked and not come back. Right now it's feeling like my breath, my body, my heartbeat aren't worth the effort it would take to lose.

Instead, I pull on socks and moccasins, heap logs on the andirons, slosh red wine into my plastic Mountaineers glass, and pull out the groceries I bought for our weekend together. I was going to make Keith and me beef stew and biscuits for tomorrow's dinner, but I think I'll cook it all up tonight.

FRISK

Hank Edwards

I sat nervously in the conference room surrounded by my partners in law and, unfortunately, crime. A slick bead of sweat ran from my armpit to the waistband of my boxers, leaving behind a track of moisture that brought on a shiver.

"What's the matter, Zack?" asked the senior partner, George, narrowing his gray eyes in my direction. "Caught a chill?"

I shrugged as nonchalantly as possible considering the situation. "Goose walked over my grave, I guess."

The seven men surrounding the fine oak conference table chuckled quietly. All of us had conspired to hide certain business transactions from the government. Now I found myself involved in a sting operation to save my hairy hide and rat out my partners. Oh, what a tangled web we weave.

A few months ago the state's attorney had shown up on my doorstep along about midnight. Midnight visitors are never good, and this one had lived up to that promise. I opened the door to a full-court press and after several hours of talks I agreed to turn state's evidence against the other partners in my law firm. The state's attorney had approached me because I was the newest member of the partners' roster and could ask the many questions that needed to be answered on tape without raising much suspicion. For this effort, I would receive a reduced sentence in a white-collar prison and lose my license to practice law. Hey, what a deal, right?

I now wore a small transmitter and microphone to every encounter I had with any of the partners. I had been doing it for several weeks, but at each meeting I felt as nervous as the first time. Would I screw up somehow and blow the whole operation? Then where would I be?

Each time I wore the transmitter I had to go through a certain procedure. It was placed on different areas of my body depending on the type of meeting: golf, conference room, travel by car or rail, that kind of thing. With two other witnesses in the office, one of the agents would meet me just before I was to leave for the appointment and tape the transmitter to my waist, back or leg. This required me to partially disrobe, a fact that forced me to start wearing boxers to better hide the fact that I was usually sporting a partial hard-on. I don't know where they found the field agents for this assignment, but I want a two-week vacation to that place.

These guys were hot hunks with buzz cuts, chiseled jaws, barrel chests with hair poking up from beneath their white shirts, and round bubble butts I longed to press my face into. Whichever agent had pulled taping duty that day would strip off his suit coat, take off his mirrored sunglasses, and get down on his knees before me. After raising my shirt and lowering my pants, he would carefully place the transmitter on whatever body part was to be used during that meeting and start laying adhesive tape. Their hands were always gentle but firm as they smoothed the tape out over my skin, their soft fingertips grazing my flesh and teasing my mind with thoughts of sex. As I have a rather hairy body, they would always try to be careful not to tape over too much hair. Some were more empathetic about this than others.

The removal of the transmitter worked in much the same way. There was, however, one exception: sometimes there would only be one agent in the room. The other two may have been called away. When only one agent was waiting, I would be frisked to make sure I wasn't carrying anything like a bribe or a weapon. The result of this search was stated into the microphone and then the transmitter was removed, usually with some loss of body hair and more than a few tears of pain on my part.

After this particular meeting wrapped up, I made my way to my office, conscious of every word or bodily emission as everything I did was being recorded for analysis later. I walked through my office door and locked it behind me. Turning, I found an agent waiting for me: the new guy, Straith. He was big and solid, an imposing mass of masculinity. His forearms were big and covered with hair, his chest broad beneath his starched white shirt. I longed to pull the buttons off his shirt with my teeth and expose the mat of hair beneath. His square jaw was marred by a slight indent centered beneath his full, soft lips. His eyes were the green of summer grass and I marveled at the contrast they provided to his short, dark hair and olive complexion.

"What are you doing here? Are you crazy? They could see you!" I snapped, panic driving my pulse up a few points.

"Relax," he said casually, a smile playing along his soft, pink lips. "I snuck in when no one was looking. I had to tell you the others were called to an emergency staff meeting and I didn't want to wait in the van." He shrugged the indifferent shrug of a hotshot agent who felt impervious to any outside influences. He made up his own rules and ignored everything else. Oh, I knew his type. He was the type I always went for: hot, masculine, and distant.

I tried to put the flood of sexual images out of my head, but my dick was twitching like a divining rod, sniffing out manmeat. "Oh. Well, it seems a little foolish if you ask me."

He shrugged again. "I didn't ask you." He smiled as he crossed the room and I felt more blood rush to my groin. Straith had only been with the operation two weeks, but I had gotten used to his big body; wide, green eyes; and that high, round ass. Or at least I thought I had gotten used to him.

"Where'd they stick it this time?" he asked as he knelt before me. I could smell his mildly sweaty scent mixing with the starch in his laundered shirt and fought back the urge to say, "Way high up inside my ass, go looking for it." Instead I directed him to the spot on my thigh.

"Okay, this is Special Agent Straith Anderson. I am in the process of patting down Zack McCallister after a meeting on the..." He turned to find the wall calendar hanging by my desk and stated the date.

Starting with my ankles, he began feeling my body, being careful around the transmitter and very thorough everyplace else. When he got to my crotch, he placed a large, warm palm directly over my almost fully erect cock and squeezed slightly. As he measured the size and rigidity inside my pants, his eyes darted up to meet mine and I felt a high-voltage spark of attraction arc between us. My cock sprang up into full readiness and he dragged his palm along its length as he stood to frisk the upper half of my body.

Starting with my arms, he squeezed each muscle, gauging its tone and firmness like a personal trainer. His hands cupped my damp armpits, digging into them as his eyes remained locked on mine. He was inches from my face; I could feel his breath on my cheek and see his lips part to expose the tip of his wide, pink tongue. His hands moved over my chest and his thumbs pressed down slightly over the center of my nipples. My stomach quivered as his fingers slid down along my waist and then over my belly, his fingertips leaving traces of heat in their wake.

Stepping around me, Straith ran his hands over my back, kneading the tight muscles that stretched along my spine and shoulders until he came to the curve of my ass. I blessed myself for spending longer than needed on that cursed StairMaster as his hands quickly gripped the globes of my ass, slightly spreading the cheeks. Before I knew it, he was done and had stepped in front of me again, his eyes falling to the unmistakable outline of my now fully locked-and-loaded erection as it extended down my right thigh.

"This is Special Agent Straith Anderson. I have completed the pat-down of Zack McCallister and have found nothing unusual on his person. I am now going to remove the transmitter."

Kneeling down once again, Straith reached out and unbuckled my belt, then carefully eased the zipper open, keeping his eyes on mine the entire time. He unfastened the clasp on my pants and they collapsed around my ankles, exposing my bulging boxers and the glistening head of my cock sticking out the right leg just above the small black transmitter.

Straith cocked an eyebrow at the sight of my prick and nodded appreciatively. He winked up at me, then set to work removing the transmitter. The tape came off slowly, pulling several hundred hairs with it, and I attempted to maintain what remained of my dignity by stifling my cries. Straith switched the transmitter off then leaned forward and grazed the head of my cock with the warm tip of his tongue. He caught the precum pooling at the piss slit and leaned back, taking a strand of it along with him, his tongue now connected to my cock by a thick, quivering thread of semen. His eyes rolled up to mine and I stared down at him.

He leaned forward again, slowly taking the precum into his mouth, then took the head of my cock in as well where it jutted out the leg of my boxers and sucked the juice from it.

"Oh, god," I groaned and leaned my head back, letting my suit coat fall to the floor as he gobbled up my cock. He stuck his face as far up the leg of my boxers as it would go and began milking the precum from me, his full lips clamped tight around my tool. I put my hands on the back of his head and felt the soft, short strands of hair part between my fingers.

He grunted and slurped as he worked my cock, his tongue wrapping itself around my shaft inside his hot, endless mouth. Leaning back, he pulled my boxers down and my cock sprang free, pointing directly into his face. He opened that talented mouth of his and swallowed me whole, taking my dick down to the root and leaving it wet with his spit as he slid his mouth up and down.

While he sucked me, Straith removed his tie and unbuttoned his shirt. He shrugged it off and sat back long enough to peel the T-shirt off his wide, hairy torso. He was damp with sweat; it gleamed beneath the lights in my office, and I groaned at the sight of his pecs brushed with a dark coat of hair that traveled down along his stomach and dropped into dark mystery beneath the waistline of his pants.

"Get up and drop those pants," I demanded, and then watched him shuck the rest of his clothes as I removed mine. His cock was thick like his body, and olive colored, standing up at an almost ninety-degree angle from the dark patch of pubic hair surrounding its base. His balls hung low and were covered with the same thick, dark hair.

I directed him to the Italian leather couch across the room and turned him around to lean over the arm with his ass sticking up in the air. My cock was so hard it ached as I knelt behind him and massaged the round globes of his ass. Dark hair covered his asscheeks and disappeared into the tight depths of his crack. I dug my fingers into the pale skin and moved up to plant my mouth and nose in the center of his ass. With a breath I brought the musky, manly smell of him deep into my nostrils and moaned.

"Oh, yeah," Straith groaned. He lowered his head and pushed his ass back even further, spreading his thick, muscular legs. "Eat my ass."

Happy to oblige, I spread his cheeks wide and dove in, licking and slurping at the dark pink pucker nearly hidden by hair. I felt like a jungle explorer making his way through the last bunch of twining, entangled vines to see the lost temple I had up to now only dreamed about. The dark, puckered ring of his hole twitched beneath my tongue, squeezing shut and gaping open as I suckled at it. Beyond the circular muscle lay the damp, hot passage that I longed to invade.

"Oh, fuck," he gasped. "That feels so good."

I slid my tongue into his sweaty hole and let my spit coat the slick lining inside. Twisting my head, I rubbed my face in the crack of his ass, smearing his masculine scent on my cheeks, nose, and chin and hungrily nibbling on his twitching anus.

Straith stood up suddenly and turned around, his lips mashing down over mine and his tongue invading my mouth. We kissed sloppily, tongues slapping and licking as his hands reached down to grip my solid rock of a dick, squeezing and stroking as our tongues swirled around each other. Breaking the kiss, Straith lay back on the couch and pulled me around so that I straddled him in a sixty-nine position. He reached up and spread my asscheeks apart, then set to work on my hole with his mouth. I groaned, riding his face like a penny pony, then leaned over and gulped down his hard dick. I wrapped my hand around the base of his cock, amazed at the width and the fact that my fingers would not meet. I fought with his hard, tall cock for several minutes, swallowing it partway down my throat and then easing it back out to work on the fat, pale head.

Running my tongue along the vein-covered shaft, I nuzzled his hairy balls and took each one into my mouth. His crotch was damp with sweat and the smell of him made me dizzy with lust. I wanted to suck, lick, and touch every inch of him.

Moving further south, I lapped again at his dark, hair-covered anus, earning a groan of pleasure as he moved his attention to my balls and then my prick. He raised his legs, clasping his ankles behind my head and squeezing my shoulders with his muscular thighs as I bent to work on his asshole.

"Oh, fuck," Straith grunted. He pulled my cock from his throat and began beating me off. "Eat that fuckin' ass. Get that tongue up there. Oh, yeah!"

I flicked my tongue up into his asshole as he jerked my dick, his cock twitching against my stomach. Sliding back, I planted my ass firmly on his face and he eagerly set to work on my asshole, putting that magical mouth and tongue to work once again. His tongue rolled up tight and plunged into my hole, penetrating me like a small cock. He tongue-fucked my ass as he beat me off with his right hand and finally I could take no more. I had reached my limit.

Sitting up straight over his face, I rode his fist to a beautiful, gushing climax. My load shot out over his massive chest and flat stomach, coating him with cum. A line of it dribbled down my cock and over my balls and he sucked it up, licking my balls clean and then pulling my hips back so that my dripping cock plopped right into his mouth. He sucked up every drop of cum left on my dick then sat up and pulled me down onto my back on the couch. Turning around, he straddled my chest and jerked himself off as I pulled his hairy balls taut and slipped a finger up his ass.

His load hit my chest and face and I opened my mouth wide to catch as much of his spunk as I could. I swallowed the hot, white load down and guzzled the rest of it from his dick as he leaned forward to stuff his still-oozing cock into my mouth. His cum tasted sweet and I ached for another helping.

Once I had sucked him clean, he pulled back and leaned down to kiss me hard and deep, his tongue swapping cum and spit with mine as our lips opened to each other.

"Now," he breathed into my mouth, "I want to ride that cock of yours."

A few moments later I sat upright on the couch and he crouched over my lap, facing me as he guided my condom-covered dick to his entrance. He eased down along the length of my cock, the hot, wet muscles of his ass tightening around me with a loving grip.

"Oh, god," I grunted. "You have got a nice, tight ass."

"You have no idea," he replied and with that he plopped himself down fully onto my lap. I let out a gasp as my cock slid deep into his body. Sweat ran down his face and stood out along his chest and I leaned forward to lick it off. As I ran my tongue through the salty beads beneath the hair on his stomach, he rocked back and forth along the length of my dick. I grunted into the hairy furrow between his firm pecs and worked my lips, tongue, and teeth around each hard, dark nipple.

I let him ride me for a while, then dug my fingers into his hips and began pounding up into him, my cock steadily battering his ass. Straith opened his mouth in a silent gasp, tilting his head back as I fucked him hard and deep. I could feel my balls pulling up, a sure sign I was getting ready to blow my load, and I closed my eyes as I hammered up between his furry asscheeks.

With a grunt I shot my wad into the condom buried deep in his ass and Straith leaned further back, his cock pulsing against my body. Hot, sticky semen blasted up against the bottom of my jaw and along my chest, drenching me with cum as the rangy odor of his seed filled my nostrils. With each burst of spunk I felt the muscles in his ass squeeze around my cock, gripping it tightly as he ejaculated. He hadn't even touched himself and he had shot his load almost three feet. Where had this man been when I was in college?

He fell forward in a heap on top of me, the sharp odor of his sweaty armpits engulfing me and making me hungry for him all over again. But we had things to do and we needed to get cleaned up. Luckily, as a partner in the firm I had a private bathroom in my office. We washed up and got dressed, playfully reaching out to touch each other and snap the elastic on our shorts. I sprayed an odor neutralizer around the room just as a knock sounded at the door. When I unlocked and opened the door, trying to look as innocent as possible, the assistant director of the area FBI office stepped quickly inside, eyeing us curiously.

"Do you have the transmitter?" the director asked Straith, and then took it from him. "Well, Mr. McCallister. It looks like your recordings may give us just the edge we need to go up the chain and catch the top dog in all of this. You're doing so well the prosecutor has mentioned shortening your sentence even more. But I think you may be in danger. I am going to assign Special Agent Anderson here to stay with you in your apartment until this trial is over. This could take several months; I hope you two feel you can get along all right cooped up in your apartment for that amount of time."

I looked at Straith and found him grinning at me. Nodding, and smiling slightly myself, I looked back at the assistant director and said, "Well, if you think it's in my best interest, I guess I can't refuse."

KLEET

Mark Wildyr

I pushed through the door of Biggs Gym for the first time in over a year. A police exercise hangout and boxing club, the place was no Stilman's New York or Johnny Tucco's Vegas, but neither was it an automated Gold's although there were a few new body-shaping machines in the back. Nonetheless, it looked the same and smelled the same and Jimmie Biggs still propped up a corner post of the boxing ring. He probably hadn't moved since the last time I was here. The grizzled old retired cop pried himself off the ropes long enough for a grimace that passed for a smile and a hard handshake.

"Hal! Long time, no see. Heard you got shot. You okay?"

The blunt, gruff greeting brought a genuine smile. "Caught one in the side, Jimmie. Nothing you haven't gone through once or twice."

"Yeah. Comes with the territory. But you okay now, right?" The old cop barely waited for my nod before turning back to the ring. "Got something you gotta see. Look at this kid!"

He didn't need to be more specific. A tall, dark young man sparring with his partner was the "kid." The boy dominated the ring, pushing his heavier opponent around virtually at will. As I watched, he loosed a furious series of jabs and rattled the other boxer with a right cross to the jaw. Jimmie immediately called a halt to the session.

"Come here, Kleet," the manager called after making certain the other boxer was okay. "Meet Detective Lieutenant Hal Marcus outta Downtown. Hal, this here's Kleet Drum, cycle cop outta the Far North District. Kleet, Hal useta be my best boy 'fore he got hisself promoted to Lieutenant and claimed he was too busy for the important stuff." Jimmy pried the kid's mouthpiece out.

"Lieutenant," the boy greeted me, touching his gloved hand to the fist I offered. "Nice to meet you. I heard of you. They say you're pretty good."

"Was," I acknowledged. "Time and circumstance caught up with me."

"Don't let 'im bullshit you," Jimmie cut in. "Youngest lieutenant on the force. What are you, twenty-eight…nine? That ain't old. So what if you got shot up a year ago and ain't put in your time? Bet you're still damned good."

"Be glad to go a round," the boy offered, holding out his hands for the trainer to take off the gloves; then he ripped off the headgear Jimmie insists his boys use in practice, and I almost gasped. The kid was as handsome as sin. No wonder he was so dark, he was an Indian. At about one-sixty his body was compact, despite his five-ten frame. The chest was probably forty-five inches. Hell, Charles Atlas's was only forty-seven. Heavy pecs, defined lats, flat belly, good thighs and legs. The kid's biceps and triceps rolled with controlled power every time he moved. There wasn't a hair on his smooth, dusky body that I could see, although an ebony mop plastered down by the sweat of his efforts covered his head. The broad forehead was smooth and unmarked except by finely curved brows. Sensitive black eyes danced restlessly. Black eyes are hard to read, and his were doubly so for some reason. The nose was straight and a little fleshy, as were the lips framing the wide mouth. He had a firm jaw, slightly rounded; skin that looked Hispanic with a rosy overtone.

In the nanosecond it took to size him up, I flashed on my ex-partner when we were his age, probably not much over twenty-one, and for the first time in five years I suffered a hunger I'd not experienced since Bryan resigned the force and moved away.

"Let me get back in condition," I said, slapping my lean belly, "and I'll take you on."

"Fair enough. Let me know when you're ready. I'm here most nights." The boy turned away, giving me a good look at the wide, tapering back.

"Gonna enter the departmental bouts," Jimmie's voice interrupted my inspection. "Take the belt most likely. He's good, Hal. And that's why I'm glad to see you."

I looked at him suspiciously. "Why's that?"

Jimmie placed a hand on my arm and motioned me to the side of the room, although there was no one within hearing since Kleet left the ring for the light bag. "I...uh, I got a problem, Hal. I...uh, I gotta go in the hospital. Put off taking care of a damned hernia, and the doc won't let me stall no more. Got me scheduled for the fifteenth of next month. Kleet's first fight's that night. Need you to stand in for me. Maybe for the next bout, too."

"Me? Hell, get somebody who's been around, watched him, knows his moves."

"Ain't nobody I'd trust like you. Kleet don't know about it

yet, so don't say nothing, but I sure need you to back me up on this."

"Give me a week," I sighed, mentally rearranging my schedule. "Let me see how I come along."

"Good enough," Jimmie smiled, knowing he'd suckered me into it. "Do your stretches and hit the rope. Then take the heavy bag." He gave orders like I was a kid who'd just signed on.

A little later I was on the bag, beginning to get back into my rhythm when someone steadied it from the other side. Although I couldn't see clearly through all the sweat in my eyes, I knew it was Kleet Drum. He leaned into the bag while I punished it with everything I had for five minutes. Then I stepped back.

He came around the bruised bag and gave me a grin. "You've done this before," he said. "You a southpaw?"

"No, why?"

"Hitting it harder with the left."

"Got shot in the right side. Guess I'm holding back. Thanks for pointing it out." I went at it for another ten minutes. He stayed and watched, until I finally gasped and gave it up.

"Not bad for the first workout in...what?" he asked.

"A year."

"Not bad at all." He gave me a crooked smile that lit up the room and turned his back on me. "Gonna hit the showers."

"Me, too," I panted, "if I don't collapse first."

I consider the shower room one giant, fucking trap. I grew up in shower rooms, first in public schools, then in college and on the job. They never made me uncomfortable, until Bryan Shalter that is. Like most street partners, we became friends in the cruiser and buddies at bars and ball games. Neither of us was married, so we bummed around; joined at the hip, some of the guys used to claim. They didn't know how true it was. Our second year together, he broke up with the girl he planned to marry, got drunk, and came over to my place where we ended up in bed. The next morning we swore it would never happen again, but when we showered in the locker room after work, our eyes betrayed us. I followed him home and butt-fucked him with both of us stone sober.

We never moved in together, but we spent most nights with one another. If social activities dictated dates, we'd meet after taking them home. Fucking the girls merely seemed to whet the appetite for what we shared. We loved one another without words for two years. A week after I verbally declared my devotion, he turned in his badge and moved to the West Coast. He tried to tell me why, but never quite got the words right. It didn't matter; I understood. We were getting in too deep. He knew we'd eventually come out of the closet if we remained together and wasn't certain he could handle it. Beautiful, blond Bryan. I wondered how he was doing.

Ever since, I've been leery about shower rooms. Couldn't avoid them, just had to be a little defensive. Justifiably so, if my reactions now were any measure. Kleet, in the shower opposite me, was of more than passing interest. I completed my inventory of him. Lean, powerful thighs. A patch of curly black hair clustered around his long, thick, uncircumcised cock. I'm no expert on men's cocks since my experience was limited to Bryan's and my own, but this one would be a monster when roused. As he washed himself, it almost got out of hand, thickening and stiffening a little. Self-consciously, he turned into the spray, and I studied his tight buns until I felt the need to turn away myself.

I started my regimen in earnest after that, greeting the road at five o'clock every morning for a run. When I worked up to five miles, I found out where Kleet Drum ran and joined him occasionally.

The first time I climbed into the ring with him I worked the pads, holding up the big mitts for him to jab. The most important thing I learned, beside the fact that he could punch like a pile driver, was that he had developed a pattern…four left hooks before he crossed with the right. He heard my warning, but didn't really heed it until we sparred a couple of nights later. I counted four jabs, slipped the right I knew was coming and landed a hard right to the ribs. He recovered nicely, but he'd gotten the message loud and clear.

Our force isn't big on departmental strata, and the camaraderie of the gym was pretty democratic, so it was natural that we developed a friendship. This meant accepting his cycle buddy, as well. Andy Lawson was a blond kid Kleet's own age whose fair Midwestern good looks made me think of Bryan. Most of the time Andy worked out on the machines at the back, but occasionally he joined us at ringside to watch his partner work out. I soon realized the blond adored the Indian, probably more than was socially acceptable. He covered it well except when he watched from ringside; then it was there for anybody who wanted to see.

The night Jimmie told Kleet about the hospital and formally turned over the kid's training to me, we ended up in a neighborhood bar without Andy, who was on a date. Kleet permitted himself two beers three nights a week while in training. Tonight was one of them.

"Well," he ventured after the first long sip. "If Jimmie's gotta hand me off to somebody, glad it's you."

"I've gotta warn you, I'm gonna change a couple of things. You're too aggressive. You don't pay enough attention to defense. Nobody ever hurt a good defensive fighter, and they've won lots fights."

"Yeah, I know," the kid acknowledged. "I trust you, Hal. You say it, and I'll do it."

After a few minutes of ring talk, we turned to the job. He liked being a cycle cop and thought Andy was a good, reliable partner. They'd backed one another often enough to get a feel. I learned he came out of poverty on a northern reservation, which he escaped by joining the army, apparently right ahead of the local sheriff. In turn, I told of the arrest of a burglary suspect with no history of violence that went wrong, resulting in a hole in my side. I didn't realize that my leg was leaning against his beneath the table until he shifted.

"Sorry," I mumbled, moving away and glancing up into his black, unreadable eyes. He shrugged and changed positions again. The calf of his leg rested against my shin for a long moment. So help me, I got an erection.

He drained his glass and shoved it aside. "Think I'll pass on my second one," he said casually. "You ready to go?"

Suddenly uninterested in the taste of alcohol, I rose, turning awkwardly so he wouldn't see my condition. I'm not certain I was successful. We walked the block to the gym. My car was the only one in the lot.

"Where are your wheels?" I asked.

"Walked over," he said. "It's only a couple of miles. Needed the exercise."

"I'll take you home," I volunteered.

Kleet crawled into the passenger's side. "Nice car," he noted approvingly. "A detective lieutenant's pay must be better than a cycle cop's."

"Supports a bigger car loan," I conceded.

Once we were out of the parking lot, he turned in the seat to face me. "Probably should have jogged. I'm sorta restless."

Somehow we ended up at my place trying out a sweet nonalcoholic wine I'd bought earlier. The kid was wired, and I wasn't in much better shape. I kept thinking of his warm leg against mine at the bar, the sight of him naked in the shower, the look in his black eyes. My erection returned. Abruptly, Kleet put down his glass of fake wine and stood up from the table in my kitchen. Grabbing my arm, he hauled me to my feet.

He took a stance, and I slipped into my own. He threw a few light jabs that I blocked. Even his light jabs stung, so I walked into him, going into a clinch. Surprisingly, he permitted it, snuggling close and giving me some pseudo-jabs to the sides. Then he dropped his hands to his sides, head on my shoulder, body against mine. If he didn't know before, he knew now. My bone stabbed his groin. Neither of us moved. Finally, I pulled away and cleared my throat roughly.

"Need another shower. I'll leave the door open in case you wanta use the can or something." Those carbon-black eyes studied me as I spoke.

After I was in the shower, he entered the bathroom. In moments, it sounded like a horse was pissing in a bucket; my cock reared up against my belly. Through the frosted glass of the shower enclosure I saw him turn and stare at my blurred image. My cock got harder. Then he walked out. Disappointment clutched at my guts.

I dried off as quickly as I could and went back out into the living room. He wasn't there. Nor was he in the kitchen. He wasn't anywhere. He had left. Concern mingled with disappointment in my belly. Damn! What had I done?

Deciding the long walk would be good for what ailed him, I took a slug of whiskey and tossed and turned in bed for an hour before finally going to sleep.

The next morning, I made a point of driving over and joining Kleet for his run. He threw me a bright hello while we did our stretching exercises with no sign of distress over the night before. Taking my cue from him, I avoided the subject.

Andy stuck close to us the rest of the week, which was probably a good thing. The blond kid was learning a lot about boxing, and I even put him in the ring once as a sparring partner when all I wanted was to point out a couple of things to my boxer.

Friday night, Kleet surprised me by announcing he had a date after the workout. Apparently he threw Andy a curve, as well. The kid gulped a couple of times and watched his partner stride out of the door after their shower. Then the boy turned and looked at me as if to say: do something! I did; I took Andy to the bar for a drink and watched him down a pitcher and a half. When it was time to leave, I wouldn't let him drive.

"Live clear…clear on other…side town," he slurred when I offered a ride home. "Take bus," he announced solemnly and started for a nearby bench. Busses had quit running hours ago.

"Afraid not, Andy. Busses have gone beddy-bye. Come on. I've got a couch you can use. You on duty tomorrow?"

He shook his head loosely. "Nope."

I gave the kid some bed linen and a pillow and went to change into my robe. When I checked on him, Andy, clad only in his jockeys, was on his knees beside the couch fighting with a sheet. It was almost like seeing Bryan in the house again. I swallowed some painful memories and went to give him a hand. He suddenly turned his head. Whether by design or accident, his nose was in my crotch. We both froze for a second, and then his arms went around my hips, pulling me into him. He moaned as he opened my robe. I was naked beneath it.

The boy sucked the end of my flaccid cock into his mouth. One hand clasped my balls; the other steadied my growing erection as he took all six and a half inches. I braced my arms against his shoulders as he worked on me. It had been a long time, and I got there in a hurry.

"Andy!" I warned, but he kept sucking and stroking. I shot.

"Oh, man!" I groaned, thrusting at him as my load pumped through me. He took all the cum I could deliver. After I worked through my orgasm, he remained on his knees, my flagging prick in his mouth. I don't think he knew how to end things.

"Oh, shit, I'm drunk!" he managed to mumble around my glans without biting me. Then he reared back and looked up the length of my torso. "Am I in trouble, Lieutenant?"

"I don't see any lieutenant here. Just me, Hal. The lieutenant's probably at the station."

The kid breathed a big sigh of relief. "Sorry, man. Don't know what got into me. But...but...well, you're a hunky son of a bitch."

I pulled him to his feet. "So are you, Andy. So are you." He accepted my kiss hungrily. At length, I stripped away his shorts and led him into the bedroom where he flopped facedown on the bed. I stretched out beside him. His shoulders were firm and freckled. I ran a hand down his spine and over the smooth buttocks. After five minutes, I was ready again. He parted his legs as I moved atop him. He took me effortlessly, and I fucked him energetically, enjoying the freedom of this larger orifice. For a few seconds it was Bryan beneath me again. As I indulged my fantasy, I'm sure he had his own. No doubt in his own mind, it was Kleet's big cock fucking his ass.

Andy was quiet after I cleaned us with warm water and a washcloth. He was probably a cuddler, but was a little on edge after getting it on with a lieutenant. But he couldn't contain himself forever. "You do this with Kleet?"

I tousled his cap of straw. "No," I answered without thinking. "But don't ask me that again. Would you like me to discuss what we did with him?" The brief silence before he shook his head was revealing. "You love him, don't you?"

He nodded once. "How did you know?"

"By looking at you."

"It shows?" he squeaked alarmingly.

"Sometimes. Sometimes it's right there on your face."

"You think he knows?"

"No, I don't believe his mind works that way. He probably understands on some level that you love him, but he'd think in terms of 'best buddy' or 'brother,' not the way you feel it."

"Doesn't matter," Andy said bitterly. "If...if he was going to do it with a guy, it'd be somebody like you. Somebody he looks up to and admires."

I didn't know what to say, so I said nothing. Soon his breathing told me that he was asleep. I followed him to dreamland shortly thereafter. He woke me at dawn, sucking my cock so thoroughly that I abandoned the idea of joining Kleet for the morning run and fought hard to make five miles by myself.

For the remaining time until the fight, I made Kleet concentrate on defense and conditioning. We ran together five days a week. We worked the medicine ball until I thought my belly would crack open like an egg. I put on the gloves and tried to put him down, forbidding him to do anything but defend himself. The night before the bout, I turned him loose and had the bruises to show for it.

Kleet's opponent for the first match was a big sergeant from the Southwest District by the name of Butch Class. He was older by five years, but also a lot more experienced. I'd already given Kleet his instructions, so for the most part I left him alone to do his mental preparation after he climbed into the ring. During the preliminaries, Butch put the stare on him, but the kid refused to be intimidated. The bell rang, Kleet exploded from his corner...and led with an uppercut! It connected and Class went down.

Andy was acting as cutman; he and I both went nuts! Nobody

ever leads with an uppercut; even the rankest amateur knows that. But he had, and it worked. After a standing eight count, the bout resumed. Class was slightly confused. He'd heard that Kleet Drum was a savvy fighter, but he'd opened with a bone-headed move like that...even if it had decked his opponent. To make matters worse, Kleet was a peekaboo fighter and could let go with either hand. Class spent the rest of the round waiting for my boy to lead again with his right, but it never happened.

The second round was totally different. Butch Class was pissed and went on the offensive. Kleet closed up and did a magnificent job of slipping and blocking...and even ducking. Butch never managed to land a clean blow in the entire three minutes between bells.

The third round was all Kleet's. He defended, but toward the last, he turned aggressive, blocking the ring, jabbing with that pistonlike left and then crossing to land a solid punch on the jaw. Immediately, he followed up with a flurry of body blows. Class never went down again, but he was beaten. The decision was unanimous. All three rounds went to Kleet.

It took some time to get back to the dressing room because all of the fans wanted a minute with the winner. When we finally arrived, Kleet put Andy on the door and told him to keep everyone out, saying he wanted a critique.

As soon as the door closed behind him, he locked it and went wild, dancing around the room and hugging me in glee. He stripped off his trunks, got out of his cup, and threw them in the corner.

"We did it!" he almost shouted. "Man, we did it!"

"You did it, Kleet. You were great...except for the uppercut. What the hell got into you?"

"He was too confident. I had to make him more cautious. His chin was right there, so I did it! And it worked."

"Yeah, it worked. And I don't ever wanta see you do it again, you hear?"

"Yeah," he agreed, standing there in his magnificent nakedness.

I couldn't help myself. My eyes raked his fine body. He seemed half-aroused. Suddenly, he grabbed my shoulders, whirled me around, and bent me over the massage table. My trousers hit the floor, and he was on me. The entry was painful despite the fact that his cock was coated with his sweat. It felt as if he were splitting me in two. I cried aloud. His hands, still taped, brushed my shoulders roughly, moving down my back and pulling my buns apart, giving him better access. His cock bit deeper. I groaned again.

Then it was all right. He was buried to the hilt; all eight inches were inside me. He withdrew and lunged again. The excitement of the entry behind him, he settled into a rhythm, ignoring the commotion at the locked door as people tried to get past Andy. He fucked me then. He fucked me with a passion, an energy, an intensity I'd never experienced. The few times Bryan had mounted me, he'd almost been apologetic. Not Kleet! He fucked as if he had a right to my ass. He claimed me so totally that I was torn between needing to experience his climax and never wanting it to end. But the end came. He came. He came with an explosion of hard, urgent thrusts and long, hot spurts of semen deep inside my bowels.

Then he pulled me back against his body, and with his cock still inside me, beat my penis until cum poured out onto the table. As my internal muscles contracted, I felt him harden again. He pressed me flat against the table and fucked me unmercifully, beautifully. He fucked me like a man fucks his woman. Like a lover pleasures his *amorata*. Like a bull takes a cow. Like a stallion!

While he showered, I cleaned things and staggered over to open the door. The wounded look in Andy's eyes told me he knew what had happened. There was a crowd of people, mostly cops, behind him, pressing to congratulate their hero of the moment. Kleet came out of the shower naked and unconcerned, shaking hands with each well-wisher before bothering to cover himself with a towel.

All the next week, I expected Kleet to make some move after our training sessions, but it was as if he'd forgotten anything had happened. Andy stayed away from the gym for a few days, and then showed up on my doorstep late one night. "Do me like he did you," he begged.

I did my best for him.

Jimmie Biggs came back, insisting he wasn't strong enough to take over Kleet's training, but he did some nosing around and came up with the fact that the kid's next opponent out of the North Valley District was a southpaw. That was bad news. Everyone hates a southpaw…even another southpaw.

We found a left-handed sparring partner, and even though the boy wasn't that good a boxer, Kleet had trouble with him. The second night, I heard Kleet swear through his mouthpiece as he switched to a left-handed stance. They both had trouble after that, but at least Kleet was landing some punches.

I quickly glanced around the club and failed to spot any strange faces. Not willing to trust to luck, I stepped into the ring and put a stop to the session, loudly berating Kleet about switching stances. He started to give me lip, but suddenly caught himself and accepted my abuse.

Later in the shower room, he saw that no one else was around and turned on me. "You thinking what I think you're thinking?"

"Absolutely. We're going to work later so I can close the gym.

I don't want anybody to see what we're doing. Think John will go along?" I asked, meaning the southpaw sparring partner.

"You bet. Only got another week before the fight, but that's plenty of time."

When Kleet Drum climbed into the ring with Robert Hoya and took up a southpaw stance, the valley cop's strategy was destroyed. Remember, nobody likes a southpaw...even another southpaw. Kleet took the round from his strong, beefy opponent. When he came out for the second round in his regular stance, it took his foe a precious minute to reshape his thinking. By that time, Kleet had landed two hard blows to the body and a clean one to the head. The other fighter was into clinches by then, and the referee didn't like that. At the beginning of the third round, Kleet started falling into his old pattern of four jabs and a hook. When it happened for the fourth time, I could see that the other boxer had caught on. Hell, it was so obvious even Andy saw it.

"You gotta do something!" the boy exclaimed. "Kleet's gonna get clobbered!"

"He knows what he's doing," I said hopefully.

He did. He loosed two vicious jabs and followed with a hook, catching the man totally off guard. Hoya had figured that after two more jabs, he'd slip the hook and catch Kleet off balance. Instead, he landed on his ass and took an eight count. From there on, he fought flat-footed. His legs were gone. Less than thirty seconds later, a straight right put him down for the count.

Andy took up his post before the door without even being told. As soon as the door was locked, Kleet stood still long enough for me to remove the gloves and bindings before stripping us naked and pushing me flat on my back atop the massage table. Standing at the edge, he put my legs on his shoulders and pulled my hips forward, entering me without once taking his eyes from mine.

It was a rush watching him as he fucked me. His confidence was amazing. His technique was more evident this time. He started slowly, built to a tempo that about brought him over the edge, and then stopped to lean forward and kiss me deeply. Then he began again, this time holding my own swollen cock in his hand as he beat himself against me. He fucked without stopping until his eyes rolled up in his head and he shuddered through a tremendous orgasm. Once he recovered, he stroked me to a climax, enjoying once again the massage my internal muscles gave his huge cock when I came. And then, as before, he proceeded to fuck me again.

When we were both exhausted, he stood with his cock still half inside me and leveled the stare boxers use to intimidate others. "You may be a lieutenant, and me just a lowly patrolman, but your ass is mine from now on, you understand?"

"Anytime you want it," I sighed, beginning to regain my breath. "But what about Andy? He's hung up on you, you know."

"Yeah, I know. And I know you've been fucking him, too. Well, we'll just have to figure out what to do about Andy, won't we? But I'm the only guy who fucks you...right?"

"Right, Kleet. Absolutely right!"

RAISE YOUR EXPECTATIONS

Sean Meriwether

It was impossible to escape the gravitational pull of the rest stop on the highway. My Uncle Angus had warned me off the place since I was a kid, reciting cautionary tales of the degenerates he routinely busted there. He had a folder as thick as his waist of all the perps he'd sent up to the Block, and shared them as examples of how I was *not* to grow up. I devoured each case file, memorized their criminal achievements and histories of sexual abuse, both given and received. I stared at their mug shots for hours, internalizing those grainy black-and-white men, trying to uncover their secrets and compare them to my own.

I made weekly pilgrimages to my temple, hiking the five-mile path through the woods separating Kingdom from the highway. I was terrified of being arrested by my own flesh and blood, so I kept my distance, concealing myself behind a screen of trees. I'd watch the men come and go and imagine what clandestine activities occurred behind the innocuous walls. I'd masturbate through my pants, fantasizing about them forcing me into rough acts of sodomy, then squirt in my shorts and run home flushed and guilty, hollowly promising myself that I'd never return.

When I found out my uncle was taking his two boys to Florida over winter break, I nearly came on the spot. I jerked myself raw planning my seven-day orgy, anxious to end the chronic celibacy of childhood with those dangerous men from Uncle's archives.

The night my uncle departed, I begged my father to let me leave work early, noting how slow the funeral home was before the holidays. I ducked out without waiting for an answer, snagging Dad's old parka to help conceal my identity. I jogged down the snowy path, my stomach clenching like a fist. I anticipated a crowd of half-naked men loitering within the men's room, waiting for innocent boys to stray into their path; I'd make a willing accomplice to their crimes.

I ran up to the concrete structure, my shallow breath pumping impotently into the frigid air, and cursed my luck. The parking lot was a tundra of frosted asphalt—there was no one there but me. I clutched my frustrated crotch and inched toward the restroom, holding out the futile hope that it bulged with other men who couldn't afford cars. No surprise that the joint was deserted.

I sidled up to the urinal, unzipped, and awkwardly tugged my erection out of my jeans. I stalled for fifteen fruitless minutes trying to piss. Eventually the cold wilted my cock and my stream rebuffed the silence in staccato bursts. I lingered with my dick out, but only the distant hum of traffic joined me.

I gawked at the elaborate graffiti decorating the walls. There were dozens of images, a how-to guide of homosexuality: a gigantic penis speared another man's mouth, crude legs spread open to reveal the black dot of an asshole, and rocket-ship dicks exploded across the chipped paint. The text introduced the terminology of my imminent sex life: jack off, blow job, hard-on, jizz, bottom, rim job. I ran my eager fingers over the tapestry of male sex, inducting myself into the club.

Unable to resist any longer, I hid in the last stall and jerked off quickly, coating the soiled toilet rim with my virgin seed. The idea that my cum joined a history of male ejaculate got me hard again, and I sent a second smaller volley to join the first. I fought the temptation to wipe it up and hide the evidence, but decided to leave it as a calling card for the next man.

I left unsated, but the promise of the week to come lured me forward and made me wish it was already tomorrow.

The nights evaporated while I sat in the last stall waiting for something to happen. Men would come in, fill the restroom with their noise and stink; sometimes, though rarely, wash their hands; and depart. I'd grown tired of looking at the same penciled drawings on the wall, and brought a pen the third night to add my own plea for contact. As the week trickled away I feared I was destined to die a virgin, and the orgy that had taken place in my mind was never going to be my reality. I flushed the toilet repeatedly and cried out my frustration.

A deep cough from outside sidelined my despondency. "Is that you in there?"

I froze and stared at the graffitied boy's head skewered by the gigantic cock. Was that what this man would force me to do to him? Was I ready for this?

The man moved inside, his shadow inking the concrete floor like an accusing finger. "That you?" He cursed under his breath like Crazy Moe, the town drunk. "Dammit, I'm fucking freezing. Are you in here or what?"

The mug shots raced through my mind; hard and dangerous men with tattoos, greasy hair and missing teeth. I prayed silently for him to go away.

The man moved forward and banged open every stall door; I cringed with each solid report. His reflective shoes appeared beneath my door and his hand slapped against the stubborn surface, straining the cheap lock. "Who's in there, goddammit?"

I opened my mouth to speak, but didn't have enough spit to manage a sound.

"Come on, fucker. Open up." Fingers appeared at the top of the stall, then the tan hat of a cop sunrised over the edge followed by the twin moons of aviator sunglasses. "What the fuck are you doing in here, kid?"

All I saw was cop. He'd know my uncle and tell him everything.

"Did he send *you*?"

I shook my head, no, because I'd been told specifically to stay away. He ordered me to open the door, and I complied instantly. His tan uniform filled the stall, radiating winter. "What's your name, boy?"

"Sev, sir."

"What's that?" He closed in until all I saw was my tiny face reflected in his glasses, echoing my fear.

"Sev, sir. Seven Philips, the mortician's son."

The cop coughed out a laugh. "Waiting for someone, Seven Philips?" My name was a dirty joke in his mouth.

"No…nobody."

The cop dropped his huge hand onto my shoulder and leaned his face into mine; we shared one breath. "Listen you little homo. You wanna get outta this alive?" I nodded compulsively, trying to remember Uncle's advice on dealing with cops. I scanned the guy's uniform.

"You from the Block?" I managed to utter.

He grabbed my coat and tugged me to him. "You want any trouble, faggot?"

"No, officer."

His lips jerked into a lopsided grin. "That's right." He touched the rim of his hat with a firm nod. "I should haul your skinny ass in, you fucking pervert. Lookin' for cock in this here public shit house."

"No, sir, I was just..."

"You were just lookin' for cock," he mocked my whine. He grabbed the front of my coat and dangled me against him like a rag doll. "A buddy'a mine was supposed to meet me here, but you musta scared him off, cocksucker. You're gonna give me your car or I'll haul your ass down to the Block. Pretty kid like you'd be real popular down there. How'd you like that?"

"No, officer."

"No to what?"

I started to droop out of my coat and grappled against his meaty chest for support. "Please don't arrest me, sir."

He snorted over me, spraying me with fetid breath. "You're gonna do what I tell you, right boy?" I nodded as best I could. "Good."

Trouble on the horizon; the distant caterwaul of sirens. More cops who would witness my disgrace. Dry swallow, then "Is that your friends coming?" He dropped me and I toppled onto the toilet seat and smacked my head against the wall.

"*Fuck*. Where's your car?" He scoffed when I told him I didn't own one. "How'd you get here? Fly?"

"I walked. From Kingdom."

He hauled me up and out of the stall, ushered me back into the winter night. "Okay, kid, let's go there."

I led him around the building to the path, retraced my own steps through the snow.

"How far is it?"

"Only a couple of miles."

"*Only a couple of miles*," he minced. He wrestled me for my father's coat, but I jerked away. He drilled into me with his steely eyes and I stripped off the coat and handed it to him. I crossed my arms over my chest and dodged into the woods, moved as quickly as I could over the familiar route. He shouted at me to stop and crashed through the trees to catch up. "You're not losin' me, buddy." He slapped his meaty arm over my shoulder and lashed me tight against him, his bearish breath in my ear. "Now walk." The two of us struggled forward, a four-legged parka on the lam.

After an interminable time, punctuated by the cop's litany of curses and the fading wail of sirens, Kingdom's lights swam into view. Though I felt no safer, returning to familiar ground eased some of my fear and allowed me to think.

"Why are you running away?" I blurted.

The cop tightened his grip on me, his voice an explosion in my ear. "Where the fuck," he pulled me into a half nelson and choked off my breath, "are we going?"

I blinked away green stars and pointed to the funeral home at the end of Broad Street. He relaxed his grip and I leaned forward, barking out bullets of stale air. We moved slowly along the scrubby brush, scouting out the building on our approach. All of the interior lights were off except the electric candles my mother had put in each window for the holidays. The parking lot was empty save for the hearse. I pointed to the side door and we shambled out of the woods and across the deserted back lot.

We stopped just short of the door, the cop urging me to get inside while scanning the woods behind us. I reached back to grab the keys out of the jacket pocket, but he latched on to my hand gruffly. "What are you...?" The keys fell to the mat with a defeated jangle. I bent over to pick them up, my ass halving over his crotch; I broke out in a cold sweat.

I fumbled with the keys and scratched the white paint around the lock before finding the slot. The door opened and he rushed me in, toppling us onto the dusty carpet. My breath squashed out in one huff, my body crushed into the floor. He inched our tangled bodies inside and slammed the door closed with his foot.

His words came hot and low against my neck. “I need a change of clothes and a car to get the fuck outta here.” He reached around my waist and dipped two fingers into the loose top of my jeans; my cock reached out to meet him. “Ain’t no way I’m fittin’ into your skinny shit.”

I stared at the square of light on the wall across from me, the carpet’s bristles warm gravel against my face. “There’s a suit,” I said, mouth dry. “My dad’s.” The cop pressed down harder, his heat burning away the winter chill. Sweat beaded down my back and ticked between my legs.

“Where is it?” His voice was slow and wet.

“In my dad’s office.” Something ground into me as he arranged his legs to trap mine. He lifted his torso up, then quickly squatted on my butt. The cop shed my dad’s parka like excess baggage. He leaned down over me. “Where’s the office?”

“Downstairs. By the morgue.”

Fresh sirens screeched down Broad Street, coming closer. The windows flared with red and blue lights. The cop exhaled roughly, a low whistle through his teeth. “This is a fucking balls-up. No tellin’ how many of them’s after me now.”

The weight of him vanished and I floated, my body cooling where his used to be. He stooped over, grabbed my hand and yanked me up into his arms; we stood like a couple waiting for the music to begin. The cop cuffed me on the back of the head and pushed me down the hallway. “Suit. Now.” I led him into the darkened interior.

"Turn on a fucking light."

"Don't want to let your friends know where you are," I snipped. He snagged my shoulder and wrapped me into his familiar embrace, and forced me down the back stairs. I savored the heat of his body surrounding mine as we descended into the pitch black of the stairwell.

The cop's breath was fast and reedy with panic by the time we reached the basement floor. He relaxed his grip momentarily to wipe his face. I stepped back hard and slipped the lasso of his arm, and dashed around the banister. I flew into the office, his feet pounding a second behind me, and then slammed the door behind me; it reverberated with the impact of his body. "You little motherfucker!"

I inched my way across the office, tracking his slow progress by his breath and curses; he opened the door and fumbled across the wall for the light switch. The fluorescents popped on and blinded us both. I pushed back into the wall as he stomped over to me, arms hard at his sides. Without warning his fist connected with the side of my face, rolling my head. An arc of blood flew from my nose and patterned the white wall. "Don't you ever pull that shit again."

I slid down to the floor, freshly terrified of this powerful man and what he might do. Blood dripped over my lips, my mouth filled with the flat copper flavor.

"Where's the fucking suit?" His brown tie wilted to the floor, his shoes were shucked.

I pointed to the closet where my father kept his spare navy blue suit. He crossed the room, unbuttoning his tan shirt. He opened the closet and dragged the clothes out with a bullish laugh. "What's your dad, an elephant?" He tossed the suit across the back of the desk chair and yanked off his belt.

Someone knocked at the door upstairs; the bark of a police radio produced a chorus of pumped-up voices. The cop eyed me, daring me to make a sound. I stared back at him, wiping the blood from my nose. "Hey, Archie? Arch, you in there?" I shook my head slowly; my father was safe at home. The banging repeated on the side door, which wasn't locked. It was Officer Moon, my uncle's deputy; he'd come in if he had just cause.

"The light," the cop cursed, and dashed out the overhead. Gravely steps ran forward; a flashlight flared in the basement window. The cop grabbed me and pulled me to the floor, his hand covered my mouth. The salty oil of his skin tainted my lips; his sharp odor filled my lungs. The flashlight beam danced around the room, settling on the suit on the chair, then flicked away.

Another volley of sirens Dopplered past and Officer Moon's radio blared with overlapping shouts. He ran off and we were left in booming silence.

The cop settled his weight into me, breathing hard; his fingers forced my lips and teeth apart. I bit down, and he smacked me with his other hand. The side of my head swarmed with stinging stars. His saliva-slicked fingers returned, dug deeper and forced my jaws apart. "Sweet little mouth," he said, daring me to bite him again.

His rolled off and his shadow merged with the darkness, and I lay there as he crossed the room and flicked the light back on. I blinked painfully and he peeled off his shirt to reveal a hairy chest, big pecs and belly swell. He dropped his sunglasses onto the pile, his left eye a purpled halo.

"You're not a cop," I whispered, feeling stupid and in grave danger. I sat up and retreated to the corner.

The man unzipped his pants and stepped out of them, leaving only his socks and white boxer shorts so threadbare they were transparent. The head of his cock peeked out of the slit, and then retreated.

"Never taken a punch before?" He looked incredulous, as if I'd missed a rite of manhood like drinking or fucking.

I shook my head, eyes burning with humiliation. I swallowed a plug of mucous. "You escaped from the Block."

He turned away and rifled through my father's desk. "Got any cash in here?"

"You got what you wanted. Just get dressed and get the fuck out."

He snorted, "Faggot's got a pair, after all." He turned and took a menacing step forward. "I ain't going nowhere till the cops move on, stupid. You better get used to havin' me for company." He returned to my father's desk and upended the drawers, creating an avalanche of paperwork and office supplies.

The man dug through the pile and rescued a half-empty bottle of Jack Daniels. "Here's to your dad," he mock-toasted. He uncapped the bottle and took a long, hard swallow. The whiskey gurgled into his mouth, spilling a trickle down the side of his face. He held the bottle out to me, bridging the gap between us. "Have some."

I remained in the corner, refusing his gesture. He thrust the bottle at me. "Take a fucking drink, kid." I crossed my arms over my chest and approached him carefully, ready to dart back if he tried to hit me again. I took the bottle from his hand, noting the rose tattoo curled in the web of flesh between his thumb and index finger. "Drink it," he insisted, as if dealing with a difficult child. I lifted the bottle to my lips, took a mouthful of brown, and choked it down. A wet cough exploded from my mouth, fire burned a path to my stomach. He laughed heartily. "Nothin' like the first time."

He dropped a hairy arm around me and grabbed the whiskey

out of my hand. He filled his mouth, then twisted me around and pressed his lips against mine. He pushed the warm liquid into my mouth; it spilled down my face and neck. He backed off, laughing. "You're something else, kid." He paced around me, sizing me up. "Never drank, never fucked, never been in a fight. Smoke?"

I lie and nod.

"There's hope for ya' yet. Take off that shirt and shit. You and me's gonna fight." He set the bottle of JD on the floor and approached.

"What?" I backed up into the wall.

"Skinny faggot like you's gotta protect himself."

"You're what I need protection from."

He ran at me and slammed his hands against the wall, trapping my head. "Scared yet?" He jailed me with his blue eyes and tore my shirt; the buttons scattered. He yanked the front of my jeans forward, popping the top button. "These too. Skin on skin. Fair fight." He unzipped my jeans and the loose fabric spilled down my legs.

"Why can't you just leave me alone?" I stared at the purple bruise cradling his eye.

He backed off, indifferently scratched his nuts. "Let's go, kid. Jeans and sneakers off."

I faced the wall and kicked off my sneakers, shamefully stepped out of my jeans—there was no hiding the diagonal of cock in my Fruit of the Looms. I turned to face him.

"Shirt too. Skin on skin."

I dropped the remains of my shirt onto the floor; the cold bristled my pale skin.

"Come here." He raised his fists into a boxer's pose. "Try to hit me, faggot. Just once." He bounced around, his movements athletic but without grace. I shuffled over in my socks.

"No, man. You gotta mean it if you're gonna fight. Get pissed. Then it's just you and him, only two guys in the world. Come on at me, fucker."

I approached skeptically, certain he was setting me up to trounce me, but the more I looked at his smug face, the more I wanted to freshen up that shiner for him. I mirrored his sidestepping dance, my hands up in front of my chest. He threw a gentle jab at my unprotected face. "Keep your hands up, stupid."

He shifted his weight, kept me orbiting around him. I punched air and backed up, moved in and grazed his arm. He replied with a hit to my chest, knocking me back a step. I clenched my fists and dove forward. He deflected my thrusts with his arm, then delivered a killer punch to my stomach. I doubled over and retched.

"Don't stand there like a fucking sissy. Fight back."

I stared up at him through slitted eyes, wanting to pulverize every bone in his body. He continued his verbal barrage; my breath was rapid and shallow, my chest an explosive seconds from detonation. "You little pansy-assed..." I flew at him, punching everything that got in my path—skin, bone, air—a low growl burned through my lips to score the melee. He punched me hard, I hit him back with all the strength I had. Hit and return; pummeled and smashed.

He stumbled back, then leaned in and knocked his head against mine, grabbed me around the shoulders and squeezed so hard I couldn't move. We stared at each other, panting, breathing in each other's sweat, skin on skin.

"Didn't think you had it in you, man." His voice a rough whisper.

Blood pounded through my body, pumping so hard I could feel it moving beneath my skin. Drops of sweat and blood littered the floor between us. My face burned, my lip and nose were swollen, my stomach knotted like I'd done a million sit-ups. His hands locked on my shoulders, pressed down and forced me to the floor. He weaved his hand through my hair and pulled me forward, burying my face in his heated crotch. His dick lurched up through the slit, sweat-slicked and thickening against my face. "Yeah," he exhaled.

I twisted my head and opened my mouth; he stabbed blindly until he found wet warmth. I closed my lips over him, sliding down his shaft, the copper tang of him muting the taste of blood. His odor invaded my nose, filling my lungs with a wet-earthy stench. I bobbed up and down awkwardly, unable to match his thrusts. His hand on the back of my head set the pace. "Watch the teeth," he said and rode my face, my spit slicking my chin and knees. "Shit." Thick fluid filled my mouth, choking me. He withdrew and I fell forward, his cum dripping out of my mouth to join our sweat and blood.

He fixed his shorts as I lay there, feeling guilty and used, conflicted and painfully erect. "Get dressed," he said. He stepped over the debris from my father's desk and picked up the suit. He put on the pants, gathered the loose fabric and tied it off with his discarded belt. He donned the gigantic shirt and the larger jacket, which hid the ill-fitting pants.

I stood and wiped the blood, spit and cum from my face and squared off against him. I approached, stopped short to dig through my father's belongings, and ferreted out a pack of Marlboros and a book of matches. I lit one and coughed, the acrid flavor unable to drown out the taste of his spunk. I tossed the half-empty pack to the man and he caught it with a deft movement. He took one out for himself and lit it, the flame dancing in his flat eyes. We stared at each other, listening for sirens; the world only silence and smoking.

The man dropped the smoldering butt to the floor and

crushed it with the toe of his shoe. "There's a car outside..." he said, half questioning.

I took one last drag and flicked the cigarette at him; it fell short and burned alone in the center of the room. "Keys by the door."

He turned and left, no thank you or threat, no warning of repercussions should I report him to the real cops. I listened to him creak up the stairs, then tracked the heavy tread of his weight across the floor. The side door banged open, slammed shut. I heard nothing for a long time, thinking he wouldn't want a witness, would return to shoot me down in cold blood. Kill me or keep me.

The engine purred into life, revved and idled. I wondered where he would go, who it was he was supposed to have met, what he'd been arrested for. The car jerked forward in a scattering of pebbles and tire squeal, moved out of my range of hearing into the world outside of Kingdom.

I stared at the debris he'd left in his wake: desk items, our discarded clothes, crushed cigarettes. I touched my mouth, the memory of his smoky lips on mine, the spill of whiskey. His slick skin against mine, his cock in my mouth. I jerked off to the smell of his sweat, the muscular arm gripping me, his fist in my face. I came violently, spraying the floor with mute bullets.

I dressed slowly, my body a foreign country of odors and pain. I grabbed the flask of JD and a fresh pack of cigarettes and climbed upstairs. The mess could damn well take care of itself. I picked up my father's parka and pulled it on, feeling that it belonged to a stranger, had been worn by a child.

I stepped into the winter night; it was quiet, deserted and completely mine. I shivered, the cold settling over my bruised skin. I pressed my frozen hands against my face and tried to shift it back into place, remove the damage tonight had wrought there, but it was already too late.

I trailed the black tire marks he'd left behind and crossed to the center of Broad Street, balancing on the tightrope of the faded double yellow lines. He was out there, riding in the night; the flavor of his cock was still alive in my mouth. I ran forward, the pain in my face flaring with each step, frightened I'd never catch up.

HALLOWEEN PICKUP

P. A. Brown

We met in the middle of Santa Monica Boulevard, just outside of Rage. Though surrounded by hordes of other costumed revelers, he still stood out. The Eliot Ness mask covered his entire face, his police cap tilted rakishly forward, shading his eyes. The warmth of the day had lingered well past sunset and he'd taken full advantage of it, going shirtless with only an unbuttoned thin blue uniform jacket with an LAPD shield above his left breast. The jacket did nothing at all to conceal his magnificence. His broad, well-muscled chest was covered with a gorgeous mat of thick, black hair. His stomach was washboard flat and two thick nipples jutted out of his furry pecs. His legs were sheathed in black leather that clung to his rock-solid thighs and displayed a packed basket I longed to explore.

My cock immediately sprang to full mast. Under my own costume of long green leggings it was instantly on display to the whole street. A short, pudgy Tinker Bell eyed it longingly. He stroked my hardness discreetly and murmured, "Top?" When I shook my head—the feathers on my green half-mask fluttering around my face—he departed sadly, weaving through the mass of hot men looking for his own night of pleasure.

My eyes went back to the cop. He had just as clearly not taken his gaze off me. If he noticed what passed between Tinker Bell and me he gave no sign. He crooked his finger at me.

I didn't hesitate. As I stepped in front of him he slipped one big hand up under the tiny green vest that was all that covered my hairless, lasered chest. He suddenly pinched my exposed nipple, sending a bolt of pain and desire straight into my groin. I gasped.

"You like that?" His voice was as deep as I'd expected. It sent a shiver down my spine. "What's your name?"

"Chris." He did the twisty thing again and I thrust my hips forward involuntarily, offering my dick to him. A pair of big-busted drag queens tittered when they saw that.

"Oh, look, Silver, I think this pretty little queen's about to get rammed good."

Eliot Ness glanced at them and smiled with a slow sensuous twist of his lips. But he spoke only for my ears. "That true, queenie? You going to let me fuck you?"

"Yes!" I gasped, wishing we were someplace, anyplace else but here. Alone preferably, but the way I felt right now I wouldn't have cared if he told me to bend over where I stood. I'd probably have done it—and damn the consequences.

"Good," he said, then leaned down and kissed me. Now, I've been kissed at least a million times since I started letting guys diddle me in high school. Maybe a million and two. But I've never been kissed like that.

He took control of my mouth and left no doubt who was in charge tonight. His mouth bruised mine and he forced his tongue between my teeth, savaging my mouth and sending bolts of desire racing along my nerve endings. I swear every hair on my body stood up and electric sparks shot off them.

He drilled me with his tongue and I knew he fully intended to do the same thing to my ass in a very short time. My dick was so hard now it strained against the thin fabric of my tights.

"Move it along, fellas. Get a room or take it home, but get it off the street."

I turned glazed eyes toward the voice and found myself staring up the nose of a very large brown horse. My gaze moved up and encountered an amused and grinning cop.

I was too befuddled to do more than nod. Eliot Ness was a bit more on the ball. Fellow officers and all that. I nearly giggled.

"Of course, officer," Eliot Ness said. "We were just leaving."

The cop nodded and turned his horse around to keep on patrolling the crowd for people having too much fun. I turned hot eyes back to my cop.

"You didn't tell me your name," I said.

"No," he responded. "I didn't."

Then he twined his fingers through mine and led me through the costumed mob.

"Where are we going?" I asked. "I have a place—"

"Not like mine you don't," he said brusquely. "Now stop talking."

I shut up and let this hot cop guide me. A small part of me wondered if I was doing something very foolish. What if this really wasn't a good idea? Was I being too impetuous here?

Finally we broke through the worst of the crowds and my own personal policeman led me toward a silver Acura, unlocking the doors with his remote. I was a little disappointed he didn't have a black and white; that would have really been hot. I dribbled a damp path of precum down my tights at the thought of being fucked in a cop car.

Before I could move around to the passenger's side he stopped me with a hand on my arm.

"I want you to do something for me."

"Wha...what?"

He pulled a black silk scarf out of his back pocket. "Put this on."

Without waiting for my consent—like I could have said no to anything at this point—he slipped the silk over my eyes and secured it around the mask. I was plunged into darkness. Sounds were suddenly magnified—I heard the clunk of the car door opening, the whisper of his leather gear as he guided me inside. He secured my seat belt, sliding his fingers around my hips, brushing my straining dick with the lightest of touches. Seconds later he slid behind the wheel and started the engine. The car smelled of leather and his cologne—Kenneth Cole. My dick throbbed, rubbing with exquisite torture against my tights.

"Where are we going?" I asked.

"Someplace private."

We drove for maybe thirty minutes. Then the car stopped and for a full minute I listened to his harsh breathing. I was beginning to wonder if we were just going to sit there. Was he having second thoughts? I even raised my hands to take off the blindfold, to see what he was doing.

"No," he barked.

Before I could respond he rammed his mouth back down on mine.

We were both gasping for breath when we broke apart. This time I had taken advantage of our seating arrangement to explore the thick outline of his dick through the skintight leather. It pulsed under my eager fingers and I longed to taste him.

Before I could formulate the thought into action he grunted and pulled away from me.

"Not so fast," he growled. "Let's take this inside."

He guided me up a stone walk and unlocked the door, but before I could step through, he grabbed me around the middle and hoisted me over his shoulder. The house smelled of furniture polish, but all I was aware of was the warm smell of his skin and the rough material of his police jacket.

He didn't put me down until we reached a second door, which he also unlocked. Once we were inside, he locked the door behind us—giving me another moment to wonder how smart this was—then he turned on the overhead light.

I know it was overhead because he jerked the blindfold off my face just then.

I stared around the small, carpeted room in awe. I'd never actually been in a dungeon before but I didn't have any trouble recognizing one.

Black leather and black walls created a snug showcase for the *X*-style sling that hung from the equally black ceiling. The walls were arrayed with other bondage paraphernalia—cuffs, chains, butt plugs and dildos of all sizes, and even a black leather cat-o'-nine-tails.

Totally under his spell now, I let him strip me. First he removed my feather-swathed mask, tossing it to the floor. Then he drew off my vest, peeling it from my shoulders and trailing his lips over every square inch of skin as it was exposed. His movements stirred the air; it stroked my superheated skin, brushing me with his tantalizing scent. Kneeling down he skimmed my tights off, but instead of taking me in his mouth like I so desperately wanted, he simply looked, his scalding breath brushing my rigid tool and shaved balls. He stood back up and proceeded to guide me to and bind me into the sling, securing my arms and legs with leather straps, even putting a band around my head to keep it raised and motionless so I wouldn't miss a thing he did to me. I hung at roughly a thirty-degree angle, with my uncovered ass at hip level. The straps held my legs up and open, exposing my pink-rimmed hole to his greedy eyes. The setup was designed to guarantee the Dominant didn't have any strain on his legs while he fucked his submissive. My whole body trembled at the thought of being so completely in this cop's power.

Once I was immobile he began stripping. Leaving on his mask and the police cap, he shed his leather pants first, revealing a cock ring that girdled his monster dick and circled his thick balls. His dick was so hard it bounced against his flat stomach, leaving a smear of precum in his navel. As he worked the uniform jacket off his bulging biceps I could see a steady stream of pearly precum seeping out of his piss slit. His fat, uncut cock head pushed free of his foreskin and I longed to wrap my mouth around it and see if it tasted as good as it looked.

But I couldn't move. Instead he slipped down and rolled my own marble-hard dick between his lips. I moaned as his hot mouth finally engulfed me, sliding all the way down to my straining root. He circled my dick with his velvet tongue, lapping up the leaking fluid, then licked his way between my balls, then probed at my back door, prying my cheeks apart and digging into my ass.

I writhed against my bonds. My hips were twisting, humping his mouth as he ate me. Then he replaced his tongue with two stiff fingers coated in lube. He stretched and probed, opening me up for a much bigger assault.

When he pushed his cock head past my tight sphincter I cried out at the sudden sharp pain.

He reared up over me and jammed his mouth over mine, cutting off my cries. He paused briefly to let me adjust, then wrapped his big hands around my elevated thighs and worked his dick further up my back channel.

We were both drenched in sweat and our harsh gasps filled the black room by the time he finally came to rest with his balls up against my ass.

"Hang on," he whispered hoarsely as he began to move. He held me tight as he steadily began plowing my ass with smooth measured strokes.

That didn't last long. His grip tightened as he began pounding into me. His thick, uncut meat drilled my hole and the only sound in the room was the sharp slap of flesh on flesh and our guttural breathing.

He kissed me again, but the Eliot Ness mask got in the way this time. With a growl he ripped it off and I stared into his familiar pockmarked face. His mouth was hot against mine.

"Oh, David," I whispered.

"Chris, baby, you are so hot," he groaned and lost all control, slamming into me in a frenzy.

His dick throbbed inside me. With a long, drawn out groan he came, filling me with his cum.

I was close behind him, erupting all over my stomach. He collapsed against me, smearing us both with my cum, and only the sling kept us from tumbling to the carpeted floor.

"Hey, stranger," I murmured. "Fancy meeting you in a place like this."

David spread hot, moist kisses over my face and throat. He pulled his softening dick out of me with a faint pop and I sighed at the loss.

It might have been my idea to try out this role-playing, but once David embraced the idea he carried it further than I ever anticipated. I sure as hell hadn't expected anything like this. Granted, since I dragged David kicking and screaming out of the closet, he's grown more and more comfortable with who he is and I'm proud of him. He might be an LAPD homicide detective during the day, but when he comes home to me he's a hot stud with a nearly insatiable appetite for yours truly. And he's more than willing to try new things. But sometimes he surprises even me, and I've been around the block a few times.

I looked around the gadget-filled room. I eyed the handcuffs with more than idle curiosity.

"Next time I get to pick the fantasy," I said, already wondering where I could come up with the gladiator outfits and the Roman bathhouse to go along with them.

"Whose place is this anyway?" I asked. As far as I knew we didn't know anyone into bondage.

David grinned as he undid my bonds, taking me in his arms and crushing me against his burly chest, further distributing my cum over us.

"You'll never believe me," he said.

"Who?"

"Bryan."

"Bryan?" I squeaked. He was right, I didn't believe him. "Uptight, by-the-book, anal Bryan *Williams*?"

"That's the one."

"And you think you know a guy," I said. My eyes narrowed. "Wait a minute. How'd you find out about it?"

"All very innocently." David waggled his eyebrows at me. "We stopped in for a couple of drinks after a particularly nasty bust and he got a little in his cups. Started talking about how he'd paid a small fortune to have the room put in. And how it really added a new dimension to his sex life, which apparently is a lot more off the wall than I ever would have thought."

David's lips began making small forays across my sweaty skin, tickling and arousing me at the same time. "When I asked him if we could borrow it he almost had a heart attack. But he finally came around."

"How long do we have?" I asked, as his dick stood up and pressed against my hip. He reached down to readjust his cock ring.

"As long as we want. He's in San Francisco at a police conference and won't be back till next week."

"Oh, good." I raised my arms. "Let's go for round two." Just before he lifted me up into the sling I reached for his hand and brought it to my lips. "Put the blindfold back on. Let's try something a little bit different."

He was more than willing.

BREAKING AND ENTERING

Dominic Santi

Every time I look at myself, I'm reminded I belong to police Sergeant Antonio D. Virelli. The initials ADV are tattooed in two-inch-high script across my fucking abs. Tony says he wants me thinking about him even when I look in the mirror. That tells you how often I get to wear clothes. Tony says he wants all five foot four of my skinny punk ass naked and ready for him whenever he decides to use me. And I sure as fuck better keep his house clean.

I don't mind the housework. I may be small, but I'm strong and I'm organized. And that fucking heavy black leather uniform belt of Tony's has sure as hell taught me discipline. Although Tony laughed when I told him, I even like the tattoos. They look hot, and just like he said, they remind me I belong to him.

It's wearing butt plugs up my ass all day that's so fucking hard. They're the only way I can get my ass open enough to take Tony's nine-inch cock.

Submission did not come easily to me. I grew up wild and

unsupervised, a loudmouthed street kid with a major attitude toward authority. I knew how to hot-wire cars before I was tall enough to see over a steering wheel. One night last summer, I tried to steal a sporty new job from a deserted parking lot behind the gym. Tony's car. He hauled me out from under the dashboard and whipped my eighteen-year-old ass raw, then threw my sobbing body over his shoulder and hauled me home to feed me—dinner and, when I begged for it, his beautiful cock. Right then and there, Sergeant Antonio Virelli determined to both change my unruly ways and fuck my hungry ass every night until my eyes crossed. In other words, he decided to keep me.

Tony walks in the door from work at 6:15 sharp. And every night, he damn well expects to find me kneeling on the living room sofa, with my head down and my ass high, a tube of lube and a selection of butt plugs next to my knee.

"Good evening, punk," he says, fingering my hole in greeting. Last night, before he said a word, he grabbed my asscheeks in his leather-gloved hands and stretched me wide, letting his first touch be a long, wet, sloppy tongue kiss into my hole. I knew better than to move. I just lay there, panting and gasping, lost in the feel of his touch, as I blurted out, "Welcome home, S-sir. Dinner is almost ready, Sir."

"You're damn right it is," he growled, sucking hard on my asslips. "Think I'll have me a little snack to unwind a bit." He slurped loudly. "Tell me about your day, punk."

I gasped and wiggled, trying to concentrate as he worked my hole.

"Um, I picked up your uniforms from the cleaners, S-sir." I moaned when he flicked his tongue over my asslips. "Th-they got the stains out of your pants, and because I got there early, I got the two-for-one sale price. Unh!" His thick, hot tongue slid deep into me, rooting around while my asslips spasmed uncontrollably around him. As he settled into long, slow tongue-fucks, I whispered, "I did the dishes and made the bed and cleaned the windows today, and I c-cooked manicotti. Oh, Sir!" I shook as he buried his tongue deep and sucked the edge of my asshole. "I wore the plug all afternoon, Sir, just like you ordered, so I'd be ready for you."

"I can tell that, punk," he laughed, standing up and slapping my ass sharply. "I plan on fucking you hard later." He fingered my hole and I squirmed. He sure as fuck knew how much the feel of his gloves turned me on. "I want your tight punk ass loose and comfy on my cock."

I shivered when I heard the lube click open, crying out as a cold stripe of gel fell across my asshole and Tony's warm, leather-covered fingers worked it into me. He took his time, quietly stuffing me full for what I knew was going to come. "You're developing a mighty fine asshole."

I groaned as his fingers lifted, only to be replaced with the tip of a butt plug pressing against my asslips.

"Take it, punk."

I grunted, bearing down like I was taking a monster shit. Tony worked a huge fucking toy into me. It was bigger than the one I'd been wearing that afternoon, but I knew I'd have to take it and more if I wanted to be able to accommodate Tony's cock later. Tony hated having a too-tight asshole squeezing his pride and joy. When my sphincter finally snapped up around the neck, I dropped my head back onto my arms and panted in relief.

"Thank you, Sir," I whispered, trembling as my body struggled to adjust to the burning stretch in my hole. Fuck, I was turning into a size queen. I loved to feel my rectum work to take even a rubber dick. I jumped when Tony smacked my ass again.

"You're learning, punk. Now strip me down. A hungry man's got to eat!"

I was fast as a snake. Even though I felt like there was a tree trunk up my ass, I stood and peeled Tony's clothes off him, baring his fur-covered and thickly muscled chest and arms, unbuckling that heavy fucking ass-beating belt and working his tight uniform pants over his cock and balls.

He hadn't given me permission to suck him, so when his pants dropped to his ankles, I knelt and worked his boots and pants off, trying to ignore the heavenly aroma of man sweat emanating from his crotch each time his leg moved and his balls swung free. I licked my lips, inhaling his scent. Despite the plug, my dick was filling again. When he finally sat down on the ottoman, I threw myself down at his feet. My asshole twitching, I sucked his sweating toes into my mouth, one at a time, and tried to keep from rubbing my cock on the rug. From the corner of my eye, I saw him smile as he patted my head.

"You're doing just fine, punk. Just fine."

I was in heaven. When the kitchen timer sounded, Tony pushed me off him and stood up. Without a word, he slipped into the robe I'd laid out for him. I padded behind him into the kitchen to serve him dinner.

Despite my menial status, Tony lets me eat at the table with him. He says my nakedness and the plug up my ass should be all the reminder I need to let me know who the master in our house is. And he wants somebody to talk to about his day. I've always loved cop stories. I listened raptly, stuffing my food in my face as he told me about subduing some whacked-out asshole on speed and about a huge burglary bust that had finally come down after a multi-unit sting operation. With each bite, I wiggled on the plug, turned on like all fuck by imagining Tony in his uniform, manhandling punks like me, and constantly aware of where his cock was going later. When I'd served him his cheesecake for dessert, I picked up the coffee carafe.

"More coffee, Sir?" I asked, refilling his cup when he nodded. My hands jolted, but I didn't spill when he reached out and lifted my half-hard cock.

"You thinking about getting fucked later, punk?" He took a long, slow sip of the steaming brew, his eyes staring me down over the rim of his cup as he stroked his thumb up and down my shaft.

My asshole clenched at the words. I closed my eyes for a second, mortified to feel my face heating up like some untrained jerk's. "Yes, Sir," I whispered. "I'm really hungry for your dick, Sir."

Tony laughed so hard I thought he was going to fall over. "I just bet you are," he guffawed, setting down his cup. "Damn, but I love an appreciative dick!" He leaned over and sucked the tip of my cock into his coffee-hot mouth. "I may want a taste of this later." Suddenly his hand tightened viciously on my balls. "You spill one drop of that coffee, faggot, and I'll turn your ass into hamburger!"

"Sorry, Sir," I gasped, quickly setting the shaking pot down on the table. I willed myself not to come as he licked up and down my shaft, sucking me when he wanted to, pulling on my balls, carefully working his tongue into my piss slit. I stood quietly beside him, trying to control my trembling while my cock quivered against his lips. He pulled open the front of his robe, ignoring everything about me except my dick as he hefted his huge, furry balls and stroked his swollen cock. Tony worked me with his tongue until I was trembling.

"Nothing like a nice, tasty punk cock to chew on while I beat off," he laughed evilly. I shook as I fought to keep from coming. Just when I thought I was going to lose it, Tony sat back up and slapped my ass again, really, really hard.

"Do the dishes. I'm going in to watch the news."

With that, he pulled his robe closed and stood up, his cock

poking out obscenely in front of him, and left the room. I was left alone, panting, in the kitchen.

I cleaned up in record time. As I loaded the dishwasher, I tried to concentrate on what I was doing, but my cock kept getting in the way and the pressure in my asshole had me completely distracted. All I could think about was how pretty soon, Tony was going to yank that fucking plug out of my ass and stuff his huge dick up me. I wondered if he'd touch my cock again, or if he'd make me beg him to fuck me so hard I'd come without touching myself.

I couldn't wait to find out. As soon as I finished I hurried into the living room. Tony was sitting on the couch, his robe open again, stroking his meat at he stared at the TV. I stood stock-still next to him, awaiting his next command. Without saying a word, he leaned forward and started sucking my cock, his eyes never leaving the basketball highlights as he again jerked his dick. Fuck, oh fuck, his tongue felt good.

At the commercial break, he leaned back, his eyes still on the TV, and snapped his fingers once, pointing toward the couch. My legs shook as I quickly assumed my usual position on the cushions: my feet next to his leg, my ass in the air, and my head down on my arms. Tony didn't say a word, just reached over and started tapping the base of the plug. He played with it all through the weather report, pulling it back and forth and to the side, then suddenly yanking it out and stretching me even further with his fingers as they slid into me—three, then four of his long, thick digits sinking deep into my ass. His fingertips settled on my prostate and he started rubbing, all the while working globs and globs of lube deep into my ass.

"Guess who nabbed those asshole burglars they're talking about," he snickered, his thumb stroking an echoing rhythm through my perineum. "Talk about punks."

I forced my eyes open and glanced at the list of upcoming features: *Burglary ring broken by highly decorated patrolman.* I shuddered at the sensation in my ass as Tony's face filled the screen.

"That's you!" I cried out. Tony pressed hard on my hole. A hot stream of juice oozed from my dick.

"You fucking right it's me. Get up, punk!"

I struggled to my feet, Tony's fingers still buried up my ass. My cock waved toward my belly, deep red and dripping. Tony stood me in front of him facing the TV, with my back to him. I shuddered when I heard the wrapper tear open.

"Sit!" he growled.

Shaking with anticipation, I straddled his legs and slowly sank down onto his lap. Tony's fingers slid from my hole and his hands gripped my asscheeks, holding them painfully open as my trembling sphincter kissed the head of his huge latex-clad dick. Then he was guiding me to him, pulling me down mercilessly onto his rigid pole of dick.

"Take it, punk."

I yelped, shuddering, as his huge fucking dickhead popped in.

"Don't fight me, punk. Kiss my dick with your asslips like you know you're being fucked good."

"Yes, Sir," I whispered. It hurt. Oh fuck, it hurt. I felt like I was fucking his nightstick or a baseball bat or a fucking fire hydrant. Tony's dick burned and it stretched me, and fuck, I wanted it! The room echoed with the sounds being torn from my throat.

"That's it, punk," he growled, holding me tightly to him when my asscheeks finally ground against his pubic hair. "Nothing like a hot, loose punk pussy to make this cop's dick twitch." He gripped my hips and lifted me, fucking me hard onto his dick, over and over again, until my guts felt like they were being pounded to mush. I let the cries of ecstasy roll from my mouth. When he paused to catch his breath, I pressed back against him, groaning, desperately seeking more.

"Watch the TV, asshole."

I shuddered as he hugged me close, his hands stealing up to grab my nipples. The sensations from my asshole washed over me as he twisted and pinched.

"Jerk your dick, punk."

My hand shook so badly I almost couldn't lift it. I cried out, the sensations overwhelming me when my hot, sweaty hand closed around my throbbing shaft. Tony's strong hands again lifted me and fucked my sore, swollen, horny ass over his cock.

"This is what punks should do with their asses."

I was vaguely aware of Tony's voice on the TV. I opened my eyes to a shot of him standing over three prostrate burglars, his partner holding a gun on them as Tony roughly kicked their weapons aside and cuffed them, while the news helicopters hovered above. Then his face filled the screen as he gave the post-action interview.

"You learned, punk," he growled in my ear. He twisted my nipples savagely, arching his dick so far into my ass I felt it in my spine. "A good job and a good fuck keeps you off the streets, right asshole? Keeps you here where you belong!"

"Yes, Sir. Please, Sir. Please!" I begged, frantically jerking my cock and grinding back against him, writhing on his dick. My eyes were glued to the TV screen, watching Tony's lips move for the cameras. He buried himself deep up my ass, his pulsing cock stretching my ravaged hole. My ears rang as he roared out his climax. His balls emptied into me and I howled, my cock spurting wildly as my asshole sucked him deep, my ass muscles clutching his monster cock and convulsing around him. Then my legs collapsed and I fell back into his arms, unable to support my own weight. I closed my eyes and trembled against him.

The news had been over for a long time when Tony finally clicked off the remote. He laughed softly as he reached up and tweaked my sore nipples.

"So, that's better than breaking and entering, huh, punk?"

My asshole spasmed contentedly, still stretched wide over his softening cock. I snuggled into his arms. "Yes, Sir. Thank you, Sir."

"Get me a cigar, punk," he laughed, pushing me off his lap, "then get back into position. I have some reports to do and petting your open hole helps me concentrate." He reached for the stack of papers on the end table. "It's going to be a long night."

My punk ass and I were looking forward to it.

MOBY

M. Christian

Yessir, the good folks around these here parts are particularly struck by the telling of a good tale. Some like to say that it's 'cause we've not—how shall I say?—"misplaced" how to sit a feller down and spin out a damned good yarn. Others though, they like to gesture toward those there damned high and awfully wooded peaks and say that it's got more to do with the fact we all got shit-poor TV reception.

Like any collection of folks—that is, folks who knows how to put the right collection of words together to spin out a handsome yarn, or got more than snow on the local tube—we've got a few we like to tell a bit more than others. Like the one about how Old Uncle Conti done helped Miss Oleander birth her seven little young ones in the middle of that awful thunder and lightning show we had back in '60; or that time Crazy Jeb got too big a taste of the shine and went on his rather reckless excursion with Huge Henry, Mr. Larkin's bulldozer; or even when Old Jeb at the Dry Goods found himself at the business end of a shotgun in the hands of that no-good eldest Barnaby boy, and how he done turned the tables on that no-account without being able to see his wrinkled old hand in front of his dead blind eyes.

But there's no one we like to chew the fat about more than that Beast of the Highway, our Monster of Road, the Legendary Creature of the Blacktop.

Yeah, that's him, that's the man—if *man* could be quite the word to describe him. It'd be more accurate to call him a force of nature, or say he's like a tiger someone done educated enough to stand up on his hind legs, a cyclone wearing size-sixteen boots, a motorcycle-riding fiend from the deepest, darkest depths of your wildest nightmares. That's Moby.

Moby, we like to say, ain't just big, 'cause that makes anyone who'd never had…funny, but I was just about to say "the honor to see him," but you know that sure is not right, 'cause anyone who done seen Moby sure as shit would not call it anything like an honor. No sir. But anyone who has laid eyes on him would have to say that *big* just ain't the right word. Three little letters just ain't enough to describe the heights of the man. They say—and I can neither agree with such nor deny it for I've never seen such a thing myself—that Moby ducks his head so as not to hit a sun hanging low, on its way to setting; or that he's able to reach up and tire a peaceful looking cloud into a righteous twister with just the twirling of his finger. Yeah, I know that's tall for even a tall tale, but I'll tell you friend, I have seen Moby myself and I can not only say that it was not any honor, but that he's taller than even the tallest tale I or anyone else could ever tell.

Another thing that people who meet the Hog Rider from Hell say about him is—well, how could I say this, being we all in polite company? Let me put it this way, the man has a presence that announces his imminent arrival even before the ground starts to do its shake and shimmy from his size-sixteens crushing down on the hardest-packed asphalt, crushing good cement to powder, cracking stones like walnuts. Moby—and to be right straight with you there really ain't no way to say this and retain civility—has a hellish fragrance. Wherever he rides, he leaves a rooster tail of reek, a hurricane of stink, a billowing cloud of stench. I've heard it described in all kinds of ways, from the sweat off a bull's balls—and I did say there was no polite way to say it—to May Tilly's septic tank on a hot Saturday afternoon in the middle of summer. And if you know the kind of seasons we have in these here parts, and you know May Tilly, you would know that he's truly a hideous proposition in regards to fiendish aromas.

The only thing said to be more potent than Moby's emissions is the strength that courses through the big-ass muscles that you can clearly see knotting and cording around his mountainous biceps and hydraulic thighs. Some say that he's strong enough to bend quarters twice, making two bits into four bits, just between thumb and forefinger. Others like to point out how he parks that roaring hog of his: no backing and forwarding for Moby, no sir. Instead, the biggest of the big and strongest of the strong, he instead finds himself the perfect old spot to put his chrome- and grease-dripping machine and he just lifts it up in one brawny hand and drops it down right where he wants it—and what with the power of those arms and that stink, it's just about anywhere he reckons to.

Now Moby, he's quite a lot of other things—more even than his size, his aroma, or his brawn—but those are what you might call other kinds of observances, less on the great list of tales that folks like to tell about the biker. But there's another thing about Moby that's right there up on the top, even greater than his cloud-rippling height, his eye-watering stink, or his ground-shaking muscles. But for that one I've got to give you a little bit more than some homespun metaphors and back-porch similes. For that I've got to sit you right down—you comfy now?—and spin you a downright special tale, the one I like to tell more than any other about that leather monster, that motorbike hurricane, that beast on two tires.

For that I've got to tell of the time Moby came barreling down to our sleepy little town, needle tapping out a high-octane, fuel-injected rhythm against the top of his speedometer, rumbling engine like the four-stroke from hell. Fast? He was way more than fast, friend. You could even say he'd just left *fast* way behind, past blasting through *quick*, leaving *breakneck* in his dust.

That day is the one I'm talking about. The day he come through—and the day a certain officer of this here municipality decided that he'd had quite enough of this hog-riding, quarter-folding, reeking tower of a man. This, you see, was the day he decided to give Moby a speeding ticket.

Who knows why he done it? When we get just a smelliest bit tired of telling tales about Moby, someone or other will bring up that day, and ponder over some shine and a smoke just what did possess that certain Officer Langtry to take it into his head to bang his own motorcycle to life and take off in pursuit of the demon. Jeb over at the old Wicker place likes to say that the sun that day must have cooked his brains into something that may very well have resembled grits, while Miss Barlow is more given to the theory that the only thing that could explain the whys and wherefores of that pursuit of Moby is that Langtry's family tree must have had some very shallow roots.

They say what they say, friend, but I can tell you for a fact that no one, least of all that officer of the law, knows quite why he did it. But he did it—he sure as hell did it.

Right up there with the whys and wherefores of Officer Langtry's darned earnest pursuit has to be another important element to this tale of his meeting with the Moby—in other words, why in the heavens above and hell below did that Harley Davidson maelstrom look behind, clearly see the flashings and the wailings of the law behind him, pull over, and—puzzle of mysteries, strangeness of weirdness—*stop*?

But he did. He did. Right over there in fact, at the fork where the main thoroughfare curls off toward River Road, by that very same gnarled old pine. That's just where Moby glided that chrome and greasy machine to the side of the road.

Who could say what Officer Langtry thought when that happened? More than likely a sense of some kind of professional satisfaction that it was his lights, his siren that did what no one else had done. That his own bike, his own authority, had reached out to the bad craziness that was Moby and reined in that wild biker bull. But just as there was a smile on his handsome young face, you have got to know that riding right along with him was more than a bit of the old stomach clenching, jaw tightening thing you and me and everyone on this whole darned world call *fear*.

But Langtry was *Officer* Langtry, more than he was young and handsome, and for him that was enough to relax that jaw, calm that stomach, and steady his racing heart. He had his badge, the authority invested in him by his good little town, this right honorable state, and this glorious nation—and he wasn't going to let no legend, no big, smelly, or even strong biker blast through his quiet little world without paying the price for his reckless disregard for those laws of town, state and country.

And with that authority in him like a good belt of something smoky and well aged, but with a kick like a mule who woke up on the wrong side of the barn, he glided his own two wheels up next to the biker, killed the engine with a quick twist of the wrist and dismounted.

It would be honest to say that at that moment in his young life on this planet Earth spinning through space, that officer of this here town, state and good ol' wonderful country, even with the badges and nifty uniform and let's not forget that pearl-handled, brushed-chrome Smith and Wesson dangling there at his hip—Officer Langtry—couldn't have been more terrified. This was Moby, people, and don't you forget it. His rough-hewn brows parted the clouds all up on high, tufts of them vanishing like the steam over the old sawmill the day they shut it down; his hellacious aroma curled every single nose hair in the vicinity and caused more than a few pigeons to drop from that summer sky in shock as he climbed off of his grease-glimmering motorcycle. It is said by more than just me, your humble storyteller, that there is nothing more important to Moby—not putting the fear of hideous death in the minds of the citizens of this region, not the destruction of road and all wildlife foolish enough to attempt to cross it, not...other even more fiendish activities I will not even dare to mention for there are ladies here at present—than that motorcycle. And so to put it aside from even the most casual of damage, heaven help anyone who would do such a thing, he demonstrated another of his Moby attributes and lifted it up off the ground with one mighty flex of an arm and put it down as neatly as a mother putting her youngest to bed.

Fear or no fear, terror or no terror, dread or no dread, Officer Langtry of the Town Constabulary was invested with all the powers of the previously mentioned town, state, and wonderful country and as such he had a duty to perform, a higher order if you will, a task that no one in the history of the history of this town, this state or even this here country had ever managed to accomplish: he had to give the dreaded hog-driving beast of the End Times a ticket and that's what he was going to do.

And as such, there were—shall we say rituals?—that had to

accomplish the giving of a Motor Vehicular Citation for Excessive Velocity On a Municipal Thoroughfare, Payable to the Officer himself or via the Local Courthouse, and Officer Langtry wasn't about to simply shake in his boots (even though he was) and twitch his hands (even though they were) and just, simply, only hand the huge, smelly, strong biker a Traffic Ticket.

And so, even through his shaking and twitching, hoping the fear he felt did not leak out through his manner of speaking, Officer Langtry walked forward, stuck his thumbs in the belt loops of his uniform pants and said in his best Law Enforcement parlance: "Do you have any idea of how fast you were going?" I should mention to all of you that to complete the aforementioned ritual correctly, there is the insertion of a word at the end of that there sentence to fully convey to the perpetrator to whom a law enforcement officer is speaking that they are truly in the prescience of a formidable authority figure. But while Officer Langtry had those many levels of authority—and I will not try your patience by reciting Town, State and Country once again—he was still in the looming, mountainous, aromatic, Herculean and smelly presence of Moby and so, possibly wisely, did not conclude his statement of "Do you have any idea of how fast you were going?" with the word *boy*.

To this, and the absence of the word so often used by members of the law enforcement community, Moby replied with stony silence.

"Well, I'll tell you how fast you were going," Officer Langtry continued. "You were in excess of the posted limit by more than fifteen miles per hour. That's breaking the law, and there are penalties for the breaking of our laws. Harsh penalties, some might say."

To this additional commentary from Officer Langtry, Moby also did not reply.

"I say to myself that no penalty is too damned harsh that'll keep the streets of our fair city safe from reckless no-goods like yourself who seem to think that every road is their road, or that stop signs are just a suggestion."

Again, there was only tall, strong, stinky quiet from Moby.

"That's right, you heard what I said. I opened this here mouth and called you a 'no-good,' and by the Lord Above and the Laws of this fine town, noble state, and great country, I stand by that statement for, Mister, I can tell just by laying eyes on you that I may in fact have been more than necessarily polite in my description."

Moby only repeated his silence, eyes showing nothing but a steely glimmer.

Now your more perceptive listener might be thinking that our Officer Langtry might be more than slightly putting his size-twelve official shoes over the line between what a law enforcement officer should be saying and what any person who knows of the biker called Moby would say. In this I would have to say that those who are thinking such thoughts are completely right in wondering such, for even Officer Langtry himself was no doubt engaged in the back of his brain wondering just such. But the words were there, coming out before he could even stop himself, one after another like bubbles coming up from a glass of cool beer, and just like you can't put your finger through the foam and stop them from coming up to the top, neither could Officer Langtry stop himself from saying the things he wanted to say, and probably many folks have wanted to say to that monster of the motorbike for a good many years.

"Just look at yourself, son. Take a damned long, hard look at yourself. You call yourself a man? A beast, more like. Big, sure as shit you're big. Strong—that too. Muscles all rippling and moving under that tight denim vest, calves like tree trunks under those jeans, chest like mom's old washboard, hands the size of one of Old Mrs. Gator's prize sows. And the stink, Lordy, don't get me started on your foul emissions. That's the worst of all, I say; the bottom of the barrel. Get rid of the reek—and once again I can only think of one of Old Mrs. Gator's hogs, and you might, and I do say 'might', come out the other end of such scrubbing and cleanliness to be a halfway respectable sample of...masculinity."

Moby stayed quiet as an owl flying across a deep night sky, but while he did not say anything, his face spoke through the raising of one eyebrow.

"It's not too late, son. You're still not on the other side of that hill. You could be something, do something with your life aside from pissing people off and scaring the local inhabitants. Clean yourself up some, get yourself some kind of respectable form of transportation, settle down with some...girl, I guess. Do you really want to go on down the road you've been driving, end up in jail for the rest of your years or maybe dead on the side of the road somewhere, like some stinking skunk too slow or dumb to get out of the way of two pair of radials?"

Nothing again from the biker, nothing but stone silence. But his hands, great monster mitts with fingers the size of extra-large sausages made from the best of Old Mrs. Gator's prize pigs, dropped down to his waist.

"Hold it right there, son—you just hold it right there. No sudden movements now. You keep your hands right where I can see them or you're going to find out, right personally, just how fast I can draw this here gun and put a thirty-eight slug right in your well-defined chest."

But Moby did not stop, not at all, and all the time he did not speak as did not stop. Hands to his waist, thick, beefy fingers forward, a twist of the thumb to push aside a narrow strip of road-filthy denim, then a pinch of zipper and down.

Down, as they say, and out.

Smelly, it has been said, by myself as well as many others who like to talk about the biker known as Moby, is the stink that follows, making even the foulest of smelling creatures run for cover. Strong, it has been stated, like bear, like a bull, like a 4x4 truck, a locomotive, and any other thing that might come to mind when you think about things that can lift, push, or pull really heavy things. Big has also been mentioned; that when he walked, birds and light aircraft were known to move out of the way of his towering immensity, that his shadow has been known to fall across county after county stretching far out yonder.

But I have yet to hear anyone else talk about Moby's…manliness.

There's no other way to say it, ladies and gentlemen, and so I have to beg your humble apologies for having to be so blunt about such matters but there really is no way to continue to tell this tale of Moby and Officer Langtry without using words that will no doubt offend some of us with their coarseness. I shall put my all into trying to use some terminology, shall I say, that will singe rather than burn the ears of some of my more sensitive listeners. To remove the shock of such words for you long before they happen to appear in the telling of this tale, I am going to put them out into the air right this very moment. You all ready now? Prepared and cautioned enough for this? Well, then here you go, in regards to the part of Moby that hangs well below his knees, I shall call it his: privates (because that part of a man is just that), willie (because I had a pal by that name), old friend (because I dare you to find a man who doesn't feel at least that fondly for that part of himself), dick (because I had another pal with that name), manliness (as I said before), and penis (because that's what it is).

And there it was, right in front of Officer Langtry on that warm summer day. In all its...well, now, I was about to use the word *glory,* but that's not exactly what would be an accurate description of that there biker's privates.

Because, good listener, this intimate part of Moby's anatomy reflects much of what we've all learned about the man, and none of that anyone, least of all myself, would call by that Churchlike word, *glorious.*

See, upon the opening of those greasy, torn-up jeans, a powerful reek of oil, sweat, farts, and other foul body emissions wafted forth, befouling the otherwise ordinary smells of that day. Like an animal in rut he was, with that kind of aroma flowing out of his pants and into the atmosphere.

Then there was that other aspect of the man, the muscles and lifting, the sinews and strength, the brawn and potency, that was reflected in that awesome willie. Men know that sometimes the spirit may be ready to perform its duties but the flesh may be more than occasionally drunk and weak, but not for that biker, and definitely not that day.

Now if I were a coarse gentleman, I would stroll off into perhaps a bit overly long description of the biker's manhood, going into some too-exact details such as how the veins along the length of it pulsed and quivered with primal juices of pure animal lust, or how the end was as big and hard as the ball on top of the flagpole in front of our beloved town hall, or how the entire flashy assemblage seemed to be as long and as steely hard as that very same flagpole. Or maybe I'd mention, casual like, how from the tip of that mightly manliness a gleaming bead of anticipatory emissions had started to form. But, like I said and continue to defend, I am not a coarse or rude man so I won't be saying anything such.

Then there was the fact that like the man himself, Moby's... extension was just such a thing. Big, you see, doesn't touch on the immensity of the organ that emerged from the man's fly. If you think of such things, kind of ponder how big something like that could get, I can bet you dollars to doughnuts that you will not even come close to the prodigious measurements of that man. After all, he is not called Moby for just the whale of his size, but rather the whale size of the last part of his particular moniker, the word that follows Moby—I speak of course, of Dick.

Now as to what the long arm of the law thought about the appearance of that certain part of Moby's body...well, you could guess and would guess right that the man was rightfully shocked by the accusing arm of the biker's privates, jutting out at him from his fly. So, to the appearance and the appurtenance's owner, Officer Langtry—an arm himself of the law and what he hoped then and there was bigger than the penis of the dreaded Moby—coughed quickly and managed to sputter out: "You p-put that thing away right now, son, or I'll have your ass rotting in jail before you can say fucking 'Jack Robinson.' "

At this Moby maintained nothing but stony silence, though he did move, just a bit, to wrap one of those Mrs. Gator ham-sized fists around the thick length of his dick.

Officer Langtry still managed to say: "Now you stop right there. I'm only going to tell you once, put that damned big... hard...thing away. You do it right now or you're going to be spending more than just one night in my less than comfortable can...I mean jail."

Quiet again, no words—not a lone one—from Moby, but the beast did move his fist up and down the length of his old friend, a bright gleam in his nasty eyes.

"I'm telling ya again, you put that thing...that thing...away or I won't be accountable for what might happen," Officer Langtry said, licking his suddenly dry lips.

Still not a word from the huge biker, who was still lazily committing the sin of Onan standing out there in broad daylight on the main road.

"Yeah, might not...know...what could happen," Officer Langtry said, words getting all soft and sensitive like. Then it happened, folks, the thing that shocked him just as you're going to be shocked by my telling of it. You see, Officer Langtry was one of those fellers who thought he was right with himself, comfortable in the house of his life, you know? He knew just where everything was, and why it was there. His ma and pa, his work, what he liked to do on Saturday nights, his favorite sit-down meal, his favorite stand-up eating, the movies he liked, the tunes he listened to, the books he liked to read—but that sunny summer day, the day he pulled over the biker called Moby, he came to realize that while he knew what went where in the house of his mind, there was a whole other room in that house he didn't even know existed.

In that room there were two folks, Officer Langtry and Moby. Moby was just as he was there, standing with his dick out, hand around it, but here is the shock, what made that room so much more different than any other room in Officer Langtry's mind, because in that room Officer Langtry was there as well, but on his knees with Moby's penis in his mouth.

Now don't say I didn't warn you, don't you dare say I didn't prepare you for what I definitely said was a shock. Don't you go opening your eyes all wide or putting on some swoon or other. But I do understand just how much of a remarkable thing this is to hear and so I'll give you all a bit of time to sort yourselves into a state where you can actually understand what I'm going to be telling next.

Ready? You sure now? Well, then I shall continue.

So there they were, the biker and the cop, the biker with his dick out and all aroused like, and the cop who wanted nothing more in this big old world than to drop down to his knees and start sucking at that pole of manhood like a calf working his mamma's teat.

Now things would have been great, for the cop that is, for Officer Langtry, if that's what would have happened. Now I'm not one to say what one does for pleasure and all that. I'm what you'd call a churchgoing fellow but I don't think the Lord Above would fault one person for doing something mutual and fun, for the lack of a better word, between himself and even another himself. God is Love, am I right? And love can mean lots of different things to different people. So I'm not saying that what Officer Langtry wanted to do to that big, smelly, strong biker that day was a bad thing. No, sir, I am not saying that. Because I know for a fact, as one man can know anything, that sucking on that man's penis was the only thing in this wide world that Officer Langtry wanted to do at that moment in time and that his desire was good and true and free of any kind of game or cruelty. Officer Langtry, you see, had looked into that room he didn't know he'd had in the house of his soul and he realized that it was a room he wanted to spend a lot more time in, a room of love—even if it was a room of man with man love. It was still love.

But what happened next was not love, no sir. In no way. What happened next was the height of cruelty to man, an act of pure mean. Because you see, this is something else a lot of folks know about the biker called Moby, a thing right up there with his towering height, his awesome strength or his offensive aroma. You see beyond all that, Moby is one thing, one thing even more powerful than his muscles, greater than his height, even more overwhelming than his stink.

Moby, you see, is pure mean.

How mean is he? Well, I could go on for hours at a stretch telling you the various and sundry acts of cruelty this man (to be polite) has enacted upon his fellow beings on this globe, but none would say it as well as telling you all what the biker did to Officer Langtry that day, a single action that would hurt that man most of all, rub him down deep in the ground and harm him in ways that no physical injury could ever go.

For, dear listeners, what Moby did that day was to smile his most vile of grins, fold away his hard and pearl-beaded manliness, get on his bike, kick it to life, and thunder off down the highway—leaving Officer Langtry there alone on the side of the road, mouth hanging open for the dick he'd never have, an act so mean, so cruel, so vile it was like someone taking a righteous bowel movement in the room the officer had just that moment discovered within himself.

That's my story, people—and everything that happened that day between the two of those men, the peace officer and the biker. The honest man who discovered something new about himself, and the biker who was meaner than them most rabid of dogs. I wish I could say that things ended well, but to be honest with you, I can't say such. Officer Langtry, yes, did discover a new way to spend his Saturday nights, a new kind of physical affection to share with his fellow man, but that day still burns in his soul, that rejection and humiliation by the side of the road.

How do I know this? Well, friend I am pleased to make your pleasant acquaintance. Langtry's the name, Officer of the Local Constabulary. Who, after all, would know such details of that day other than the man who was involved?

And Moby? Well, to this day you can see his head towering over the tallest of trees, feel the thunder of his hog as he roars by, smell his deep beastly stink as he passes, and hear his bellowing laugh as he continues on his journey from one cruel and heartless act to another.

Tall, strong, reeking; but most of all pure, absolute, horribly mean, is that biker Moby. Most of all. Most of all.

WALKING THE BLUE LINE

Vincent Diamond

You never know what you're gonna hear when you're eavesdropping. It could be anything: the innocuous plans of a domestic duo, a hushed confession, a quick make-out session.

A low-voiced threat.

A Sunday morning, probably six o'clock or so. The rave was over, the partiers taking off in loud cars, their engines gunning and tires squealing as they left the warehouse in downtown Jacksonville. Up in the warehouse office, I heard the thump of equipment cases being slammed shut, imagined some of the guys squatting and hefting the big speakers from the four corners of the room. I should have been down there; it was my job to be humping some of that weight but I was *so* tired.

Tired of doing these damned all-nighters. At twenty-eight, I looked young, all blond hair and boyish features that let me get away with infiltrating a college dorm—or a ravemaster's street crew. But I was in over my head on this undercover op—and floundering.

That morning, I was on the sofa in the warehouse office and I heard the door rattle open. Jason's voice, a little breathless and high-pitched, and then Conrad's murmuring, low as a foghorn, sexy as hell.

Jason was one of the kids who hung around the crew. Barely out of high school, with a kid's swath of acne across his forehead and a wispy goatee. He had a crush on Conrad that was nearly painful to watch. Fixing Conrad's cranberry juice drinks, making sure the DJ booth was swept clean, rubbing Conrad's shoulders and neck if Donalita wasn't around and, sometimes, even if she was.

I lifted my head and could see them through the tangle on the equipment table and boxes stacked around the room. Jason grabbed Conrad's hand and did a twirl under his arm, giggling, off balance.

Conrad spoke, his deep voice solemn. "Jason, you are stoned, my man."

"I'm not!" Jason stumbled against Conrad's broad chest, laughing.

"Did you have a little party tonight with Marcos?"

"Maybe." Jason shrugged and pressed closer. "Maybe not."

Conrad put both hands on Jason's head and held him still. "I told you about that shit. You shouldn't be messing with Marcos and his supplies."

"Screw Marcos."

"No thanks." Conrad smiled.

"Then how about me?" Jason surged upward and planted his mouth against Conrad's. "Please, I love you so much, Conrad. I just wanna be with you."

Conrad elbowed him back. "Whoa, whoa. Jason, stop." He forced Jason away from his body and I saw the tent in Jason's pants. The poor kid was higher than a kite and as hard as a statue.

"Come on, I know you're not for real with Donalita; that's just for show."

"Maybe, maybe not. Either way, it's not something for you to worry about."

"She doesn't love you."

"I think you're right."

"*I* love you, Conrad."

"And I love you too, baby Jay." Conrad's words, soft as a feather. Hearing that made my stomach clench.

"Not like that. I really do love you." Jason angled inside Conrad's grip and kissed him again. Seeing that made me stir, knowing how soft Conrad's lips were, how hard his chest was. It turned me on, seeing two guys together like that.

"Jay, babe, no. No more."

"Please!" Jason tried to squirm closer but this time Conrad held him back.

"Enough. Get outta here. I need you to pack up the mixer for me; I don't trust anybody else. Check that the files aren't messed up, okay?" He swatted Jason on the ass and pushed him toward the door. Jason protested but settled for a clench of hands. His heavy sneakers thumped down the metal stairs.

Conrad stayed at the door for a minute, cracking his neck and easing his shoulders up and down, a broad target.

The Jacksonville police department had focused on Conrad Stalton for this op. He was a bulked-up, shaved-bald ravemaster who deejayed illegal street dances and—we suspected—fronted a team of drug runners who operated from Miami to Raleigh. I'd spent the last few weeks out at clubs all night, making the raves, drinking with the crowd, trying to worm into Stalton's good graces.

And pants. Again.

A week earlier, Conrad and I had had a close encounter of

the belly-rubbing kind, right here, on his mixing table. He'd kissed me like a storm. I was enthralled with his wide shoulders, his smooth chest, that caramel-colored skin. It was just a quickie, nothing special, except that he was the first man I'd ever touched, ever kissed, ever—wanted.

I tried to tell myself that it was part of the job, a way to get close, to get the intel we needed to make a bust. That little meeting didn't make its way onto my weekly report, but it replayed in my head, over and over. At night I jerked off, thinking about Conrad's full lips and ripped arms; in my dreams he bent me double and mornings, I woke up with wetness on my belly.

Plus, I liked the guy. A mutual appreciation for old American muscle cars, late-night rides to the beach, and mixing killer versions of new house music interspersed with riffs from Perry, Page and Hendrix let us spend hours together. We had fun. Dammit.

Conrad turned and stalked over to the mixing table. He punched a button on his cell phone, then set it on the table while he stacked up some CDs. A couple of rings came through the speakerphone setting, then Marcos was on the line, his voice froggy and gruff. "Whassup?"

"I just had a little chat with Jason. Did you set him up tonight?"

"What's it to ya?" In the background, some female giggles and the faint hum of traffic.

"I told you I don't want you expanding your customer base with my crew."

"Demand and supply, Conster."

"I mean it, Marcos. No more. Not with the kids."

"He's got the money, honey. And I've got the juice."

Conrad ran his palms over his bare scalp. It dragged his eyebrows back, pulled his face into a tigerish snarl. "Leave him alone!"

"Aaawww, is he your little homeboy now? Geez, Conrad, haven't you learned? Don't get attached. Blow 'em and throw 'em!"

"It's not like that. And it's none of your fucking business anyway." Conrad's face was flushed and I saw him clenching and unclenching his fists.

The voice on the phone turned low and ugly, throaty with menace. "Fuck you, Stalton. You keep the hell out of my business and I won't tell you how to run yours. Deal?"

There was a click and the phone went dead. Conrad stared at the phone, its blank hum buzzing in the office, his face twisted and angry. He thumbed at the cell phone, too hard, and sent it spinning onto the floor with a tinny clatter. "Shit!"

When he bent down to pick it up, he spotted me on the couch. I tried to rearrange my face into an expression of "What the hell? Just woke up..." and yawned. Maybe I could fake my way through this.

"Hey, did something fall?" My voice was froggy. I stretched and sat up.

"Just my cell phone. Did you just wake up?"

"Yeah. I'm sorry, man, I didn't mean to nod off but I've just been so tired lately...."

"It's okay. I've seen how hard you're working." He had a little smile on his face that made me nervous.

What did that mean? Was he onto me?

I swallowed and ran a hand through my shaggy hair. "You been watching me?"

"I sure have."

The moment stretched out. I was embarrassed but I couldn't stop looking at him, his eyes, the way his bare scalp gleamed in the light, the creamed-coffee hue of his smooth skin. He wore tank tops most of the time and they showed off his wide shoulders and big arms; it was a cliché but one I liked now, the tough guy in the wife-beater.

"I've been watching you, too." I meant to say the words with bluster, pretending to be tough myself but they came out as a near-whisper. An admission—to him and to myself.

He ambled over to me, his broad chest tugging his tank top in all sorts of interesting directions. "Maybe you're just fooling yourself." He sat down, his hips against mine, one hand pushing me back onto the couch.

"About what?"

"About this." He bent down and kissed me. His lips were soft and he nuzzled at my mouth for long seconds, teasing me. The heat of his torso made me realize how chilly the room was and that my nipples were hard and my cock was harder. He palmed down my belly and gave me a tweak. "Nice."

My hands were shaking, my fingers fumbling a little against his chest. Breaking the taboo of touching another man scared the hell out of me—but not enough to overcome the flood of heat in my groin or the drumming of my heart. He watched me as I explored him, my fingers under the stretchy cotton of his tank top, thumbing his nipples and smoothing my palms over his chest. So smooth, his soft skin over hard muscle. The only bones I could feel were his clavicles; every rib was solidly clad in muscle, his pectorals ripped, arms thick.

I elbowed up and kissed him, then pulled back. "Conrad, what is this? I don't know what to make of you. Or you and Donalita."

"Donalita's just somebody to dance with. Are you flexible?"

"I am now." I kissed him again, getting some tongue this time.

He pulled away and stood up. My gaze went to his pants, hoping to see him hard. He was, and he eased one hand over his erection, his mouth open as he watched my face. "You like what you see?"

"Yeah." I could barely get the syllable past my throat.

"You ready to do this for real?"

"Yeah." Lust had reduced me to panting monosyllables; there wasn't much blood in my brain, it was all pooled in my cock.

"Come over to my place tonight for dinner."

"Tonight? Why not now?"

"Tonight. In a real bed, doing real fucking." He squatted down in front of me, his face serious. "You're not gonna bail on me are you, straight boy?" Conrad put one palm against my face and held it tight.

Bail, jail, the words made me shiver. But his touch made me shake. "I'll be there."

"Seven-ish. Bring your favorite wine."

"How about dessert?"

He was at the door, one hand on the handle, and he turned back with a smile. "You're the dessert."

Thirteen hours later, I was in Conrad's kitchen, in a delicious fog: yellow rice steamed in one pot, black beans bubbled away in another. A long loaf of Cuban bread lay on the counter, cut open, a slab of butter on the cutting board next to it.

"Wow, you can really cook," I said.

Conrad stirred some sugar and eggs into a bowl and whisked it with quick, deft movement. "You'll find I'm full of surprises."

"Yeah? Like what?" False bravado again. I couldn't seem to stop myself from smart-assing this guy.

"Like this." Conrad set down the whisk, grabbed me by one belt loop and wrenched me toward him. My hands were full with the wine bottle I'd brought and my car keys and I fell against him awkwardly—magically. We bumped noses, then teeth as Conrad's mouth met mine. A sweet dry kiss at first, then longer and wetter, his tongue teasing against my lips, sucking on the tip of my tongue, flicking his own tongue inside my mouth. My senses filled up: the pillowed softness of his full lips; the smell of soap on his skin, shaving cream. The kitchen hummed around us, pot lids clinking as the food simmered, the ceiling fan blowing the warm air around us.

The kiss must have lasted for over three minutes. Just that. Just kissing, no hands roaming around—yet. I had my tongue all the way out and Conrad sucked on it, twisting his mouth from side to side, making my imagination go wild with fantasies of what it would feel like if he tongued my cock the same way.

A buzzer on the stove went off, startling us. Conrad pulled away. "Beans are done," he announced.

"I'm just about done!" I stepped back.

He smiled over his shoulder at me. "I'll get you done later, pretty boy. Why don't you pour us some wine?"

My fingers shook so much that I was afraid I'd break the wineglass; I could barely control the heavy wine bottle. I stopped for a second, my head bent low as I tried to control myself...my hands...my thoughts.

Remember, you're here to do a job. Get some information out of him—about Marcos, about the drugs, about the next pickup in Raleigh.

But beneath the forced professionalism an erotic buzz: *touch him, suck him, fuck him, rub your cock on him and come!*

"This is amazing," I said, lifting a third helping of chicken and rice onto my plate.

"Thanks." Conrad grinned and raised his wineglass. "Glad you're enjoying it."

"Where'd you learn to cook like this?"

He shrugged. "Dad's Cuban, Mom's Spanish-Italian, so we

always had good food around the house. The flan's a recipe from my great-grandmother."

"You grew up where exactly?"

"Downtown Jax."

I went on, asking him questions that I already knew the answers to. My sergeant had literally quizzed me on the team's files before I went under, so Conrad's background and schooling were old news to me. But I was playing a role, the new kid, so I asked the right questions. He asked some questions, too, and for the most part I told the truth about growing up on a farm, working cattle, wanting to get the hell away from a small town to a big city. I just lied and said it all happened in Bloomington, Indiana instead of Ocala.

The phone rang and from the living room we heard the answering machine pick up. Conrad's gruff words then a message. It was Marcos.

"Hey, Conster! We got a delivery date and I need some help driving. Let's leave Wednesday, about noon, okay? Catch you later." A click, then the phone went dead.

Conrad looked embarrassed and grabbed the bottle of wine.

I raised my glass for a refill. "Ever do anything stronger?"

"Nah," Conrad said as he poured for me. "I did some shit when I was younger but now... It just makes me paranoid and blurry. It's too hard to mix music right when I'm feeling that out of it. Why?"

"Seems like there's a lot of stuff floating around the raves."

"If you want something stronger than wine, go see Marcos. He can set you up."

"He's the man, huh?"

Conrad stared at me for a second, his brows furrowed, his mouth turned down. "I'd say so. I don't know for sure, it's not my business." He shrugged.

"Don't you guys go back and forth to Raleigh?"

"Twice a month, usually. I hit the clubs and I have a friend who runs some music stores up there. I don't know what Marcos does when we're there. I stay with Lonnie. " He gazed away, his brown eyes flicking around the kitchen. "He loves music and how he gets some of these imports, I don't know. I don't care as long as he shares it with me."

So Marcos was the real target—at least for the department. Enough work. Time for play.

I grabbed his hand, my fingers caressing his. "So, what happens now?"

"That depends on you," he answered. His low voice was flirty. He pulled my hand to his and kissed my fingers, a silly old-fashioned gesture. It arrowed straight through me. "What do you want to have happen?"

I looked at him, letting my gaze roam over his shoulders and chest, back to his face, focusing on his lips. Could I say it? Should I?

"I want..." The words eased back into my throat. What was I doing? What was happening to me that I wanted to say these things to him, that I wanted him to... "I want you."

"Want me to what?" He stood up, his broad torso blocking out the light from the window behind him; he was just a dark silhouette coming toward me.

My breath hitched. "I want you to touch me."

"Say it."

"I want your hands on me."

Conrad turned me in the chair so he could straddle my legs He kissed my forehead, my cheeks, my nose. "Say it."

"Your mouth on me. On my cock."

"Mmmm," the moan eased into a throaty growl from him. He held my face with both hands, the same way he'd held Jason.

His eyes were dark, his pupils huge. He thumbed my eyebrows and nose, gentle. “What else?”

My cock burned, ached. A wet splotch of my pre-seed oozed out of me. I grabbed him hard, my fingers digging into his ribs, pulling him down onto my lap, grinding up against him. He was heavy—over two hundred pounds—and I could barely lift up from the chair. There was something unsettling about the size of him, how he could hold me down, how he could control me through sheer weight and force.

Unsettling and arousing.

“What else?” he repeated.

“I want you to fuck me,” I said too fast, afraid that I’d swallow the words if I didn’t ratchet them out before my brain reeled them back in.

Conrad stood up, his pants tenting out. He held out one hand, an invitation. This was my choice.

The room was quiet except for the electric hum of the refrigerator. Outside, some kids played a couple houses down and from a few streets over, I heard the tacky tinkle of an ice-cream truck. The kitchen filled with the sound of our breathing.

I took Conrad’s hand.

The first time passed in a blur of tearing off each other’s clothes, grappling on the bed; me pushing Conrad down on the mattress, biting his shoulders. Little pieces of the encounter pierced at me: how tan he looked against the pale yellow sheets; panting against his neck as I pumped over him; the way he held my face in his hands to watch me come. It happened fast, not the way I’d imagined it, just me rutting against him like some horny teenager in the backseat of a car. He smiled when I came and scooped up my semen, still warm, and fed some to me and then himself.

“Tastes good,” he murmured. When he rolled over to straddle

me, I was still breathless, too fuzzy and weak to protest. He jerked off on my belly, one hand fisted over his cock—dark as wine—the other between his legs, fingers thrusting just behind his balls. He closed his eyes and swayed above me. It reminded me of a cobra, that easy movement, his hips pumping, his broad chest heaving. It was beautiful.

He was beautiful.

His semen spurted on my chest, hot. I smelled it, thicker somehow than my own, something rich and exotic about the odor. He eased down to sit on my belly and opened his eyes with a soft smile.

"Put your knees up," he said.

I did and he leaned against them. His weight on my hips sank me into the bed. I felt the heat of his ass on me, the softness of his balls pillowed against my own skin. He let me look at him in the flickering candlelight, touch his softened cock, run my thumbs over his pubic hair and fondle his balls with gentle fingers. He winced a little as I explored.

"Sensitive?" I asked.

"For a couple minutes after."

His thighs were well-muscled, solid; and he had short, wiry hair on his legs, sparse. I palmed his smooth chest; I couldn't get enough of it.

"Do you shave?" I asked.

"Just my head."

"So smooth," I said, shaking my head.

"And you're so fuzzy." He bent and nuzzled my chest, his nose tickling the blond fur that eased over my pecs and down my belly. He rolled off me, squashed the pillows up under us and pulled me over to lie on his chest. It was completely comfortable, not like fumbling against a woman's breasts and having her wince and pull away because I'd accidentally pressed too hard, but instead knowing I could rest easy. His heartbeat tha-thumped in my ear as he drowsed.

This feels—right.

The thought made me swallow and my stomach clenched as I thought about being such a two-faced liar. Or was it three-faced? Lying to him, lying to my sergeant, lying to myself.

I'm just doing my job here. This doesn't really mean anything. I'm not gay.

The accusations and excuses whirred through my brain while Conrad dozed.

After a few minutes, Conrad woke up with a jerk. "Sorry. I usually drift off if I'm someplace comfortable."

"I don't mind," I said and elbowed up to look at him. "I think it's kinda cute."

"Cute? I am *not* cute, I am a badass," he growled but he smiled as he said it and grabbed me around the waist. Within seconds he'd wrestled me halfway down the bed.

I fought back—a little—but I liked his hands on me and the feeling of his control and his strength. He tugged me to the middle of the bed and spread my legs apart. My cock started to fill with blood again, snaking up my belly as I looked at him bent over me. His face was easy to read, filled with lust and yearning and nothing more than that, just that primal want for another's body.

Conrad flipped me over. I gasped when he touched me and got a lungful of fabric softener. The sheets beneath me were smooth and time-softened, a little faded. He slipped one finger between my cheeks and I clamped down and pulled away. Too much, too soon.

He stretched out beside me, his chest against my shoulder. "Try to relax, Steven."

I nodded and put my face in my arms, looking away from him.

He rubbed my lower back for a few minutes, massaging and

kneading the muscles. I tensed up again when he touched my cheeks; he sighed and moved to straddle my legs. The full weight of him on me made my heart quick beat—a jolting spasm of unease that made me swallow.

Can I do this?

"You're thinking about this too much." His deep voice rumbled through my back as he leaned over me. Conrad kissed my ear and neck. "Just let your body feel it, that's all."

"Just do it."

"No."

I raised my head and looked up at him. "Why not?"

"Because this is the only first time you'll ever have. I'm not gonna push you so you can justify it later that I forced you. I don't play that game."

I flushed, feeling caught and embarrassed. That's precisely what I wanted him to do—to grab me fast and hard and just fuck me and get it over with so I didn't have to think about it.

"I'm sorry...." I looked away from his dark-eyed gaze, my face warm. "I guess you're right."

"Stop thinking about what it *means*. Just let it happen, let me touch you, feel you."

Conrad's warm breath in my ear and sexy voice made me stir against the sheets. "Okay, just...go slow."

"I will, babe." He kissed my neck again, then my shoulders and lower, his lips soft against my lumbar and then—*oh yes!*—on my ass. He used his knees to spread my legs apart and I felt his broad thumbs open my cheeks. And then more kisses, up, across, all around my anus; and me feeling it tighten as he got closer, his tongue now just behind my balls, flicking me *just there, oh yes, higher, higher, oh god yes, right in there!* I groaned as his tongue licked me open, my knees involuntarily spreading wider, and I pushed back against him.

I was disappointed when he stopped tonguing me. He leaned over to the nightstand and grabbed a tube I hadn't noticed before. He slicked his fingers, then lay down beside me again.

"Look at me," he said.

I didn't want to, afraid that my face was too full of trepidation and want and raw emotion. He palmed my face gently. "Steven, babe, look at me."

And when I did, it was all right. His gaze was even and calm, his eyes were soft and understanding.

I elbowed up to kiss him. "I'm ready."

He nodded and then held my gaze as one finger fondled me outside, slicking the lube around me, then just inside, in, out, in, out. My hips twitched with each stroke and my cock stretched up against my belly. He pushed one finger all the way inside me, just slowly, letting me get used to it and I did relax—*this isn't so bad*—until he pressed against something inside me that made me gasp and jerk upward and back against him. Fiery hot, a burning jolt of pleasure.

"What is that?" I gasped.

"Where I want to touch you, babe, right there." And he did it again, his finger slicking in and out of me, the hot arc making me squirm on the sheets.

"More," I gasped. "Please, more."

He used two fingers next, then three and by then I was on my knees, my face pushed into the mattress, my ass up, and I'd never felt so turned on. My cock bonged up against me, hard, heavy, and I looked down between my legs for a second to see Conrad kneel behind me. The mattress indented from his weight and I heard the quick rip of the condom packet. I closed my eyes and waited, wanting him.

His thumbs spread me open. "You ready, babe?" His voice was husky, wet with arousal.

"So ready." My whispered words melted into the mattress.

The wet slick of the condom lube was cool against me and then the pressure of his cock, thick and hard and wet, a steady push up, up, partly inside—*oh god too much! He's too big!*—and he felt me tense up. Conrad stopped. "Push back against me, babe. It's all right, just push back."

When I did, it released that tight muscle and the stretch of him inside me wasn't so much about pain but sheer fullness and his weight on me and in me and I stopped thinking about what he was doing to me and let myself feel his hot thrusts as he grew harder and wetter, his hips pumping, his thighs rubbing against mine. The bed squeaked as he pumped in me. Someone was gasping, crying out, screaming, *Oh fuck me, Conrad!* and he reared back and pulled me up with him, my weight impaling me on his cock and he thrust harder, his groan filling my head. My voice then, hoarse and raw and needy as I came again, came from inside as his cock filled me up and rubbed me just there. The warm spurt of my semen jetted up on my chest and belly. Conrad thrust slower, his lips wet on my neck—I'd have a bruise—and then he gave a soft sigh as he orgasmed. I felt it, his cock pulsing inside me. I held him still for a few seconds as we balanced on our knees.

It scared me.

I'd never thought that being with a man would be this way—gentle and tough at the same time. It scared me to think about taking undercover too deep.

And it scared me how much I wanted this.

I covered my face with one hand. What was happening to me? What the hell was going on that I'd *let* this happen to me?

Conrad held me for a few seconds, his cock soft. He slipped out of me with a little groan. "You okay?"

I squatted back on the bed and nodded from behind my hand.

He sat down on the bed, the mattress tilting me against his leg. I heard him sigh. When I looked over at him, he had his head back, face pointed to the ceiling, lips looking oddly thin and twisted. As if he were in pain.

I put one hand on his sweaty neck. "Are *you* okay?"

He looked at me, eyes full. "Is this the part when you smack my face and call me a fucking faggot?"

"No, of course not. What makes you say that?"

"It's happened before. Some straight guys get weirded out afterward and then they get pissed."

"Maybe I'm not so straight."

"Maybe it just means you're one of those guys who likes some strange now and then." His gaze held me, a questioning look on his features.

"I don't think so." I drew a shaky breath. "I like you."

His full lips stretched into a gorgeous smile. "I like you, too."

I ran my hand over his chest again, feeling shy and bold and scattered. "Can we spend some more time together?"

"Like I'm gonna let you leave tonight." He shoved me back on the bed and wrestled me up against the headboard. The pillows fell over on my face and Conrad laughed and pushed them down on me, then pulled them away, squirming in between my legs. He lay his head on my chest and I held him for a long time.

When a cool breeze made us both shiver, Conrad pulled the comforter over us. I tucked it over his broad shoulders and stroked his face with the tips of my fingers.

They weren't shaking anymore.

IN THE HEAT OF THE ARMIES OF THE NIGHT

Simon Sheppard

That's right, boys, you g'wan in there. One at a time. All—how many of you cocksuckers are there? One, two…six. All six of you. Yep, that's it. Right in that fuckin' cell, cocksuckers.

Okay, Duane, you go on and take their cuffs off. You there, stop squirming or else the fuckin' handcuffs don't come off. Pissant troublemaker…

I hope you kids have learned a goddamn valuable lesson. You outside agitators don't come into a nice little town like ours and start making trouble. Not while the President is here. He's the fuckin' President of the United Fuckin' States, and you pieces of dogshit figure you have the right to come in uninvited and start making trouble? Fuck, you try that in some other goddamn country and you'd be in big fuckin' trouble….

Good, Duane. Yeah, you can leave us here. I'll be fine with these little faggots. Just close the cell door behind you when you go.

Now, then, as I was saying…you can't embarrass the President without consequences…not in my town, you can't. You little pukes, I'll show you what embarrassment is.

Take your pants off.

That's right, boys. Pants off. Don't give me those looks. Shoes off and drop trou. Now.

Fuck! You, fuckin' hippie. No underwear, huh? What's your name? Rosen? Sounds Jewish. You Jewish, boy? You...look Jewish.

Don't give me that fuckin' expression, Jewboy. What's your problem? You got a fuckin' problem? You hiding something? I bet you're concealing something. Turn around.

I said TURN AROUND!

You want more of that, boy? You fuckin' want to hurt some more? Nope, I'm betting you don't. Now that we understand each other good, you just turn around and bend over. Yeah, like that. Grab your fuckin' ankles. And you, tattoo-boy, you spread Jewboy's cheeks and let me see that he ain't hiding nothing up there.

Do what I fuckin' say, tattoo-boy, unless you want some of what I gave Rosen. That's it, spread that ass. Let me see clean up that dirty shithole.

What's *your* problem, nigger? Oh, excuse me..."African-American boy." Almost forgot my fuckin' sensitivity training. You boys wouldn't want me to forget that, now would you? My sensitivity training? Cause if I went and forgot that, heaven only knows what I would do....

Did I *tell* you to let go of his ass? Keep 'em spread. And you, the skinny one, you go over there and look up his hole. Just to make sure he ain't hiding nothin' in there.

Do it! And don't start thinking you're going to get to call some goddamn Jew lawyer, probably some relative of Rosen's. This is my jail, and what I say, goes. This ain't someplace like Jew York. Got it, skinny? Now go look up his butt.

Anything up there you can see? No? Okay, tattoo-boy, leggo of his cheeks. And you, Rosen, stand up and turn around.

Hey, was your Jew dick as big as that before? It can't be that somebody touching your ass got you *excited,* now can it? Only faggots get excited when someone touches their butt. You ain't a faggot, are you boy? A faggot *and* a Jew? Jesus, what's this world's coming to? No wonder you fuckin' disrespect our President. Your parents must be so proud....

You, black boy, go on over and check on Rosen's dick. Do it. Don't make me go over there and give you what I gave Rosen. That's it. Good boy. Now check it out. Put your hand on it. Give it a feel. You think it's any bigger than it was?

That a "no?" Hmm. Well, maybe you're not the best judge of that, 'cause I hear you people are kinda abnormal when it comes to size. Right? I *said*, "Is that right, darkie?"

Lemme see. See your black cock. Don't give me that look. I mean it, take your underwear off. Now. You don't like it, you go complain to the ACLU.

Fuck, that *is* a good-sized dick. Not as ginormous as some, I'm betting, but big enough. I wonder—just as a matter of scientific curiosity, mind you—how big it gets when it's hard. Big? Real big? E-fuckin'-normous?

You over there—old dude. Jesus, what the hell are you doing with these young punks? I guess you're anti-American, too, huh? You probably spit on my brother when he came back from 'Nam, didn't ya? So you like being around all this young anarchist shit? Does it get your feeble old dick hard? Fuck, I bet you're a cocksucker, a real cocksucker. And I bet you want to suck that big black dick over there, don'tcha, grandpa?

Go on. Let me see you suck it. I said DO IT, you fuckin' old fuck. See this? It's real. And I'll use it. You think I won't? Go on, call my fuckin' bluff. Who you think is gonna stop me? *Duane?*

That's right, go on over to Malcolm X there and get down on your knees. And let's see how good you suck dick. Go ahead, get that black piece of meat good and wet. You like watching that, Rosen? Let's see you stroke that Jewboy dick. And the rest of you, too. You all get your underpants off. Now. And beat off. Beat off for the sheriff. I said *Beat off!* Are you fucks deaf or something? That's it, boys. Stroke those goddamn commie dicks.

Hey, Rosen, looks like your prick *is* getting hard. So you *are* a faggot, after all. And you, gramps, back off that black dick. Yeah, you *do* know how to suck cock. Man, it's true what they say about you fuckin' liberals, ain't it? Bunch of sick cocksuckers, the whole pathetic bunch of you.

Okay, the rest of you, go on and get stiff. Yeah, you too, Pancho. Make that beaner cock of yours hard. Or fuckin' else.

Duane *got* to see this. YO, DUANE!

Hey, gramps, did I tell you to stop sucking? You keep smoking that black pole till I say to stop.

Hey, Duane, see, what'd I tell you? Just a bunch of faggots, huh? Yeah, Duane, c'mon back here in the cell with me.

Hey, blond boy, you with the fuckin' little piece-of-shit beard. C'mon over here. I think Duane's got something for you. He has a *nice* piece of law and order for you. Show him, Duane. Whip it out and fed it to this fucking commie cunt.

See, blond boy? That's what real American dick looks like. May not be all that big, but hell, Duane's an ugly fuck, anyway. Now get down on your fuckin' knees and make my deputy feel real good. Do it or I swear I'll blow your fuckin' head right off.

And you, skinny kid. Yeah, you. Take the rest of your clothes off. Strip all the way naked for me and then come over here.

Yo Duane, that feel good?

Hey, blondie. Do what Duane says. Take that little bit of meat of his all the way down your throat.

Yeah, over here, skinny, get your fuckin' ass over here. Hey, you got a big dick for such a scrawny guy. You ever been fucked before? But you've always wanted to get fucked, right? Right?

Hey, gramps, back off that dick now, let skinny here see that big fuckin' African-American cock, see what he's in for. Must've been hard to sing "We Shall Overfuckingcome" with your mouth full, anyways.

You think you could take that big black dick up your ass, skinny boy? Don't give me that look, like you're so fuckin' innocent. Soon as I saw you fuckin' parading around with that anti-American sign, I knew you wanted to get fucked. And now you will be. Long and hard. Down on all fours, cunt. Not such a big man now, are ya, down on the floor like a skinny bitch? Spread your fuckin' legs, show me your balls. I said SPREAD 'EM! Duane, you want to take your dick out of blondie's throat for a minute, take care of this skinny bitch, make him shape up? Aww, never mind, Duane. Skinny little bitch decided to behave. Sorry to disturb you.

Okay, bitch, keep them spread. Big dick, big balls. Bet those balls are sensitive, huh? Well, *this* is for making me disturb my deputy.

Fuck, you want more? You want *more?*

No? Then stop your fuckin' whimpering.

Hey, you with the tattoos, mind your own business, keep jackin' off. What the fuck did I tell you? Did I say you could stop? Damn right I didn't.

Okay, Mr. Malcolm X, let's see you over here, on your knees behind this scrawny commie bitch. Now get some spit on that big black thing and shove it up scrawny boy's ass. Do it *now*, darkie, unless you want this to be your very last day on Earth. Yeah, get that fuckin' thing up there. Shove it, just shove it.

Fuckin' hell, the kind of shit I have to go through to keep

this world free of dope-smokin' scum. It ain't easy being a cop, right Duane? Hey, that blond boy still sucking you good? Yeah? Feel good?

Hey, blondie. Spit out my deputy's cock and come on over here. What's your name, son? Okay, Pete, I'm gonna have to find out firsthand what a good cocksucker you are, you commie anarchist piece of shit. On your knees. Yeah, you like my dick? Like the way it smells of fuckin' cheese? You just go on ahead and put your mouth around it, then, Pete. I said SUCK IT!

Hey, Duane! You thought this cocksucker was *good?* Maybe it's 'cause your cock's so much smaller than mine, hey? Jesus, I've had underage hookers with little tiny mouths in here that sucked lots better than this.

What are you looking at, ni—I mean, African American? You just keep fuckin' till I tell you to stop. And you, blondie, you better start in sucking my cock a fuckin' lot better, bitch, or I'll have Rosen come over here and plow your—OW! Mother*fucker!* You fuckin' bit me, you little... Get the fuck off me. Back *off!*

Man, I'm fuckin' bleeding. Duane, come over here, this little cunt bit me. I said OVER HERE, deputy. Stop playing with tattoo-boy's ass and give me an assist. Aw, shit, he bit my fuckin' dick. Now I'll be out of fuckin' commission for days.

Oh, Jesus, Jesus. I sure hope he didn't give me nothing. Fuckin' AIDS. Fuckin' faggot AIDS. Hey, Duane, come have a look at this, see if you can patch me up. Duane! I said come over here! Fuckin' deputy...never around when...

Hey, gramps, what you doing? Get your saggy ass back there. You too, Pancho. Get the fuck away from me. Don't you dare fuckin' put your greasy brown hand on me. All of you, back the fuck off. I got a—unhh.

Leggo of me, gramps. Leggo of my cock. Ow! Fuck! Leggo of my arms, nigger. That's a direct—unff.

Oh, sweet Jesus. Leggo. Leggo.

All of you, get the fuck away from me. Get the fuck back! I'm warning...

Duane! *Not you, too!*

Duaaane...

HARD CELL

Adam Ryder

After finishing college, I hitched from New York to California. I made good time until Nevada, where I got stranded in a small town in the middle of nowhere. There were a few mostly run-down houses and trailers, a gas station, liquor store, luncheonette, and some small offices.

There was nothing to do. It was hot and dry, augmented by a bright sun. I decided to wait until early evening to hitch, rather than stand on the highway in the heat of high noon. I found a shady spot behind a shed to sit in, and must have dozed off. I was wearing worn jeans, white leather sneakers, and a white T-shirt, and carrying a knapsack. When you're a kid, you're naïve. The tight jeans and T-shirt highlighted my lean swimmer's body, full pecs and tapered waist. I thought I looked cool, but I probably stood out like a sore thumb. I was a city boy with long hair and that lean, faded look that is common among college students. Late in the afternoon, I was awakened by a cop in crisply pressed khaki trousers and a creased short-sleeved khaki shirt. He tapped me with the tip of his black cowboy boot to rouse me.

"I'd like to see some ID please."

The cop had a sexy baritone voice, and spoke slowly, with a slight drawl. He was polite, but his voice had a threatening undertone. He looked distinctly unfriendly. He also looked distinctly attractive, which registered at the back of my mind as I squinted up at him against the bright sky.

I was groggy from sleep. "Why?" Suddenly I was a lawyer. "I have as much right to be here as anyone else."

He repeated himself: "You've been loitering where you've got no business. I'd like to see some ID." However, his stance changed. He spread his legs apart, and braced his hands on his belt, placing one disturbingly close to his pistol.

As I became more awake, fear tempered my indignation. I debated whether to insist on my rights or simply show him some ID and get the whole thing over with. Prudence won out. I didn't drive, and had no driver's license, but I had college ID, credit cards, and a photo ID showing my age. I reached into my back pocket and gave them to him.

He looked them over for what seemed like hours, his expression completely blank, and then said, "These aren't proper ID. We need to go to the office." As he said this, his right hand moved to his gun barrel. He gestured for me to get up. By now I was terrified, and in no mood to argue. Carrying my knapsack, I meekly stood up and preceded him around the corner of the shed to a waiting police car. He did not cuff me, but directed me into the backseat, placing his hand lightly on my left shoulder to push me inside the car, and closing the door behind me. I had never been in a police car. The backseat was like a cage: there were no handles on the door, there was no way to open the windows, and there was a plastic barrier between me and the front seat.

It took about ten minutes to drive to the police station. It was a wood cabin with an asphalt roof, in a dirt clearing surrounded by tall trees. An unrailed front porch with a gently sloping roof ran the length of the cabin. As we pulled up in front, I noticed a cinderblock extension on the back, with high barred windows and an antenna on the flat roof.

It was not until I arrived at the sheriff's office that I began to fully take in the sheriff himself. He was suntanned and big, about six feet three inches tall, and broad in the shoulders to match. His uniform fit like a glove—khaki trousers and a matching uniform shirt with a badge on the pocket. The khaki brought out the deep brown of his eyes. He had a slim waist, thick thighs, and a firm ass. His hair was light brown, cut just long enough to brush down, and he was clean shaven. Some tufts of hair showed just above the open neck of his shirt. His trousers were tightly tailored, showing off the contours of his ass and a hint of a bulge in his crotch. He had enormous hands. He was wearing black western boots, shiny where they were normally covered by the uniform trousers, but with a light coating of very fine dust where they were not. I could not tell his age, but if pressed would have said he was in his late thirties. The rough features of his face made him look like a movie star, handsome but not pretty. He exuded an air of competent authority and control which was intimidating and, disturbingly, sexy.

"Come inside." He ushered me in, holding open a wood-framed screen door covered in chipped and peeling paint. The place was empty. We went down a short hallway to a room in the back with an air conditioner in the window. This seemed like a real police station. The floor was covered with institutional gray linoleum, there were wanted posters on one wall, a calendar and a picture of the state capitol on another, a row of filing cabinets and a metal desk with a telephone and some kind of radio. There was a metal door to the rear of the room, behind the sheriff, which presumably led to the cells.

"I've had a complaint that someone fitting your description is selling drugs. I need to be sure about you before I let you go. We don't tolerate drugs in this state." That was fine with me: I didn't do drugs, and didn't even smoke. However, it gave him an excuse to open my knapsack, dump the contents onto a table, and rifle through them.

My misplaced legal sense roused itself again. With outrage, I said, "Hey, you can't do that. You need a search warrant."

"Why, boy? Hiding something?"

I could feel myself blushing with a mixture of shame and anger. Suddenly, I was a criminal, even though I had done nothing wrong. At the same time, a little voice inside my head wondered if hitchhiking was legal in Nevada.

As the cop pawed through my gear, he kept making faces of disgust, and from time to time he would make some snide crack about my clothes or possessions.

"Turn out your pockets," he ordered. Again, I complied.

"Don't seem to have a lot of money or any way to support yourself," he mused, staring directly into my eyes.

"For god's sake," I responded. "I have a credit card and a checkbook. What more do I need?"

"For all I know, these are false or stolen."

My frustration got the better of me. "What is this? I was just sitting in the shade until it got cool, and wasn't doing anything. Suddenly you're treating me like I'm some kind of damn thief!"

"First of all, boy," the sheriff drew out the last word, saying it long and slow, "you may not speak that way in my office. If you do it again, you'll spend the night behind bars. Second of all, I don't know you from Adam, but I know you match the description of someone selling drugs."

"For god's sake, what the hell does that mean? I showed you some ID."

"I warned you once. You don't get a second chance." The sheriff advanced toward me, and the next thing I knew, he had gripped my arms and fastened them behind my back with a pair of cuffs. I had not realized how big he was until he got close. He towered over me, even though I am just about six feet tall. His height and broad shoulders made him intimidating but, at the same time, he had a sexy smell of aftershave, the outdoors, and cigar or pipe tobacco.

"You bastard. What do you think you're doing? You can't arrest me!"

The sheriff laughed, and pushed me through the door to the cell block. Maneuvering me into a cell, he locked me in.

I was terrified. Suddenly I was in a bad movie about a southern sheriff in the middle of nowhere. My hair was too long, my jeans too faded and tight, I didn't have a lot of money, and I was completely at the mercy of this man. Strangely, my fright made me intensely excited. For the first time, I discovered that fear was like an aphrodisiac, making my cock hard. Wearing just jeans and a T-shirt, my hands cuffed behind me, I was locked in a cage with an amazingly sexy man as my captor.

"You can't do this!" I shouted.

I stood panting with fear and anger. The sheriff spread his legs apart. Looking at me in a knowing way, he coolly ran his eyes over my body. His eyes slowly traveled from my head to my toes, pausing on my crotch. I felt violated, as if he was undressing me with his eyes. He replied in a low voice, "I sure can. And, if you keep talking back, I'll gag you." My cock surged at the thought, but I cursed it for doing so. I was in serious trouble, and had no idea what would happen next.

"You can stay in there until you can keep a civil tongue in

your head. I have the option to give you thirty days for your behavior but I'm gonna sleep on it overnight and let you do the same." As he talked, my eyes were drawn to the triangle made by the curve of his left and right pecs straining against the tight fabric of his shirt and the suggestive bulge around his crotch. He stood there for a few minutes, shifting his left leg as if he were adjusting his cock, then walked slowly out of the cell block, closing the heavy metal door behind him.

The sound of the closing door brought home my helplessness. I was completely at the sheriff's mercy, and had not even thought to ask for a phone call. Giddy with panic and anger, I sat on a bunk and put my head on my knees. At the same time, I was disturbingly turned on by the sexiness of the cop who was abusing me. My cock kept getting hard, only to soften again each time the gravity of the situation came back to me. I did not realize it then, but looking back with the eyes of experience, I recognize in that cop the unself-conscious arrogance of the truly attractive man. He walked with a slow swagger that showed his meaty thighs and long legs in front, and the firm rounds of his ass straining through his trousers behind.

As night fell, the cell became steadily dimmer. I became reconciled to the situation, telling myself that sooner or later I would be released. Toward evening, the sheriff reentered the cell block. As I heard the door open, I looked up with a mixture of fear and hope. Perhaps the sheriff had changed his mind, but then, perhaps things had gotten worse. The lights came on and the sheriff stood outside the bars of the cell.

"Okay, boy. I'm going to let you out of the cell to piss, then give you something to eat before I go home for the night. However, I have to leave your hands cuffed. And, I'm warning you, if you curse or speak disrespectfully, I'll leave you in there 'til tomorrow, with no food and no chance to use the bathroom."

I held my tongue, but was truly nervous about being left alone for the night. I was wiser now, and hungry, and I badly needed to piss.

"Well, boy?"

"All right".

"All right, *Sir*. In my jail, you address me as Sir. Is that clear boy?"

I cursed myself and the sheriff, but my cock swelled at this exchange. I could not control it. Moreover, with my hands cuffed behind my back, I could not hide it. My cock bulged out under my too-tight jeans, and my arousal would have been obvious to a blind man.

"Yes, Sir." I said it grudgingly, hating his slight smile as he heard me submit. I was sure he was turned on by this.

"Good." The sheriff led me out of the cell and down the corridor to a toilet. First unzipping my fly, he momentarily unlocked the cuffs and told me to pull out my cock and piss. I was mortified: the incidental pressure of the sheriff's hand-on my dick as he unzipped the fly had given me a roaring hard-on. It would have been hard for the sheriff to avoid noticing. "Don't miss," he added, "or you'll clean it up."

The sheriff watched impassively as I reached my tingling hands around to hold and aim my cock. Despite myself, my cock stiffened further: I was pissing in front of this masculine figure who literally held the key to the rest of my summer. At first, I could not piss because my cock was so hard. The more I willed the piss to come, the more I was aware of the sheriff silently watching. Pissing was even harder because I had been holding it for so long. Finally, piss started to flow, growing in intensity as my bladder released its load. Finished, I attempted to push my cock back into my jeans, and then allowed the sheriff to cuff me once more and lead me back to the cell. Once I was back inside, the sheriff left and returned with a couple of sandwiches on a plate, which he placed on the floor of the cell before locking me in again.

"Come on man, you can't expect me to eat like this."

The sheriff gave me a sharp look. "Please, Sir," I began again, "I'm locked up behind bars, can't you let my hands loose?"

"Sorry," replied the sheriff, "but I'm on my own, and can't release you. I'll leave the plate there," he added. "You can eat or not as you choose." The sheriff turned around to leave the cell block. I called out, "Wait a minute." He turned back. "You're not just going to leave me here? What if something happens?"

"Nothing has happened here since I've been sheriff."

There was no toilet in the cell, no basin, not even a bucket. "What if I need to piss?"

"You had your chance. You'll just have to wait until morning."

"What about something to drink?"

The sheriff thought for a moment. He disappeared, returning a short while later with a soup plate filled with water. "This is the best I can do. Stand at the other end of the cell." When I complied, he opened the barred door and put the plate on the floor, then turned around again, and walked out. I heard the click of a lock falling into place as he turned the key in the door. Then the lights went out, all but a weak bulb in the hall.

I was starving, but hadn't wanted the sheriff to see that. It was humiliating, but as soon as the cell door closed, I was down on my knees trying to get my mouth around the sandwich. Finished, I wiped my mouth on my shoulder and lay down on the bunk.

I could not sleep. I was too nervous. Each time I started to drop off, the cuffs cut into me, or pins and needles in my arms woke me up. Finally, in desperation, I sat on the painted concrete floor with my back to the wall, resting my head on my knees.

Toward morning I finally dozed off without even realizing it.

When I awoke, the inside of the cell was dim, but some early morning light was coming through a window in the corridor. I had to piss, but there was nowhere to go. I sat there, still tired, but nervous and uncomfortable enough that I could not fall back asleep. The growing need to piss would have kept me awake anyway. Finally, despite my efforts to hold back, a small amount of piss escaped my cock, and I felt a stab of moist heat as it soaked through my underpants and jeans. I managed to stop it, but as time went on and the sheriff did not appear, it became harder and harder to keep it in. Finally, my bladder seemed to empty of its own accord, the warm piss pouring into my jeans, first pooling inside, then soaking the material and dripping through to the floor.

"Shit," I thought, and was close to tears. It wasn't my fault, but I knew this would cause trouble when the sheriff showed up. Strangely, I had been holding it for so long that pissing felt almost like an orgasm. The hot liquid washing over my crotch and thigh was an incredible turn-on. The relief and release left me feeling sleepy. I must have drifted off, since the next thing I knew, the sun was up.

The sun had been up for a while when the sheriff finally arrived. I heard the roar of a motorcycle, and a short while later heard the tapping of heels on the floor as he slowly walked toward the cells. If he was attractive yesterday, today he was a wet dream come to life. He was dressed in motorcycle policeman's breeches, short-sleeved shirt, and high leather riding boots. The boot shafts had a mirror shine, but the feet were slightly dusty from the road. I was sitting on the floor when the sheriff entered. He stood watching me as I slowly stood, using the wall as support to ease myself up. I noticed that he shifted one leg slightly, and put his hand briefly in his pocket. Standing in my worn jeans and T-shirt, smelling of piss, my hands cuffed behind my back, unfed and unwashed, I felt helpless and angry, but could not keep from staring at his taut breeches. They were rounded against what seemed to be massive balls, and clung tightly to the thick sausage shape bulging up from his crotch. Despite the circumstances, I felt myself getting firm. The more I willed my cock to stay soft, the more it grew, straining against the worn fabric of my jeans. The sheriff glanced over the cell, taking in the empty plates, licked clean. If anything, his cock seemed to get thicker as his eyes swept over me and the cell.

When the sheriff spoke, I raised my face and our eyes met. I felt a strong sexual current as he stared at me, and could not break eye contact until he turned away. A knowledgeable, strangely sophisticated expression passed over his face, a mixture of lust, seductiveness, and power. It was as if he was looking directly into my soul, reading all my hidden thoughts.

Unfortunately, my cock became harder, and I fought the impulse to get down on my knees before this big, sexy man, despite the unfairness of my imprisonment.

"I hope you thought things through." I stayed silent.

He noticed the damp patch on my jeans extending from the area around the cock down my right thigh. "I see you pissed yourself, boy. For your sake, I hope you didn't piss on my mattress."

"No Sir," I replied. "It was on the floor, over there." I pointed with my head.

"I ought to make you clean it up."

"Shit, I mean, please." I stumbled over my words, took a deep breath, and started again. "Please, Sir, I didn't get any on the floor, it was all in my jeans."

The sheriff removed his gloves, got a rag, poured some cleaning fluid on it, and passed it through the bars. "Clean the place you were sitting." I had to kneel and lean backward to wipe the floor with my cuffed hands. The sheriff stood there, legs spread apart and hands on his hips, and watched impassively as I squatted down in the corner where I had spent the night and rubbed the cloth behind me. The breeches showed his muscular thighs beautifully, and the tight shiny boots showed his bulging calves. I was tempted to taunt him by suggesting that I clean his boots, half hoping and half fearing he would take me up on the offer, but discretion won out, and I followed his orders to clean the floor.

"Make sure you clean the entire area. Raise yourself so you don't rub your filthy pants on the floor." I obeyed, but it was hard to clean the floor with my hands cuffed behind my back, and even harder with my cock still rigid. I kept my balance with difficulty. When I finished, the sheriff told me to pass the rag back to him.

At this point, I heard a car pull up. The sheriff turned away to return to the main office, giving me a glimpse of his rounded muscular ass, tightly encased in the uniform fabric. He returned with another man, opened the cell, and led me out.

"I've decided not to charge you. Jim here is going to give you a lift to the next county, and I never want to see you around here again."

Jim was sexy too, built like a traditional cowboy. He was clean shaven, slim, tall, and suntanned. His hair was cut short and sun bleached. His eyes were a brilliant blue, his face lean and his cheekbones high. He was dressed in a faded blue denim Western shirt, dusty brown Western boots, a light-brown suede jacket worn shiny in places with use, and tight-fitting faded jeans that showed a big cock. Like the sheriff, he had broad hands with large, long fingers. Like the sheriff, he had a knowing grin on his face. He was in his late thirties or early forties, but looked lean, fit and supple.

The sheriff unlocked the cell, and the two men led me out to an old-model car, covered with dust from the dry dirt roads. I was unprepared for the heat outdoors that hit me like a slap in the face. It had been cool inside the cell block, and the sheriff's office was air-conditioned. The sand of the parking lot was uncomfortable through the soles of my sneakers, and I remember smelling the resin of the pines. Just walking to the car, I broke out in a mild sweat.

"If I was you, I'd put something down on your car seat before he gets in," advised the sheriff. "He pissed himself last night, and there's no telling what he might do." I squirmed in embarrassment and annoyance at the unfairness of the statement. "Who knows when he last had a bath?"

Jim responded by getting a tarp from the trunk and draping it on the passenger's side.

"Get in" he said, holding the door open.

"What about my hands? What about my knapsack?"

The sheriff went back into the office and returned with my bag. He tossed it into the backseat and said, "For now, your hands remain cuffed." As he spoke, he shifted his legs a bit, adjusting his crotch as if his hard cock was bothering him, again making me aware of his arousal and his sexiness.

"Jesus Christ," I burst out. "What's going on? You said I wasn't under arrest!"

"You're not," he replied, "at least, not right now, but keep up your behavior and you will be. Jim will release your hands when he gets to the county line."

I eased myself into the front seat. The inside of the car was like an oven. Despite the tarp, the seat was hot against my back. Jim reached over and closed the door. The realization that I was cuffed, belted in, and completely helpless made my cock tingle again. As Jim was fastening the seat belt in place, his hands just brushed against the strained fabric covering my cock.

Once he belted me in, Jim walked back inside the sheriff's office. He was gone for a while—ten or fifteen minutes. Finally, he returned alone and got into the car. As he put it into gear, his hand brushed the side of my thigh. Aside from that there was no more contact, and no conversation for the half hour or so it took for him to drive me to a deserted road in the middle of nowhere, with a county sign on it. He unbelted me, helped me out of the car, released my hands from the cuffs, and tossed my knapsack onto the ground.

Getting back into the car, he said. "A car or truck will be along soon." Then, gunning his motor, he disappeared in a cloud of dust. I had no idea if he was lying or not. He might have left me in the wilderness to starve or die of thirst but, after a while, a large semi came by and the driver offered me a lift all the way to Bakersfield. I vowed never to go to Nevada again. Funny, but only when I was safely in the truck did I realize that my balls were aching from unspent desire.

At the time, I hated myself and my cock for getting turned on by the arrogant bastard who had clapped me behind bars for a night and laughed at my discomfort. I hated the way my cock dominated my brain and betrayed me in an incredibly frightening situation, but my fright and helplessness were part of the reason for my hard-on. I hated the knowing way the cop looked at me.

Once I was safely out of the state, my terror (and self-hatred) ebbed. I began to wonder what had been going on. I was extremely inexperienced—I'd never been to a gay bar or club, and had only had a few brief sexual encounters—some kisses, some groping, and being sucked off a few times. However, I had an extensive fantasy life peopled by hot men in uniforms. In Nevada, my sexual fantasy figure became real.

Within a week, I was jerking off at the memory of his shiny

boots and tight breeches, cursing myself for not seizing the opportunity when it was offered. Maybe I had misread the cop's arousal. Yeah, I might have ended up in bigger trouble—arrested for sodomy, or abused in other ways.

He could have had sex and then shot me, accusing me of resisting arrest. On the other hand, maybe he did this often, stopping hitchhikers or motorists he found attractive, keeping them in jail overnight, getting a blow job, making them lick his boots, or using them in some other way.

Maybe he just got off by dominating and controlling his victims, keeping them in cuffs and behind bars, and making them humiliate themselves. Maybe he regularly went to Las Vegas or San Francisco to cruise the bars and clubs, strutting his massive, muscular frame, showing off his immense dick, fucking and being sucked. I'll never know, but I've thought about him for over a decade, going over his black boots, tight shirt and breeches in my mind's eye, smelling his aftershave, and thinking about the brief touch of his hand on my cock. I wonder what might have happened if I had done more than show a hard cock. I am increasingly convinced that he was looking for sex—his choice of uniform that morning, the tight breeches that showed off his sausage cock, his boots; even his stance as he watched me clean the floor....

He was my police fantasy come to life. Whatever I felt for cops and uniforms before, I felt it ten times more afterward. The mixture of fear and arousal I felt when I was his captive became a staple of my fantasies and later of my scenes. Even today, when I am having sex, sometimes I close my eyes and think of him. I have never seen anyone quite like him, but I can always hope.

THE RUBBER ROOM

Zeke Mangold

The sun had nearly baked the hunger out of Dell's stomach, but since breakfast had consisted of nothing more than a can of Coke and a remicrowaved, deep-fried "pizza nugget," he made his way to the tiny employee dining room of the Baja Palace Hotel & Gambling Oasis in search of greasy nourishment.

Located about five miles east of the Las Vegas Strip, Baja Palace was one of the nicer casinos on Boulder Highway. Dell had felt lucky to get a summer job as a lifeguard after 9/11. He had exerted very little effort with the pool manager, but landed the job anyway. He'd spent two hundred dollars on his hair at a salon inside Fashion Show Mall that morning, and arrived at the interview wearing an Urban Outfitters T-shirt, ripped jeans and sandals. The pool manager instantly liked him, even flirted a bit by sharing what she herself called "a risqué anecdote" about using sunscreen as lubricant. Dell smiled through it all, and received a call later that afternoon. He was no longer flipping burgers for minimum wage. He'd reached the big time at seven bucks an hour.

The Baja Palace pool was vast and perfectly blue. Dell didn't have to mess with chemicals or handle a brush. Instead, he donned his red trunks and Maui Jims, and perched himself in a white-vinyl bucket seat atop an aluminum platform near the diving boards. He avoided the pool manager. He watched locals "sneak" poolside to work on their tans. God, they were hideous.

Yes, the worst part about Dell's job was that it was a total dick-shrinker. There was nothing at all for him to admire. It was an infinite parade of sunburned potbellies, greasy comb-overs, and assorted cottage cheese. It made him sick to the point that by his third day he was bringing stroke mags to work so he'd have something to enjoy after lunch in the antiseptic-smelling restroom stalls of the spa. There was another male lifeguard, Pete, but his acne-ravaged skin and odd smells were off-putting. Dell quickly made friends with London, a female coworker with whom he could converse about the Hollywood hunks who appeared in the pages of *US Weekly*, *Life & Style* and *People*. London drove a Dodge Magnum her father had bought for her, and she and Dell took it out for lunch at P.F. Chang's.

But London had called in sick today. So Dell entered the employee dining room with a cheeseburger and fries on his mind and a pang in his gut. Before stepping up to the grill, however, he had to run the gauntlet of the hot line, which always featured plenty of steamed-to-death vegetables. He noticed the towering security officer in front of him, an old paperback edition of Norman O. Brown's *Life Against Death* on his tray.

"Isn't that out of print?" said Dell, indicating the book.

"Could be," said the good-looking officer, who offered a disarming smile. "The guy's ideas are pretty fascinating."

Dell closed his eyes for a moment. " 'The dynamics of capitalism is postponement of enjoyment to the constantly postponed future.' Or something like that."

"Yes, exactly. How do you know Brown?"

"My mother's a psychology professor." Dell reached for a soup ladle, then thought better of it. "No one reads Brown anymore. Except Camille Paglia."

"Paglia?"

"She's something of a postfeminist, and a Freudian." Dell wondered if the guy was a 'mo. "And very much a raconteur."

"Sounds interesting." The line surged forward, and the officer swiveled a tad dramatically to catch up with it.

Definitely a 'mo, thought Dell. *But a good-looking one who, at middle age, is just starting to get in touch with his 'moness. Probably has a wife and kids. Recently learned that Old Spice smells like shit. Of late, has discovered hair gel.*

"Does she—your mother, I mean—teach at the college here?" asked the officer.

Dell nodded. "For twenty years."

"I used to be a campus police officer. Name's Gus." He extended his hand, which Dell found to be a little rough. A real working-class hero, this one.

"Dell. You're up, Gus."

"Oh, thanks."

The cook stared at them with a bovine expression, his apron smeared with oil, awaiting instructions.

"Hank!" said Gus, spreading his arms as if to embrace the portly chef from across the sneeze guard. "Thank you for feeding the animals, sir."

After work, Dell couldn't wait to tell London about Gus in the smoky darkness of the Roadhouse Saloon, a redneck dive just a few blocks from the Baja Palace. London struggled valiantly to remove an eyelash that had been scratching her cornea since she woke up that morning, which was why she'd called in sick.

She said, "Yikes, you're not going to do the nasty with a retired cop, are you?"

"Why not? You know, you shouldn't wear—"

"—so much eyeliner. I know, asshole."

"Well, it's just that the sun melts it. You're liable to blind yourself, and guess what? There's no market for sightless lifeguards."

A cruel smirk came to London's lips. She finished off her bottle of Pabst Blue Ribbon and belched with aplomb. "Look who's talking about blindness, Mr. I Jack Off at Work."

"Can't help it. I'm eighteen, and I'm so horny I'd hump a board full of rusty nails if I had to."

"That what Gus is to you? A board with nails?"

Dell paused in honor of Boston's "More Than a Feeling," the signature riff of which began blasting via the bar's Internet jukebox. He raised his fist in mock approval. "I don't know. He's sure big, though. Big and burly like Chuck Norris."

"Barf! Chuck Norris is, like, an ancient dwarf." London successfully dislodged the eyelash, made a wish, and ordered another round. That's what Dell loved about London—her fortitude in the face of hardship.

"I want to learn about authority figures," Dell said. He felt content and full of grand sexual designs.

"Huh."

"He's literate, you know. He's reading Norman O. Brown."

"Sure he is."

"Did I tell you about his 'feed the animals' line?"

"Twice. Feed 'em before you fuck 'em, Dell."

The next morning was chaos. Dell had been dozing off in his lifeguard throne—and trying his best to dream up a glory hole fantasy involving the construction worker plagued by awful tattoo work who modeled a gnarly Speedo and relentlessly performed somersaults off the high board—when a pudgy wreck of a sunbather approached, limping, leaving a trail of tiny blood drops behind him and along the length of the pool. Dell stared down at him from behind his sunglasses and said, "Are you hurt, sir?"

"Yes, I am," said Pudge, using his hand to ward off the sunlight. "Your swimming pool cut me."

During orientation, Dell had been advised to report non-life-threatening guest injuries—abrasions, broken bones—to security. "Okay," he said. "Give me a second." Dell picked up the walkie-talkie and called for an officer. As they waited, Dell noticed a perfect slice just above the Pudge's right ankle—if you could call it that. Pudge was such a whale his ankles were invisible. It was Gus who finally showed up.

"You look familiar," Gus said to Pudge.

"Have we met before?" said Pudge, his face adopting an ashen appearance. Dell removed his shades and threw a look at Gus, which was ignored.

"Nah, couldn't be. Let's file an incident report, sir." He and Pudge headed to the security office, leaving Dell to dream about nibbling Gus's cojones.

At the end of his shift, Dell stopped by the security office. Gus was filling out an incident report.

"So who sliced Fatty?" said Dell.

"He did it himself. With a razor."

"Really. Why?"

"To sue Baja." The expression on Gus's face made Dell uncomfortable and horny. What was he up to? Dell wondered.

"Happen a lot?"

"Oh sure. A couple once tried for an on-the-spot cash settlement after claiming someone had broken into their room and dumped in their toilet. They had flushed the evidence, of course."

Dell shook his head. "So the fat guy, what'd you do with him?"

"Let me show you," said Gus, standing up from his desk. He led Dell to the back of the office and into a small room with a few benches pushed up against the walls.

"Whoa," said Dell. "Interrogation room?"

"Rubber room. This is where we go to town on a sonofabitch with rubber mallets. They don't leave visible bruises."

"You beat Pudge with a mallet?"

"Well, no." Gus reached for Dell's cock, and the lifeguard didn't flinch. "But I sure roughed him up a bit."

Without much fuss, Gus guided Dell onto one of the benches and yanked down his trunks. Gus knelt and began sucking him off. It was a classic sitting blow job, and not the standing skull-fuck Dell longed for. That had to change.

Dell stood up, grabbing the officer forcefully by his short hair so that Dell's dick remained in Gus's mouth. Standing with his legs part, Dell began thrusting harder, faster, pumping his hips against Gus's head. He felt his balls filling with semen even as Gus gagged, saliva dripping from his chin in long strings. It failed to discourage the older man, who hungrily—voraciously—suctioned Dell's throbbing prick.

"I'm going to cum in your mouth," the lifeguard announced, his voice thick with lust. "Don't you dare spit. Swallow every drop." He tightened his grip on Gus's hair and plunged deeper.

Gus moaned in response and went to work. He placed his mitts on Dell's chest, relaxed his jaw and throat muscles, and let the young man pound away.

Suddenly, Dell pulled out, slapping his cock on Gus's forehead. He placed his balls on the officer's mouth. Gus, still on his knees, licked them with gusto. Bored with this after a minute,

Dell turned around and bent over so that Gus could lick his asshole clean, which he did with even greater vigor. Meanwhile, Dell stroked himself—his dick slick with the officer's saliva—and allowed the warm tongue to swab his anus. He thought about reaching orgasm this way, but he wanted to see Gus's face as he ate a load of cum.

Dell turned around and re-inserted himself into Gus's hot, buttery mouth. He pumped and pumped.

"I'm coming. Look at me as you eat my cum." Dell loved the sight of the officer's stretched lips around his fat cock. He intentionally held off to watch those lips do their excellent work. Gus's grateful eyes locked with Dell's own as Dell shot his thick load.

"Mmmm," said Gus, swallowing Dell's semen in a series of gulps. The lifeguard was already tugging at the officer's belt. As soon as he touched Gus's cock it exploded with hot, sticky jizz. *Christ,* thought Dell. The guy needed this badly, no Viagra necessary. Dell wiped the semen on Gus's pants. Cum continued to ooze from Dell's own slit.

"There's more here," said Dell. "Eat it up."

Gus did exactly as he was told. He used both hands to squeeze Dell's dong until more cum gathered at the tip. Gus scarfed it down like it was whipped cream on a sundae.

Shocked by what had just occurred—by his own sexual ferocity—and worried they'd be discovered, Dell quickly hiked up his trunks and exited the room without saying a word to Gus. He looked back to see the officer wiping his mouth and giving a loud, throat-clearing cough.

By the time he reached the employee parking lot, he realized Gus hadn't locked the door to the rubber room. Had someone spied on them? *Of course not,* he thought. *Stop being paranoid. Get it together.*

He stared at his reflection in the rearview for a minute.

Finally, he turned the key in his Honda's ignition and drove home, allowing the soft piano rock of Rufus Wainwright to soothe his nerves, even as his cock once again swelled with blood at the memory of Gus's lips. He pulled into an empty lot behind an abandoned strip mall and milked himself to another satisfying orgasm. At some point, he turned down the music and picked up his cell phone.

"London," he said. "Guess what?"

"You fucked him," she said.

"Well, not properly. I don't know if I ever will. I'm angry at him."

"Because you enjoyed it?"

He had to think about that one.

The next morning, Gus walked right up to Dell and invited him to dinner. Gus wore shades, too, which for some reason made Dell feel silly. Here they were: two guys looking cool by the pool, and talking around the fact that a turbulent erotic encounter had taken place.

"Stop by tonight," said Gus. "I'm making duck."

"I don't know. My mom needs her garage boxed up. She's moving to Aliante at the end of the month."

"That's your excuse?" Gus beamed his patented, impossible-to-resist smile with those white teeth and tender lips, and Dell felt his loins stirring. Goddamn his dick; it had a dirty mind of its own. The sun's heat began to irritate him. He wanted to exact revenge upon this security officer for nearly getting them busted yesterday. Being fired was something Dell could handle, but being embarrassed was excruciating and intolerable. He would make Gus pay for his carelessness.

"All right," he said, swatting at whatever was buzzing his shoulder. "What time?"

They lunched together for the first time in the employee dining room—or, as Dell jokingly called it, the Ebola dining room. Gus shared his law-enforcement background. He'd worked for three years as a patrol officer for the Los Banos department, where he investigated auto-theft crimes. To supplement his income, he opened a water-purification company in California. When his business partner began insisting on making bad decisions, Gus sold his half of the company and moved to Las Vegas to start a new one. In the meantime, he needed a steady source of income, so he went to work at Baja Palace. He never returned to the water-purification industry, and he never married. Though he had dated a male stripper or two over the years.

"I love what I do here," Gus explained.

Dell leaned back in his chair and folded his arms. "And you do what, screw the staff?"

The officer gave a toothy grin, took a sip of coffee. "Just you, beautiful. Are you going to show tonight?"

"No, I'm going to watch a movie instead."

"Be careful, Dell. 'Art seduces us into the struggle against repression.' "

Norman O. Brown. God, he loved this ex-cop. Dell made a note to douche and shave his balls tonight.

Dell knocked, and Gus answered his apartment door in the nude. The ripped muscles on his tanned chest, back and stomach—oh, that supertight six-pack—caused Dell's heart to skip a beat. Maybe two.

Gus immediately led him into the bedroom, kissing Dell's neck and ears, biting yet not breaking skin. On the way there, Dell stripped off individual articles of clothing, until he too was buck-naked. Dell lay across the bed to allow for a partial sixty-nine. What he got instead was a bed's edge face-stabbing that gagged him with the first few thrusts. It was pain mixed with sweet pleasure.

The sweaty musk of Gus's shaved balls almost caused Dell to instantly ejaculate. He tilted his head in such a way that his esophagus straightened out, allowing Gus deeper passage. Balls slapping his eyes and forehead, his throat full of cock, Dell began moaning loudly, knowing the vibration would make Gus's cock stiffen even more. Gus reciprocated by leaning over to give the lifeguard the sixty-nine he'd been hoping for. Those lips screamed out for Dell's cum; they demanded loads of it.

"You're going to taste your own ass this time," said Gus. "Bend it like Beckham."

Now it was Dell's turn to be bossed around. It wasn't what he'd anticipated, but he loved it. Who was the more aggressive lover, he wondered?

"I douched," Dell submissively admitted. He spread his cheeks, giving Gus a complete view of his pink bung.

He almost came again when he heard Gus hawk a loogie and felt the cop's hot saliva seep into his anus. The force of the man's cock dug right into Dell's prostate, even as his O-ring burned from being penetrated. Gus began with shallow thrusts, then pushed deeper until Dell could feel the knob deep in his guts. Dell swore he could feel every vein in the man's iron-hard erection.

"Ready to taste ass?"

"God, yes!"

Gus pulled out and hurdled Dell's body, inserting his glistening cock into the younger man's eager mouth. Dell couldn't taste anything except Gus's tangy precum.

"Pump my ass and cum in my mouth," Dell pleaded.

"No. I'm going to cum in your ass. Then you'll drink it like a milkshake."

"Yes."

Gus got behind Dell and spit again into his open asshole, lubricating that hole even more. He started pumping right away, the friction quickly resulting in Dell's own ejaculation, causing the length of his body to shudder, his slender back to arch, his tight young bum raised in the air. As Dell spurted, Gus remained inside and reached between the lifeguard's legs to scoop up the cum with his fingers. He shoved his cum-sweetened digits into Dell's mouth.

"Taste your own cum before you eat mine."

Dell thought his cum tasted sweet, but good. He was about to orgasm again, but Gus beat him to it.

"I'm coming now. Clench your butt so that it all stays inside."

Dell scrunched and felt the cop's hot semen flooding his chute in large spurts. "It's boiling," he said. "Oh god, I want it in my mouth."

Gus already had a glass ready for him. "Now sit up and pour the cum into this."

Dell sat up on his thin haunches and placed the glass beneath his red, swollen anus. A long, thick trail of white spunk slowly bubbled its way into the cup.

"Drink it," said Gus.

Dell put the glass to his lips and downed it like a milky shot. The cum was still hot. Hot and salty with a nutty tang. He felt it coat his throat, giving it a thick sheen of malty cum. He wanted more and said so. He used his mouth to polish Gus's cock, tip to balls.

"Let's watch a movie now," said Gus with a sly grin. He got up from the bed, his mule cock waning, and left the room.

Puzzled, Dell grabbed a towel from the bathroom and wrapped it around his waist. He entered the living room where the naked cop was watching what looked like security footage.

It was a video of Gus giving Dell head in the rubber room.

Dell felt a sickly sensation creeping up his spine.

"I want you to have this," said Gus, stopping the film and ejecting the DVD.

"You sure?"

"Absolutely." He handed the disc to Dell. "Use it to jack off."

"Is this the only copy?"

There was a silence. "I'm not blackmailing you, Dell. I'm giving you the DVD, and I have more to lose here. This is my job we're talking about." Gus's face was a mask of utter seriousness.

"Sorry. I expected you—oh, never mind."

They showered together languidly, and afterward dined on a succulent roasted duck with a lovely chardonnay. They talked a great deal about modern psychology, as well as gay marriage and healthcare reform. That night Dell went home with the DVD in his jacket, his balls completely drained, his throat bruised, and his ass still leaking jizz.

He called London as soon as he pulled into his mother's driveway.

"What did you learn?" she asked.

"Cops have issues," he said. The taste of Gus's spunk was still discernible on his tongue despite the wonderful duck. "And I can't help them."

BLOWING IT

Neil Plakcy

It all started with a pog.

If you've ever been to Hawaii, you probably know that a pog is a pineapple-orange-guava juice drink, and you get one any time you fly between islands. I was returning to Honolulu from the Big Island after a police training class, and I had to hurry to make the last flight back. I didn't get a chance to visit the men's room at the Kailua-Kona airport before boarding, and as soon as I drank that pog I had to pee like a racehorse.

I didn't even slow down long enough to bolt the door behind me, just kicked it closed with my leg as I was unzipping my pants. I stood and peed, and man, it felt good. I was just finishing when the door to the tiny bathroom opened and the male flight attendant, Keoni, slipped in. I shouldn't have been surprised; he'd made it clear to me that he knew who I was when he served me the pog. I've got my fans, you see; I'm the only openly gay detective on the Honolulu police force, and my picture's regularly in the *Honolulu Weekly* and gay bar rags like *Da Kine*.

He was a cute guy, and I admit I'd entertained a brief fantasy as he handed me the pog and our eyes met. He was a few inches shorter than I am, about five-nine, and we both had dark hair, tanned skin and hairless forearms. I'm thirty-three, and he was probably about five or six years younger, but we had the same slim build. The little porno movie had played in my head for just a minute, and then he moved on, and I drank the pog, and suddenly all I could think about was getting to the lavatory and emptying my bladder.

Keoni clearly had other things on his mind. There wasn't much room in the tiny lavatory, but he squeezed down in front of me, pushing me against the back wall, and I balanced myself, one hand against the sink and the other against the side wall.

My dick wasn't hard, and there were probably a few drops of urine still dribbling out, but Keoni didn't seem to mind. He took me in his mouth as he unbuckled my belt and opened my pants, dropping them to my knees, then reached up through the leg of my boxers (the ones with tropical fish in neon colors, not nearly as embarrassing as some in my drawer) and fondled the underside of my balls.

It was like he flipped a switch and my dick immediately responded, inflating to its full six inches. (I'm a cop, after all; I don't lie, even about the length of my dick.) His finger kept working me, stroking the sensitive area between my ass and balls as he sucked and licked, and all too quickly I felt shudders rising.

But he pulled back, and I didn't come. I was still hard, my mouth was dry and my groin was roiling, but I didn't come. Keoni said nothing, but his index finger found my asshole and started wiggling, and a minute or two later his mouth was back on my dick. He deep-throated me, then pulled back to lick me like I was an ice-cream cone. The tip of his tongue penetrated my piss slit and goose bumps rose on my arms.

I felt the pressure build—but so did Keoni, and he backed off. Three times he brought me nearly to the point of explosion and then backed off. By the fourth time, though, I was ready to beg. I couldn't tell how much time had passed, but I was sure there was somebody else with a full bladder waiting outside the lavatory, and my arms had grown so weak I was having trouble keeping my balance—and I needed to come.

Keoni knew that, too, without my having to do anything more than utter a few inarticulate moans and whimpers, though I tried my best to be quiet and keep what we were doing in there a secret from anyone standing outside. As the pressure increased inside my groin for the fourth time, Keoni didn't let up, and it felt like every nerve ending in my body became electrified as my cum exploded down his throat.

I have to admit that I don't get as much sex as you might expect for a reasonably good-looking guy with a uniform and a pair of handcuffs. Maybe it's the long hours I work, or the fact that most of the guys I come in contact with are in the process of committing a crime or being arrested, but it had been quite a while since a cute guy's mouth had come anywhere near my circumcised dick. So I was reeling and had to sit down on the toilet—after fortunately having had the presence of mind to flip the lid.

Keoni wrenched himself to his feet. "I need your help," he said.

"You could have just asked," I said, after catching my breath. "You didn't have to blow me first."

"I did that because I wanted to," he said. "Can you stay in your seat after we land, until the rest of the passengers get off?"

I started to laugh. "Don't tell me you're going to blow every one of them?" He gave me an evil look—which made me like him even more. "Okay, sure," I said.

"Keep the door closed after I leave. Stay here for a couple of minutes and then come out."

He slid the "occupied" sign on, opened the door and stepped out. "I'm sorry, there's a problem with this lavatory," I heard him say. "Can you please use the one at the rear of the plane?"

By the time I'd flushed the toilet—I had peed, after all—closed up my pants and washed my hands, there was no one waiting outside, and no one even seemed to notice that I'd come out of a lavatory that was supposedly broken. A guy got up out of his seat as I sat down and went in, as if he'd never even noticed Keoni coming out and making his announcement.

True to my word, I waited in my seat until the rest of the passengers had left. I followed the last couple, an elderly man and woman in matching aloha shirts, and Keoni fell into step behind me as we exited the jetway. "I have a stalker," he said. "I need you to help me get rid of him."

"Let me guess," I said. "You gave him one of those world-class blow jobs and he keeps coming back for more."

"Something like that," he said. "Listen, I need to clock out. Can you wait for me at the front of the terminal?"

I agreed, and after I'd been waiting only a few minutes, Keoni arrived. "If you can give me a lift to Waikiki, I'll explain the problem," he said, and he began his story as we walked to my truck. "I don't usually give blow jobs on the plane," he said. "I wouldn't want you to get the wrong idea. But I do occasionally slip a napkin with my phone number on it to a cute guy."

We got to my truck, which was parked in the short-term lot—I'd only been to the Big Island for the day. "Jerry called me as soon as he got off the plane, and we met outside Lappert's ice cream. I took him into a back corridor I know, and blew him. I figured that would be it, but he called me the next day. He found out my schedule from the airline, and he looked me up on the

Internet and found out where I live and a whole bunch of other stuff about me."

"It was a hell of a blow job," I said. "I can see why somebody'd want another one."

"You help me get rid of Jerry, I'll give you all the blow jobs you want," Keoni said. "As long as you don't turn into another stalker."

"Stalking's not my style," I said. "What do you know about Jerry?"

He didn't know much. He gave me Jerry's phone number, though, and a general description. After I dropped Keoni off at his apartment, a low-rise building in a run-down area of Waikiki, I called Jerry on my cell phone. "Hey, my name's Kimo," I said. Fortunately, Kimo's a pretty common name in the islands; it's the way the early missionaries translated the name James when they were converting the Bible into Hawaiian. "Keoni told me you've got a big dick and you like blow jobs."

Keoni actually hadn't said anything about the size of Jerry's dick, but I've never met a gay man yet who wasn't flattered by the compliment. "Keoni's a great guy," Jerry said. "Nobody gives a blow job like he does."

"You can only say that because you haven't gotten one from me yet," I said. "You want to give it a try?"

At the time, I didn't have any plan to go down on Jerry; I was just trying to get him to meet me. "Sure," he said. "Where can we meet?"

Yes, I know having sex in public places is illegal. Remember, I'm a cop? But I know this gay bar on Waikiki with a couple of rooms in the back, and if you slip the bartender a ten-dollar bill (or if you're a regular customer, like me) he'll give you a key for one of the rooms.

It's not like the baths; you can't sit there with the door open and your dick waving in the wind like a rainbow flag. But if you meet somebody at the bar and you just can't wait to get to his motel room—or, more likely, if he lives with his mother in some distant suburb—you can both discreetly stroll down the hall, slip inside, and close the door behind you.

You can't leave used condoms on the floor, and you can't howl like a wolf when you come, but pretty much anything else goes. I told Jerry to meet me at the bar, and to head down the hall and knock three times on the third door. "Give me a half hour to get there," I said.

I parked my truck back at my apartment building and walked over to the bar, which is only a few blocks away—very convenient when I'm either thirsty or horny. And despite the world-class blow job from Keoni, my accumulated sexual drought had left me still on the horny side. I was leaning against the wall, with my badge pinned to my shirt and a pair of handcuffs in my hand, when Jerry knocked.

I opened the door, let him see only my face, and ushered him inside. He was a good-looking guy, with a chiseled face and slicked-back hair that reminded me of a young Arnold Schwarzenegger. He was just a little on the stocky side, but that happens to be how I like my men—with some meat on their bones.

He was wearing flip-flops, a tank top and compression shorts, and his hard-on was clearly visible against the nylon fabric. Then I moved behind him and locked the door. That's when he turned and saw the badge.

"What the fuck?" The hard-on quickly deflated.

"Keoni says you've been bothering him," I said. "That true?"

"Dude, you gotta understand," he said. "I never had a blow job like that before."

"How long ago did you meet him?"

He frowned. "About a month ago, I guess. I went over to the Big Island for a couple of days, and I was flying back when he slipped me his phone number."

"How often have you seen him since then?"

The room was small, with a single bed jammed up against one wall and a rubber sheet stretched over it. There was a drain in the center of the concrete floor, and a flip-top trash can with the word *mahalo,* which means thank you in Hawaiian, on the flap. I motioned him to the bed, and I leaned back against the door.

"The first week, I saw him every day when he got off work. I knew when his last flight arrived, and I used to hang around at the airport waiting for him."

"And he gave you a blow job every day?"

He nodded. "Then he started avoiding me. I guess I got a little obsessive about calling him."

"You know that's stalking, don't you?" He nodded. "And you know that's wrong?"

"But dude, he does stuff no guy has ever done for me."

"I know. He blew me in the lavatory on my flight."

"So you know."

"Yeah." And suddenly, I knew how I could get Jerry to stop bothering Keoni.

I grabbed the single pillow from the bed, threw it to the floor, and got down on my knees in front of Jerry. I reached up and jerked his compression shorts down, causing him to jump a little. His limp dick tumbled free, and I reached up under his balls the way Keoni had done to me. In a moment, his dick came to life.

It was thicker than mine, and a little shorter, but it tasted just fine to me. I tried to remember everything Keoni had done to me. I began by licking his dick from the root up to the tip, like a it was a lollipop. Rotating my head, I got the whole thing glistening with my saliva. I wrapped my hand around the bottom of his dick and started slowly jacking him, while nibbling and sucking at the top.

Jerry seemed to like it, and I willed myself to go slowly and pay attention to his reaction. I deep-throated him a couple of times, relaxing my gag reflex enough to go down so far his pubic hairs tickled my nostrils, then pulled back and licked him a few more times.

My nose was filled with the rich, earthy locker-room smell of a dick in heat. I stroked the area behind his balls as I took each of his goose eggs in my mouth. He groaned. As I licked and sucked, I listened for those little signs that he was losing control—quickened breathing, slight moaning, a stiffening in the loins.

As soon as I felt his body responding, I pulled off.

"Dude, don't stop," he panted.

I ran my index finger along the inside of his thigh, and he shivered. After a minute or two, when it was clear the moment of near-ejaculation had passed, I went back down on him. My own dick had begun straining for release, but I knew that as soon as I started touching myself, I'd forget all about monitoring Jerry's excitement level. So I left my dick stuffed awkwardly into my shorts, and focused only on Jerry—on his solid, beefy thighs; his hairy, low-hanging balls and his fat, juicy dick. Twice more I brought him nearly to the verge, then pulled back.

He was starting to whimper a little, begging me, trying to hold my head in place over his dick. At that point, I abandoned my strategy. I fumbled with my pants and finally gave my dick the open air it had been craving. With my right hand, I pulled some saliva and precum from Jerry and used it to lubricate myself.

Then I began furiously jacking myself while sucking him strong and fast. It didn't take long for us both to erupt. Jerry's whole body shook as the semen coursed out of his dick and down my throat. Mine spurted up like an eruption from Mauna Loa, spilling onto the concrete floor.

"Dude, that was awesome," he said, when we'd both caught our breath. I struggled up from the floor and sat next to him on the bed, both of us slumped against the wall.

"But not as good as Keoni?"

"Keoni never got himself off at the same time," he said. "That was major hot, watching you jack off while you were sucking me."

About a month later, I checked in with Keoni. I thought I was about due for another one of his special treatments, and I wanted to see if Jerry'd stopped bothering him. "Yeah," he said. "He called me once, a couple of weeks ago, and we got together. But he promised not to stalk me, and he's been pretty good about it."

We made plans to meet. I wanted to ask him about a couple of techniques. I'd been getting a lot of practice lately, but I knew there were a few things I needed to improve. I was lying back on my bed, naked, just thinking of seeing Keoni and stroking myself lightly, when my cell phone rang. I looked at the display, and then answered.

"Jerry, you've got to stop calling me every day," I said.

COPS AND DOCTORS

T. Hitman

Me, I'm nobody. A thirty-year-old with a slight gut who volunteers at the local city-run animal shelter when I should be getting laid; who works as an attendant in the Ellis General Hospital Emergency Room. *Attendant*, that's a glorified term for an ER orderly. I transport patients, splint broken fingers, clean up the messes left behind by the doctors and nurses and insert catheters into the pee-holes of old men who can't piss due to swollen prostates or young Turks who've just rolled Daddy's SUV over the embankment along Route 459. Nobody.

Fox Burgess, he was somebody. Thirty-five. Six-foot-two. When he entered a room, you couldn't help but notice him, find yourself struggling to catch your breath at the sight of him. Fall in love with him or at the very least in lust. A week before the shooting, the ten-year vet of the Ellis Police Department sat in a chair in the nurse's lounge filling out paperwork, his painfully handsome face unshaved for a day or two, maybe longer, and from the ajar door of the narcotics supply closet, I heard two of our nurses verbally masturbating over him.

"Can you imagine how that scruff'd feel on your clit?"

"I just want him to fuck me hard from behind until my cunt explodes."

I tipped my gaze into the nurse's lounge and caught sight of Fox's grinning face, which was quickly turning red. Our eyes met—his remarkable, hypnotic chocolate browns, mine your average everyday shade of hazel—and his smile widened.

"What the fuck," he chuckled under his breath, slowly shaking his head.

Arms folded, dressed in my hospital white pants and the deceptive blue scrub shirt that nearly hid my stomach, I leaned against the door to the nurse's lounge and fired back the first thing that came to mind. "Heartbreaker."

Fox nodded and adjusted the bulge in his crotch-hugging black uniform pants as he rose from the chair. I fell into his shadow and deeper under his spell. He was magnificent, with hair buzzed nearly to the scalp, classically handsome face, perfect lips formed into a smile that curved slightly downward at the corners, his eyes looking perpetually wounded like a puppy dog's that's just been scolded, no matter whether he happened to be smiling or was seriously pissed off.

"I know, poor me," he sighed, tucking his clipboard under one arm, clapping the hand of the other on my shoulder and briefly massaging my flesh through the flimsy fabric of the scrub shirt with long, strong fingers. "Be good, buddy."

And then he breezed out the door, fired off a "Good night, ladies," and was gone.

The next time I saw Officer Burgess came after the telltale squawk of harsh musical notes tore out of the intercom connecting our ER with the paramedics, shattering the night's relative calm. I was polishing the stainless steel arms and frame of an empty gurney with rubbing alcohol when it happened. Two of the third-shift nurses, one of them part of that same duo that had wanted to drop their pussies on Fox Burgess' cock, were taking a smoke break outside in the ambulance bay beyond the sliding doors, which stood open. Doctor Vern Lucas was making notations on a chart.

That fairly routine early autumn night quickly spiraled from order into chaos after Doc Lucas pressed the intercom button and identified himself.

Officer down. Gunshot wound. Patient unresponsive.

The cop who'd gotten shot was Fox Burgess.

There's a secret, special relationship between cops and the healers who inhabit an emergency room, and that relationship extends beyond just the doctors and RNs to the attendants, the phlebotomists, the psych counselors and even the secretaries who answer the phones. The bond is unspoken, unwritten, and unbreakable. Half the nurses in any ER are married to cops. It's just one of those symbiotic relationships that has always been, always will be. They're the soldiers of the law maintaining order throughout the night, but we're the keepers of life. We're the ones who'd give anything to fuck or marry them, but when it comes right down to it, they look up to us. They have to, because when one of them pulls over a nut-job in a stolen car and that twenty-one-year-old bad-ass who's looking at serious jail time gets desperate, reaches for the gun tucked in his belt under cover of a baggy basketball jersey, and fires, striking one of them in the chest…

Well, we're all the hope they've got left in this world.

The next few minutes stretched into something that felt more like hours, and time wasn't the only element distorted out of context. Space, too, seemed to fall apart. The air inside the emergency room took on a hazy quality, as if an undercurrent of electricity was rippling throughout it, through us. Voices screamed from every direction as Special Care Room Four, the main venue for trauma victims and heart attack patients, was rapidly transformed in preparation for the paramedics' arrival.

In Special Four: Doctor Lucas, two nurses (one, the RN who'd wanted to feel Officer Burgess' thickness inside her cunt, standing with tears in her eyes), the respiratory therapy techs who always traveled in pairs like religious zealots, the EKG tech off to the periphery, a phlebotomist, me.

Strobing lights the color of blood shattered the darkness outside the ambulance bay doors, but we had heard the high-pitched wail of the siren well in advance. Bile rose in my throat; a sour taste ignited on my tongue. An invisible, leaden weight pulled my stomach into knots. The air inside the ER, temperate as autumn was settling in across New England but not hot, grew suddenly strangulating. By the time those double doors clacked open, unleashing a wall of much-cooler night air, sweat was pouring from my scalp.

It all happened very fast.

One ambulance attendant at the head of the stretcher turned the corner into Special Four. A paramedic was at the side of the stretcher, his gloved hand pressing a blood-soaked square of gauze over the naked flesh of the downed officer's chest. Fox's uniform shirt and white undershirt had been cut off his body and lay in shreds at his side along with plenty of blood. Christ, the blood.

The two ambulance attendants lined up their stretcher with our gurney. Fox was on a backboard, an oxygen mask over his face. The stink of rotten eggs, sulfur from the gunshot, clung to his body. The paramedic holding pressure braced his side of the backboard, I assumed the other from across the gurney, and with the help of both the ambulance attendants, we four slid the backboard over.

From there, the action ramped up into overdrive: the blood pressure cuff was applied to the bare flesh of Fox's muscled arm. I noted the chain of barbed wire tattooed around his biceps, silently marveled in secret at the lush, dark nest of armpit hair, briefly drank in the dense *T*-shape of matching fur that cut Fox across and down his chest. A split second after the BP cuff was on, one of the nurses scraped a disposable razor through the hair just above the tiny pink nipples protruding out of that dense forest, as well as the intercostal region between his fifth and six ribs on the left. Gummy pads were slapped over the clear-cut circles and then attached to the wires feeding up into the cardiac monitor. I yanked the oxygen hose out of the portable cylinder hidden beneath the ambulance stretcher, jabbed it into our wall-mounted nozzle and cranked the valve open.

"Fox, can you hear me? This is Vern Lucas. You're at Ellis General," the doctor bellowed. He waved a penlight over the policeman's wide, wet eyes. "Fox, do you know what's happened to you?"

"What happened is that some piece of shit shot Foxy!" answered an angry voice from the doorway.

I glanced over to see Officer Mike Doogan and the chief of police standing at the open curtain. Mike, who was my age, made no attempt to disguise the pain in his sharp blue eyes. Chief Daniels' tears looked barely held in check.

"Come on, guys, it's crowded enough in here," the EKG tech urged. She took the men by their arms and led them into the nurse's lounge.

I automatically pulled the curtain shut and was thanked by one of the nurses as the other told me to undress the patient.

My location at the foot of the bed now put me in the perfect position to see Fox Burgess and what had been done to him. He lay prostrate before me, his handsome face a mask of pain, blood soaking the rags cut off of his chest. I was at the end of the gurney, staring up at his big booted feet, his uniform pants, and for a split second, I froze. A chill teased the small hairs at the base of my neck. And then I went on automatic.

Unlacing Fox's boots. Pulling them off. The white socks underneath, their toes damp with a reverse bas-relief of sweat.

The hot, buttery smell of a real man's feet filled my next shallow breath. I peeled off one sock, my fingertips vanishing into the coarse hair just above his ankle. The warmth of his naked flesh proved intoxicating; my heart galloped in my chest. I drew down the other sock over ankle, instep, and finally, toes.

While stuffing each sock into its well-traveled matching boot, and then the boots into a large white plastic patient's belongings bag, some unaffected register in my mind noted the perfect shape of his feet. Thin black strands of hair capped his toes. The second digits were slightly longer than his big ones, like the feet on classical statues. Fox's were the type of feet that passionate artists fell madly in love with.

I hung the bag on a hook, opened another, and maneuvered between the crowd of bodies that were drawing his blood, checking his heart rate, peeling back the hastily-applied bandage over the bullet wound that had ripped through his upper right chest area. The coppery odor of fresh blood assailed my nostrils as I reached for the policeman's belt.

Fox's holster sat empty, the gun gone, no doubt handed over to Officer Doogan for safekeeping. I fumbled the buckle and top button open and then unzipped his uniform pants. One of the RNs took hold from her side of the gurney. I grabbed a handful of pants and together we stripped him to his ankles.

While most of this happened at breakneck speed, that register in my thoughts recorded the events at a much slower pace, observing the incredible contour of the policeman's outer thighs, solid and hairy; his calves, equally impressive. He'd been wearing a tatty pair of tight whites when he'd gone on shift that night, not the kind of underwear you want to be caught in should that mythical accident all boys are threatened with while growing up actually land you in the hospital. A tear along their left side revealed the hair-covered orb of one swollen ball.

I eased his pants off completely. By the time I made it back up there, the nurse had cut his underwear into shreds using her bandage scissors.

"You'll need to cath him," Doctor Lucas said.

"Yes, sir," I answered.

Again, I did what needed to be done without question. Male catheterization kits are fairly easy to use once you know what you're doing, at least in clinical if not emotional terms. I mean, you're sticking a tube into an opening that's not designed for such an invasion. A man's pee-hole is meant to be one-way only, unless he's just been shot and you need to know how deep the damage goes.

The loud rolling sound of the portable X-ray machine's wheels ground to a stop outside the door. The strapping ex-army X-ray tech poked his buzz-cut crown into the room. His frown mirrored everybody else's.

"We're out here when you're ready," he signaled to the team.

The last thing I'd ever expected to find myself doing at the start of that night's shift was performing a cath job on Fox Burgess. *Is this for real? Am I holding his cock in my hands, about to shove a rubber hose into it?*

"Fox, we have to insert a tube into your penis to measure the fluids we're putting into you against what's coming out. Also, we need to make sure there isn't any blood in your urine. You're going to feel some pressure," Doc Lucas said, his tone soothing, if not his words.

Yes, pressure.

I stole a bottled glance at the policeman's cock. Though limp, it still rose up impressively over my now gloved hand, thick, with a network of veins, ridges, and dings. Dark hair lined both sides of its shaft. The head was shaped like a fireman's helmet, as classically perfect as those long second toes.

I swabbed Fox's dick with iodine solution, dipped the catheter's tip into lubricant, then eased it into his piss slit. Fox jerked beneath me, resisted. That silent pop that tells you that you've done your job with precision followed and the catheter slid the rest of the way in. I hastily inflated the balloon that holds it in place with a syringe of sterile water and hooked the bag attachment to the gurney's lower side rail. Clear, pale yellow urine flowed out of the catheter and down the tube into the bag, from which I gathered a sample for those all-important lab tests.

Less than an hour later, the surgical team was in place on the third floor, awaiting our arrival. I guided the gurney down the corridor, flanked by an OR doctor dressed in blue scrubs who studied X-rays as we moved, his operating room nurse, the anesthesiologist and an RN from our ER. The cold overhead fluorescent lights raced with us to the elevator, blinding, consuming, swallowing us whole.

I didn't break down until Fox had been transferred over to the OR team, unhooked from our equipment and reconnected to theirs, until I was alone in the elevator on my way back down to the ground floor, riding with a gurney whose sheets were soaked in blood and the cut-away remains of Fox Burgess' uniform.

The solemn reality of what had happened hung over the ER like a shroud.

I parked the gurney outside the big double doors to spare anyone in there from seeing the blood, the shreds. I gathered the sheets together and dumped them in a laundry bag. Fox's uniform shirt...I discreetly put that in the trash, washed the stretcher, and returned to the hub.

More cops had gathered in the nurse's lounge. Seeking a much-needed cup of coffee, I made it inside the room where Doogan, Chief Daniels, and their brothers-in-arms sat in silence, not making eye contact with anyone. The coffee pot had been drained dry.

"How is he?" somebody asked.

I didn't realize it at first, but the comment had been meant for me. Going through the motions, I emptied coffee into a filter, filled the carafe with water, poured.

"He's up there now, and just so all of you know, he's in the best hands possible. That's a great team they have in our OR."

The coffee began to percolate, and although I hadn't said much, my words seemed to comfort the cops collectively. One of the officers clapped a hand on my shoulder. Another thanked me.

"Coffee's on the way, guys," I said, exiting the room before drinking a single drop of it.

Mike Doogan pulled Fox's keys out of his uniform pants. "Dude," he said, taking me aside. "Got to ask you a huge favor."

"Sure," I answered.

"Fox has this big old mutt named Buzz. Great dog. Somebody's got to feed him, walk him. I know you volunteer over at the town shelter, figured since you love animals and all..."

The words were out of my mouth before I could stop them. "I'd be happy to."

I accepted the keys. Officer Mike gave me the directions to Fox's house, and at half past seven in the morning, bedraggled and emotionally drained, I drove to the far side of town, to a small brick ranch house with a weedy, overgrown lawn.

Buzz and I became fast friends. Buzz was a fat, neutered male husky-shepherd mix Fox had rescued from a chain in a dirty backyard after his previous owners had skipped out on the rent, abandoning him without food or water during the dog days of a New England August several years before.

I let myself in through the kitchen door, was greeted by nervous yowls, but spied an open box of dog biscuits on top of the fridge. By the time I clasped a leash onto his collar, we'd bonded. I led him around the yard, fed him from a can I found in the cabinet, and filled his water bowl. Then, exhaustion and the weight of the past night's heavy emotions overwhelmed me.

I knew I'd never make the ten-mile drive home alive. And I can't say I've ever passed out in my work scrubs before taking a shower, washing my body clean of the filth that comes from working in Ellis General's ER.

When I bolted awake on the couch in Fox's living room, I had no idea where I was—hell, *who* I was. Nothing about the living room with its big TV and mismatched furniture and sheets tacked over the windows for drapes was familiar. Buzz had fallen asleep lengthwise on the floor beside the couch and jolted up with me, his nervous yelp anchoring me back to my location. I was in Fox's house on the outskirts of Ellis, Massachusetts. Fox was likely in post-op, headed to the hospital's intensive care unit.

If he was still alive, that is.

My clothes stuck to my body like a layer of dead skin. Sweaty, the taste in my mouth foul, I staggered into the head to piss.

I didn't set out to open the medicine cabinet and remove the tube of toothpaste, brushing my teeth using a length of mint gel squeezed onto my right pointer finger. I'd started out cupping a hand under the bathroom tap to rinse my mouth, but it wasn't enough to remove the foul taste on my tongue. I washed my face, mesmerized by the thought that Fox had been the last to touch the bar of green soap, which smelled clean and masculine.

In a trance, I undressed. I opened the shower curtain, ran the water moderately hot, and stepped in under the spray. Another bar of soap waited in the caddy, along with a bottle of generic shampoo and a razor. Dark hairs clogged the drain. The air possessed a slightly mildewed smell. I washed, both mystified and plagued by guilt over the erection I'd popped. But I didn't masturbate, not that time.

"It's very important that when you go in there to see him, you keep your emotions in check," I said. Judging by the expressions on their faces, Mike Doogan and another young cop whose name I didn't know looked to be on the verge of busting up the ICU's waiting room. "There's a good chance that even though he's still unconscious, Fox will pick up on what's being said or emoted. So go in there and talk to him about good things. Fun things. Normal things. That's the best medicine now, to give him a reason to come back from the abyss."

Doogan nodded. "Thanks, man. And thanks for keeping an eye on Fox's house and that mutt of his."

"No problem...."

I exited the shower, toweled dry, and in a trance, moved into the bedroom.

Fox's bed was a mattress and box spring on the floor. A TV sat atop a dresser covered in scars and old decals of baseball teams and rock groups, probably the same dresser he'd owned while growing up.

Like the nights, the days had started to take on the first cool bite of autumn. Naked and feeling chilled, I slipped beneath the blanket, which still smelled of Fox, a sour-sweet muskiness of perspiration likely sweated out over the recent summer mixed with a trace of cologne and feet. As had happened so often in the previous two days, I proceeded in a daze, only partially aware of my actions.

I pressed my face into the pillow and breathed deeply until high on his smell. In the middle of the bed, I discovered spatters of dried semen on the sheets, and like a man possessed, I licked at them until the salty tang of Fox Burgess' past ejaculations tingled across my taste buds.

I jerked off while tonguing the piss stains he'd left on a pair of white briefs I found in a pile of dirty clothes at the side of the bed, and came again several minutes later with my nostrils shoved into a pair of sweat socks whose toes stunk of the policeman's foot odor. After a third eruption beneath the stale bedclothes, I slept, while miles away, Fox Burgess drifted in a state of limbo, trapped between this world and the next.

On my fourth day at the house, I mowed the lawn.

I washed the pile of dishes he'd left in the sink, stacked them neatly in the cabinets, and cleaned the rest of the kitchen. I swept the floor. I brushed the dog and was rewarded with a look of pure gratitude and devotion.

I cleared out the fridge, drove to the grocery store, and

stocked up on fresh milk, orange juice, eggs, and fruit.

I vacuumed the living room. I scrubbed the bathroom. I washed and dried Fox's dirty clothes in the basement laundry area, which sat adjacent to a weight bench and the skeleton of the motorcycle he was restoring.

As twilight crept in, earlier now that summer was on the wane, I carried his clean underwear, socks, T-shirts, and blue jeans over to his dresser. I discovered Fox's stash of porn in the sock drawer.

With the same trancelike movements I'd displayed for the past four days, I withdrew the pile of magazines. I flipped the top rag open to its centerfold, but found the pages stuck together, doubtless from a wad of Fox's cum, so I backtracked through images of naked, hairy men; boners, swollen testicles, and bare muscle; registering all that I saw, but still not completely understanding it. That revelation came after an unmarked VHS tape slipped out from between the stroke magazines, clattering to the floor and shocking me out of my spell.

Though my dick throbbed in my pants, I was barely conscious of it as I slid the tape into the VCR and hit the PLAY button.

A grainy picture shimmered into focus, of two wide eyes trained upward at the man who was holding the camera. The eyes were attached to a mouth. The mouth was wrapped around a magnificent erect cock. And not just any cock, but *his* cock.

"Fuck, dude, play with my balls," I heard Fox growl. "Yeah, just like that...."

The image shook as the big hand holding the camera wavered.

Fox was completely naked, seated on the couch in the living room, bare legs and big feet spread. A stocky, hairy troll knelt hunched between them, slobbering up and down on his stiff cock. The troll and I shared the same body type; he was a nobody, just like me.

"Oh man, that feels so fuckin' great. My favorite, man..."

I watched as the nobody tugged on Fox's nuts, rolled them around in their loose sac, and briefly regurgitated the cop's impressive column in order to suckle each ball.

"Nothing I love more than having my bone sucked and my nuts worked on at the same time."

The nobody resumed sucking Fox's dick. Less than a minute later, Fox growled out a blue streak of swears.

"I'm fuckin' gonna bust, dude—you ready?"

The nobody moaned his approval around a mouthful of hard lawman dick. Fox bellowed and the camera shook.

"Lemme see it," Fox ordered, his voice weaker.

The nobody opened his mouth; as he did, a river of creamy white liquid oozed from between his lips and ran over his hairy chin.

"That's fuckin' sick, dude," Fox chuckled. The picture went dark after the troll swallowed down the remaining semen in his mouth.

I hadn't realized it until I reached into my pants to adjust myself that I'd shot my load without having touched my dick.

The next day, Fox came to me in a vision.

I had watched the tape for probably the hundredth time, had crawled into the bed's freshly-laundered sheets and blankets and closed my eyes when, seemingly an instant later, I felt the mattress sag under the weight of another body. I glanced over to see Fox's head resting on the pillow beside me, turned in my direction, a sad scowl on his handsome, unshaved face.

"Limbo, land of lost souls," he whispered, his eyes weighted down by that scolded puppy-dog look. "The ferryman is coming soon. You know what you have to do if you want me to stick around, dude."

I nodded, choked down a heavy swallow. "I love you."

"I could love you back, pal. Especially if yours is the first face I see…if I wake up."

I nodded. Our eyes locked and I felt myself falling deeper into his pull. But just as our lips moved close enough for the brush of a kiss, Fox's gaze darted toward a corner of the room.

"The ferryman!"

I shot awake to find that I'd soaked the pillow in tears, and that I was again alone in the bedroom of a doomed man.

I tore back the covers and quickly dressed. I showed up three hours early for my shift at Ellis General, but no one seemed to take much notice. After all, I'm nobody.

The intensive care unit, an oblong region of shadows on the same floor as the OR, was kept mostly dark regardless of the time of the day. Respirators wheezed and automated IV pumps chimed throughout the false twilight created by those few lit fluorescent bulbs over the nurse's station, a smaller oblong box located dead center of it all. Limbo, land of lost souls.

I approached the nurse's station and was greeted by a sharp, practiced smile.

"Hey," I whispered in a solemn voice.

The ferryman, dressed in pale blue hospital scrubs, glanced up from her paperwork, a hefty manifest of checks and balances, the life stories of every lost soul in the unit. "What can I do you for?"

"I wanted to check in on Officer Burgess. We're friends."

She tipped her chin toward the bed at the station's immediate left. "Don't suppose you have time to change his catheter while you're in there? The house attendant called out sick today."

"Sure, Rita, I'd be happy to," I said.

Heart pounding in my chest, I found a fresh cath kit on the ICU's supply cart and trudged the hundred or so steps to Fox's hospital bed, my feet altering from flesh, blood and bone to blocks of lead.

Fox lay on his back with his head and shoulders raised, a pristine white blanket covering him up to his bare pectorals, the breathing tube still in his mouth and a collection of tubes and wires anchoring him to this world. But he wouldn't remain here much longer, I knew.

I drew the heavy hospital curtains shut then opened the cath kit, but didn't waste time pulling on gloves or opening the iodine packet. Leaning close to his left ear, I said, "Fox, it's me. I'm here."

I lowered the blanket and did my best to avoid looking at the bandages on his upper chest. From the periphery, I caught sight of the dried blood that had soiled the gauze pads around their edges.

"I've been taking good care of Buzz. He and I want you to come home," I continued, uncovering Fox's lower abdomen, crotch, and those amazing hairy legs. "We love you and need you to stick around, 'kay? The house is clean now, and there's plenty of food in the fridge. I even mowed the lawn."

I pulled a syringe out of the kit and drained the bulb of sterile water I had injected into the catheter to hold it in place inside Fox's urethra. Holding his flaccid cock in one hand, I carefully removed the tube. When the tip slipped free of his pee-hole, a spurt of pale yellow piss surged out with it and rained down, showering his tight, leathery balls. I tossed the old catheter and its collection bag into the waste barrel, wiped off Fox's dick with a square of gauze, then pressed my lips to the side of his face, offering featherlight kisses.

"I know your secret passion. The thing that makes you happier than anything. I want you to come back, Fox. Follow the passion and find your way home to me."

I lowered my head between his legs, opened my mouth, and accepted his flaccid maleness between my lips. A bitter cocktail of piss and latex tingled across my tongue, but I ignored it and began to suck.

Images from the videotape played in my thoughts, only in my imaginary version I was the nobody kneeling between Fox's spread legs. I was the one pleasuring his needs while he held the camera, recording the encounter so it could be relived in private again and again. I reached for his damp balls and massaged them, gently at first but with increasing force the longer I worked at conjuring his cock out of its coma.

I'm not sure how long I remained in that position, leaning over one side of the hospital bed, toying with Fox's sac, nursing on his limp dick, because since the night of the shooting, linear time had lost most of its meaning to me. I do know that it was longer than it should have taken an attendant to change a patient's catheter.

I sucked, ogled, and massaged his legs and his crotch, running the fingers of my free hand across the treasure trail cutting him down his abdomen.

Please don't make him leave, I silently prayed to any deity who'd answer.

I sucked harder, rolling Fox's manhood between my tongue and the roof of my mouth. And just as I was about to give up, I felt something push back.

It couldn't be! But there it was, I quickly discovered. The mass between my lips was responding. I yanked on the policeman's balls and found their tightness loosening. On one plunge down to the root, I felt Fox's dick pump up to a half-hard state. On the next it was fully engorged, and that same magnificent boner I'd seen in his homemade porn video now filled my mouth with raw, fierce power.

Yes, Fox, I'm here!

I lifted his nuts, draped them over my nose, breathed in their pungent, wonderful stink and completely swallowed his cock. In concert, the gently rolling musical note beeping on the heart monitor above me began to increase its cadence.

I tasted precum.

Working harder, faster, I thought I heard a throaty groan from deep within Fox's chest. He grunted again, and I knew it wasn't my imagination playing tricks.

I lapped at his pee-hole, which had been stretched open by the catheter, and savored the raw, pure taste of his fluid.

"I love you, Fox," I said aloud, pulling violently on his nuts, now loosened completely. Moments after that declaration, with his thickness again in my mouth, Fox rewarded me with the first squirt of his semen.

I milked the shaft of his cock while sucking down the hot, sour liquid as his balls jettisoned half a dozen shots into my mouth. I was still sucking and he was still unloading when I felt the hospital bed shake. His legs—Fox had spread his legs!

I spit out his cock, forced my eyes from his dick to his abdomen, his abdomen to his chest, and from his chest up to his face. And at that moment, as our eyes met, Fox Burgess woke up.

PARTNERS

Dale Chase

When I get the call about Stan Perello I cannot remain at my desk. Two of my detectives sit opposite, waiting, and I look past them as I hear the word "dead." There are other words like "heart attack" and "quick" but they just roll off.

"Excuse me," I say and I rush out. My chest is tight, my stomach churns, and I don't know if I'm going to have a heart attack or throw up but then I'm outside gulping fresh air which helps except people are around and they start to look. There's nowhere to go but my car. I sprint toward it like I can outrun the facts.

In my car I absorb the awful news and, try as I might, I cannot hold back my feelings. I press my forehead to the wheel and go back to the beginning: that night twenty-four years ago, Perello and me in the car on the wrong side of Los Angeles. I let it play because him not being alive is impossible.

We're patrolling just after midnight when he suddenly swings the car into an alley as if he knows something is going down.

Nothing has been said but I know better than to question anything since I'm the rookie. Three guys scatter in the headlights and Perello corners one with the car, tells me, "Stay here," and jumps out.

This goes against procedure but in my brief time alongside this fourteen-year veteran I've learned not to question his methods, so I do as I'm told and stay put, don't even radio in. The guy he's cornered is maybe twenty and talking a mile a minute but so is Perello and then I see something that blows me away. When Perello turns the guy to the wall—to cuff him, I'm thinking—he yanks the guy's pants down. I then see my partner fumbling at his own crotch and seconds later he's riding the guy's ass. The radio crackles, it's dispatch saying we're needed elsewhere, and I respond with an affirmative, wondering what in the hell I do now, but then Perello is done. He zips up his pants and the perp runs past me.

I need to tell him we're responding to a call but what I've seen has rendered me speechless. So Perello, veteran that he is, says it for me. "Look, kid, you're gonna see things riding with me, okay? Only you're *not* gonna see, if you get my drift. This is life on the street and you'd better get used to it."

"Right," I manage, then tell him there's been a break-in four blocks over. "I told them we're on the way."

"Good boy."

The rest of the night I'm in a kind of fog, trying to figure things out. Perello sits two feet away and acts like he didn't just fuck a perp and let him go. I was thrilled when I got to partner with everybody's favorite cop but suddenly I don't know him. He's got a wife and kids at home; what the hell is this?

The shift ends at 6:00 a.m. and he leaves me with nothing but a nod. I get home and crawl into bed with Aaron, my businessman partner of two years. He awakens, murmurs as he wraps his arms around me. "Anything exciting?" he asks like always.

Usually I tell him, but this time I can't.

"Rough night?"

"Yeah."

He gets up and heads for the shower and I lie quietly, trying for sleep that I know is not going to come. Not when the sight of Perello doing the perp keeps playing in my mind. All I can see is his ass as he pumps in and out; all I can think of is his dick up that butt. My own stiffens and by the time Aaron is out of the shower and dressing for his day, I'm doing myself under the covers. He kisses me good-bye then huffs, "I don't see how this night shift is ever going to work," but he doesn't wait for a reply. He's gone and I roll onto my back, kick off the covers, and start to work my cock.

It's easy to visualize what I didn't see: the perp's butthole with Perello's cock buried in it; the perp's own dick that, I don't care the circumstances, has to be hard; Perello's come shooting out of him and into the guy. As I think about Perello coming, I do it myself, spraying jizz all up my belly. God, it's a good one, probably because it's been churning all night, but then my mind kicks in again and I wonder what Perello is doing now. Is he fucking his wife or does he just do guys, realizing marriage was the biggest mistake of his life? This man I admire is turning into a mystery.

I sleep half the day then hit the gym, watch some TV, and when Aaron gets home around seven, I have dinner ready. He's full of himself and his work so I mostly listen to corporate stories and then, as I'm clearing the dishes, he starts in about the cop thing. "You could be so much more," he says like it's a new idea and he hasn't already said it a hundred times. "Study law, go to night school. Do you know how many cops do that?"

"Do you?" I counter, tired of his trying to remake me. I've told him over and over that I've wanted to be a cop since I was five. "I'm doing what I want to do," I tell him again.

"You aim too low," he snaps.

"Please don't do this, Aaron. Do you know how it feels to hear that?"

"I just want what's best for you."

There is more to say but I leave it unsaid and we pass our usual weeknight half-evening. He gets several phone calls—all business—and at nine I dress for work. He's still on the phone when I leave so I just wave and head out. I'm eager to get back on the job.

Perello is larger than life. When he arrives at the station he pretty much takes over. Briefing room, locker room, john, doesn't matter, he's what you'd call a presence. Large, well built, solid, he exudes masculinity. That plus rugged good looks and a booming voice make him irresistible. I watch as people give way willingly. I've been told more than once I'm lucky to be paired with him.

This night, things are quiet and I'm starting to see Perello doesn't like that. He's a man of action; wrestling a perp to the ground probably gets his dick hard. We stop for tacos around midnight and he's antsy as hell.

"Quiet tonight," I offer.

"Nah, they just want you to think so. There's action on every corner, you just can't see it. Look up any alley, some punk's shooting up or fucking up or maybe just fucking." He says this last "fucking" with emphasis, then stands up, tosses his soft drink toward a can ten feet away. It misses. "Fuck," he says. He starts to the car and I toss the rest of my meal and follow.

We cruise our usual neighborhoods, keeping an eye out for trouble, but I soon realize we're circling one particular block. I start to ask why, then catch myself and wait. Sure enough: "Look over there," Perello says, nodding at a leather-jacketed guy slinking along with hunched shoulders.

"Yeah."

"He's holding."

"How do you know?"

"I can smell it."

We drive up the block, turn right and park. "Stay here," Perello commands and he gets out, walks back to the guy. I look into the rearview mirror.

He approaches the suspect, shows his badge, spreads the guy against the wall, does a quick pat-down, pulls something from the guy's pocket, flips him around, and starts talking to him. He's holding up what's probably a nickel bag and I think the guy is arguing the point but suddenly Perello is pushing him into a doorway and I can't see what's happening. I last about two seconds before I get out of the car, hurry past a couple storefronts until I can see through the glass into the doorway. The perp is on his knees with his back to me and there's Perello with his dick in the guy's mouth.

I watch the crotch-bobbing head and then Perello suddenly looks skyward, arches his back, and I know he's coming. He turns frantic and I can tell the guy is choking but he's also taking it. Then it's over and Perello pulls out. I see his cock, bright against the dark uniform. He leaves it out while he pulls the perp to his feet, says something, then shoves him out of the doorway. Perello shakes his head like he's trying to clear his mind and zips up. I run back to the car.

"So what was that?" I ask when he joins me. "Did you let him go?"

"Fucking punk. Waste of time."

I wonder then if Perello knows these guys, if maybe this is a regular thing, consensual in its own way, and he's been doing without for a while to break me in gradually. I don't question him about letting the punk go and the rest of the night he's in relatively good spirits until around five a.m. when the sun starts coming up. He obviously wants it again. "When I'm on days, this time of morning I'm fucking the wife," he offers without any prompting. "Wake up hard, roll over, give it to her whether she wants it or not, sometimes up the ass. Nothing like a fuck to start the day. You do that, Colby? You fuck to start the day?"

"When I can, yeah, sure."

"Trouble with the night shift. I get home, she's got the kids and won't let me near her. Man needs to get off, ya know?"

"Yeah."

"One time I busted this hooker only instead of taking her in, I did her in the car, fucked her up the ass. She didn't like me putting it up there but I tell her she don't have a choice and I ream her butt so she can barely walk after. That's what not getting it at home does to a man."

I know he's not talking about any female hooker. He'd done some guy and now he wants to do him again. We keep driving, keep looking, but all we get is a robbery attempt. Watching Perello disarm a perp is something because he talks the guy out of it. This is the bigger side of him and I never get tired of seeing it, which only adds to the confusion.

When Aaron gets home that night I'm naked and when he gets a call as I suck his dick and actually reaches for the phone, I let go of him, grab the receiver and toss it aside. "I'm sucking your cock, for chrissakes!" I yell. "What could be more important?"

"Sorry," he says like I'm being rude. I look up at him from where I'm kneeling and shake my head. "Forget it."

"No, Kevin, come on, I'm sorry. It's just that Mel said he'd call and this is important, you know that, but I want you too." He pulls me to my feet. "Let's go into the bedroom but first I need to call Mel back."

I laugh, it's that absurd. "Fine." As I start down the hall I hear him say, "Mel? What's the word?"

I pull back the covers and lie down but instead of anticipating my partner, I think about my other partner. It's not that I haven't considered the fact that I have two of them, I've just never compared them sexually, but now I do: Aaron with his priorities in the other room and Stan Perello sticking his cock into a perp's mouth. By the time Aaron finishes his call I'm hard and when he rolls me over and pushes in, I'm still thinking about my other partner.

So Perello has sex on the job several nights a week and I wonder if he did this when he was riding with his former partner or if he's just taking liberties with a rookie he knows won't say anything. And does he even know I'm gay? I haven't said a word about my personal life, let everyone believe I have a girlfriend, which is easy as all you have to do is nod when they talk pussy. Before me he'd partnered with Ed Morgan for something like eight years but Morgan was older and then he retired. Had he tolerated the younger cop's antics? Had he maybe initiated them?

One night about a month after I first see Perello having sex on the job, we break up a domestic dispute which involves a raft of people. A fight has broken out, people are bloody, we call for backup, and in the melee I lose Perello. The old broken-down house has two stories and about a dozen rooms. While I'm downstairs taking statements, Perello is upstairs doing the same—only he's not. I know this because he chased two young guys up there and sure enough when he finally comes back down he wears a look I recognize. "I interrogated them both," he says. "They've got nothing. The shit heads down here, they're the ones caused it all."

Hours later we're back on the street. "You take it where you can," Perello says out of nowhere. "You want to do somebody on the job, I don't see a thing just like you see me getting some, you don't see it either, ya know?"

"Yeah, sure."

"Don't know how you do it, kid."

"What?"

"Riding around all night, dick not even hard."

"How do you know it's not hard?" I snap.

There's a long pause. He nods but nothing more is said.

The next night is a busy one. After just about everything in the book—two domestic disputes, a botched robbery and a successful one, a brutal three-car traffic accident and some drunks carted off to jail—we get a disturbance call and find two guys coming out the back of a liquor store. "My uncle owns the place," one says as we confront them.

"Then why you coming out the back?" Perello demands.

Our guns are not drawn. I've got a flashlight and Perello has his baton in hand. "Cause he won't give me the key, man," the guy replies, laughing.

"You think this is funny?"

"No, man, I don't."

"Empty your pockets," Perello says as I shine the light on them but then one guy bolts and I drop the flashlight and start after him while Perello detains the other. We sprint down the block and I land the guy when a bum sleeping on the street trips him. I cuff the perp, give the bum a dollar, and go back to Perello. I put my guy into the car, then join my partner who is still talking to the first guy. I can't figure why he's not in custody. I pass Perello a look but he ignores me.

"Marvin here says his uncle really does own the store but he can't seem to prove it, can you Marvin? I think you are gonna do some serious time."

I notice that Perello's baton is back on his belt and I realize what is going to happen. He's gonna fuck the guy. I don't see how but knowing him, he'll find a way. He backs up, grins at Marvin, who, fool that he is, takes the opportunity to run. "Fuck head," Perello says and he takes off after him. I take off after Perello.

There's no bum to help this time. Marvin leads us on a good chase but I finally overtake him, leap onto his back and bring him down. We're in a vacant lot behind a warehouse and he is seriously resisting. I take an elbow in the throat, which throws me off balance, but then Perello gets an arm around Marvin's neck while I struggle to get the cuffs on him. None of this works. The three of us scuffle and in the dark it's just bodies against bodies. Perello manages to land a good punch to Marvin's gut which drops him like a rock but then Perello is suddenly up against me.

The scuffle continues but there's just two of us now, wrestling like we're in combat and yet it's far from that. We twist and grab and then Perello pulls me to him and starts to grind. I feel his hard dick and that, plus the excitement of the moment, does it. I start grinding back. Marvin, meanwhile, is forgotten.

Perello claws at my belt and I start in on his. We are in near total darkness in a deserted lot full of rusted cars, weeds, and god knows what and we get out our cocks, get our pants down because we are going to do it here and now. We are going to goddamn fuck.

"Bend over," he says when my ass is bare. He pushes me forward and then he's in me, going at it full out, muttering "Fuck yeah," under his breath. He doesn't last long, he's too worked up, and then he's grunting and snarling like the pig he is.

I am aware of everything around me just as he is not. I hear city sounds, cars and trucks and sirens, but here on our forgotten scrap of land the fuck slap and Perello's noise are all that matter. I am also aware my partner's dick is shooting spunk up my butt and this arouses me to no end but he's done now and pulls out. "Shit, man," he says between gasps.

I raise up and turn toward him. I'm stroking my cock and he watches as I shoot come onto the ground.

"You're too fast," he manages as I spew. "I would have sucked you off. I like the taste of it."

When I'm empty I become acutely aware of what I've done. I can't see Perello's eyes in the dark, just his teeth because he's grinning. He shoves his dick into his pants, zips up and so do I. We walk to the car in silence. Marvin is long gone, and we let his accomplice go with a warning.

We finish the shift like we didn't fuck. Perello stops for donuts to take home to the family. At the station nothing is different. We go our separate ways like always.

I don't go right home because I can't deal with Aaron right now plus I have to figure this out because tomorrow night I'll be back in the car with Perello. Will he want to fuck? Will I?

I drive out to the beach and park in a deserted lot at Playa del Rey. It's overcast, never mind it's summer. I try not to think for a while. I watch seagulls fly in and land on wet sand; I watch waves pound the beach; I look for something solid because everything feels seriously off-kilter.

The sea finally calms me and I allow Perello back in. I try to apply labels—predator, renegade, there's no shortage—but partner is in the mix so I think about us then, riding together, me learning from him, making arrests, bull-shitting—and now fucking. When I get to that, I feel a surge so I lean back in the seat, shut my eyes, and let it happen again, trying to see just how it did happen: Marvin struggling, us thrashing around with him—and without—and Perello grinding against me and me not resisting. I try to recall what I was thinking but all I get is what happened and that makes my dick hard. I can feel him in me and see him afterward, cock out, grinning.

Dick in hand now pretty much says it all. I get serious with myself, pumping my swollen meat like it's him doing it. Hell yes, I want him again. I think about the night ahead when it's hardly day and I come big-time.

Aaron is long gone when I get home. I crawl into bed and sleep much of the day, exhausted by the turn life has taken. I get up around five, go to the gym and stay there because I don't want to deal with Aaron. When I finally get home it's almost eight. "Where have you been?" he asks, pausing in his phone conversation.

"Gym," is all I say and I head for the shower. Soaping myself, I think about the night ahead and I spend time on my dick. When I get out I hurriedly dress.

"You're early," Aaron says, finally free of the phone.

"Yeah, extra duty. I'll eat later."

I kiss him good-bye and hurry out, wondering if it will ever work between us, but I set this aside when I reach the station.

I catch up on paperwork until nine when Perello sweeps in. It's different now, watching him with other cops, and I know why but it still surprises me. I enjoy his easy camaraderie with the others but when he talks a long time with Roberts, I wonder if they ever got up to stuff and suddenly the whole squad room looks different and I think maybe everybody's fucking everybody else. There are enough hot guys to make quite a scene but then I get a tap on my shoulder and it's Creston. "Hey, man, wake up." It takes me a second to connect with reality, then we're talking shop but I'm still watching Perello.

He's surprisingly quiet in the car and outside of busting up a teenage party and rousting a few drunks, the night is uneventful. Perello shifts in his seat too often and I realize he wants me to know he's restless. Then we get a call of suspicious activity and head for a warehouse where we find everything quiet. After inspecting the perimeter we radio in but instead of getting into the car, Perello heads back around the back. "C'mon," he says.

Rusted barrels sit next to a dumpster but there's a gap in between. This is where Perello bares his dick. "Let me fuck you," he says, stroking himself. His big honker is already up and I enjoy the sight. I move toward him, drop my pants. He bends me over a can and spreads me. His wet cock head pokes around then hits home and he pushes in with a satisfied grunt, then starts to thrust—and to talk. "This is gonna work out, you and me," he says and he grinds into me for emphasis. "You got one sweet ass, Colby, and I'm gonna make fucking use of it, fuck you every fucking night and then some."

His talk is working me into a lather and I'm frantically pumping my dick and ready to come. He keeps on talking, going on about his dick up my butthole. I shoot come onto the barrels. Now he's riding full out and when he's there he makes it known. "Holy fucking mother of god, shit, fuck, oh, shit, fuck." He unloads both dick and mouth until he's spent and pulls out. When I turn around he's holding his cock. "Fuck yeah," he says.

After that there was no turning back because doing it a second time meant the first wasn't some spontaneous fit of poor judgment. Coming back for seconds said something—and believe me, I listened—but now he's gone and life has turned to shit.

We kept on with each other as long as we partnered but we never became what you'd call friends because we lived in different worlds. But on duty we were a couple. We'd do some great police work, then go off and have a good goddamned fuck. I stayed with Aaron, probably because I had Perello.

Then, ten years in, he got shot during a routine traffic stop and retired. We had still been fucking and in the end we'd been like some old married couple, able to read each other like a book.

His retirement party was bittersweet. I was happy for him but sad for me, for us, because it would never be the same. We eyed each other all evening and finally, when everyone was well into drunkeness and his wife was yakking with the women, we slipped away and did it in his truck. The same urgency; pants down, him on me. He huffed and puffed befitting his age but he got it done and I came in buckets. I had tears in my eyes when we walked back to the party.

We tried a couple more times to keep it going but it wasn't the same. I met him at a remote spot up in the hills one Saturday morning and we did more than usual, taking time to explore, which turned things into a kind of lovemaking that was maybe our undoing. The MO had always been a quick one on duty. Set us free and it morphed into something I think maybe scared Perello. I only saw him once after that and we did it standing to mimic old times but it was too late. We'd crossed over into foreign territory and there was no going back.

Now I want to start the car and drive it into a wall. I want to cry; I want to fuck. God, yes, that's what I want. I pick up my cell phone and call Aaron. He's in a meeting so I leave a message. I've never told him about Perello but maybe it's time. After the fuck, though. "Hi, it's me," I say. "Something bad has happened and I need you in the worst way. Come home, please."

SENTENCING

Steve Berman

Monmouth County Codes

10-0 Officials Present

10-1 Stand By for Phone Call. When he heard the distinctive chirp of his cell phone, the officer pulled his patrol car into the nearest parking lot, that of an abandoned cinema still showing *Played* on the marquee.

10-1 Phone ——. "Catch anyone interesting?" came a gruff voice that sent a shiver of anticipation through the officer's body.

10-3 Go to HQ. "When you're done, why not come over?"

10-4 Received. "Maybe," the officer said softly into the phone, glancing at the dashboard clock and figuring he could be at the gruff man's apartment just before midnight.

10-5 Repeat. "You say that every time and yet you always show at my door."

10-6 Stand By. A second incoming call came on his phone, the tiny screen blinking his home phone number.

10-7 Out of Service. He ignored the interruption from his wife.

10-8 In Service. "I want to feel you inside of me," whispered the officer, aching for the gruff man's arms to pin him down to the mattress as he thrust his way deeper and deeper into the officer's ass.

10-9 Arrived at Scene of Call. By the time he pulled up to the apartment complex, the officer found himself so hard—nipples, cock, even the hairs on his arms goose-bumped—that his uniform chafed his entire body.

10-10 Assignment Complete. The sex was rushed, forceful, raw with brush burns from the gruff man's thick red sideburns, and demanding, and the officer groaned loudly as he pounded out a load that cemented their flushed bodies together.

10-11 Prepare to Copy. After showering away the sweat and spunk, the officer arrived back at his tidy house just shy of two a.m. and slipped into bed next to his wife, who murmured and moved up against him, nearly arousing him once more but only nearly.

10-12 Record Check. Days later, when she asked him who all the 609-410-7390 calls were on the cell phone bill the officer brusquely answered, "The new guy on duty."

10-13 Look Up. She came over to where he sat on the sofa watching the Eagles game and rubbed his shoulders, like she used to do back when they first dated, and he forced himself to smile at her.

10-14 Assignment Complete. On a lunch break, he ate the gruff man's thick cock and drank his cum.

10-15 Accident. One of his wife's friends waved the officer down coming from the gruff man's apartment complex; his face still smelled of the man's sex.

10-16 Hit & Run. The officer forgot the woman's name—he always thought of her as the loudmouth with the bad dye job and the lipstick on her teeth—and pretended not to see her while stepping on the gas.

10-17 Request Wrecker. His wife mentioned in a curt tone over leftovers that her friend saw him on the other side of town.

10-18 First Aid. He muttered between bites of sour lo mein that he had dropped off some money to an old friend for lottery tickets.

10-19 Fire. When she rummaged around in a kitchen drawer and pulled out a pack of cigarettes—she quit nine months ago—he remembered what a terrible liar he was.

10-21 Abandoned Vehicle. That night he prepped the living room couch to sleep on, remembering how often his father had retreated to the couch when the officer was a kid.

10-22 Stolen Vehicle. But he could not sleep—instead he lay looking up at the ceiling and wondering when he had allowed passion to steal away all rational thought and end normalcy.

10-23 Suspicious Vehicle. He knew his wife suspected something, perhaps even an affair, but he doubted she ever conceived he only wanted to be in another man's arms.

10-24 Intoxicated Person. Not that he had anticipated it either; and he could not blame beer or bad cards or losing to the handsome guy the sergeant had invited to the summer poker game.

10-25 Escort. The officer had discovered the gruff man could be gentle; too drunk to even piss straight, let alone drive home, he had let himself be coaxed into returning to the gruff man's apartment.

10-26 Alarm. He had sat in a leather recliner, slowly sobering, and found himself staring at a glimpse of the man stripping down to shower away the cigar smoke.

10-27 Meet——. The morning had been awkward, as the officer felt uncomfortably aware of the man's near-nakedness—worn flannel boxers that had a habit of showing too much in the front—but the gruff man fixed him a breakfast fit for a king.

10-28 Homicide. The taste of steak and eggs still in his mouth, the officer had stood by the door, dawdling a bit as he suddenly wanted to stay the whole day with the gruff man, and it felt so welcome when they slapped each other on the shoulder good-bye.

10-29 Deceased on Arrival. When he had pulled into his driveway and realized that his day at home would be like every other day spent there with his wife, he had felt heavy inside, understood he was dead inside there.

10-30 Assault & Battery. Enough of memories; he received a call from the gruff man saying that his battery had died, but when he pulled up to the man's car he saw it was a plot; the pickup was idling fine just outside a bar, a gay bar.

10-31 Domestic Problem. He nearly drove off—what if someone saw him even in the bar's parking lot and told his wife?

10-32 Disorderly Conduct. The gruff man dared the officer to step out of the car and into the bar, to have some balls and admit what he really wanted.

10-33 Sex Crime. He refused and then broke, leaning his head against the man's truck a moment for strength before stepping in with the gays.

10-34 Fight. Home later than ever, he was met with the click of the lamp and his wife sitting on the sofa in her bathrobe.

10-35 Suspicious Person. "Just tell me, do I know her?"

10-36 Vandalism. Her reaction to his stammered excuse was to pick up the full ashtray beside her and throw it at his chest.

10-37 Mental Case. She began an interrogation, rattling off questions, demands, her voice rising to a pitch he had never heard before, a volume that only the crazies brought into the station could match.

10-38 Armed Robbery. "You stole my life with your lies!"

10-39 Larceny. He let her scream, throw things, even slap his face, all because he knew deep in his heart he had robbed her of all the promises he had vowed to years ago.

10-40 Breaking & Entering. Without saying anything else—his mouth felt so empty—he went to the bedroom and grabbed a change of clothes, but left his wedding ring behind on the dresser.

10-41 Prisoner/Subject. He slept in his patrol car, feeling both safe and yet trapped by all the metal.

10-42 Bomb Threat. He would not answer his cell phone—neither the calls from home that soon stopped nor the ones from the gruff man—out of fear both only wanted a final word with him and nothing more.

10-43 Riot. But that weekend, he returned to the club and lost himself in a sweaty moving crowd, first on the dance floor and then at some guy's basement, when countless hands and mouths explored every inch of his body.

10-47 Subject Armed. But even as they stroked and licked his skin, the officer could not stop thinking about the gruff man, how his hands knew his muscles and holes far better than these strangers did.

10-48 Officer Needs Help. Later, spent, he showed up at the gruff man's apartment, his uniform askew, face unshaven, feeling lost until the door opened.

10-49 Urgent. The officer fell into his lover's arms and sobbed and burrowed deeper, pressing his damp face into the gruff man's neck, pressing his body tightly and needing to be held until the tears stopped.

10-50 Use Caution. "Can I stay with you?" the officer asked, and though he left it unsaid, his eyes and lips made it clear that the request was an open-ended one.

10-51 Use Speech Privacy

THE GUARDS OF GOVERNOR'S SQUARE

Shane Allison

I could feel the sweat cascading down my back into the ditch of my ass. Not to mention my face, forcing my glasses to slip and slide from behind my ears. I stuck the last orange and hot-pink flyer in the windshield of some piece of shit Ford Tempo. My green T-shirt was soaked. The acid wash jeans stuck to the skin of my thighs. My bare, sweaty feet slid around in the confines of my caramel-colored Rockports. The cool air of the mall ran across my hot face as I entered through its glass double doors plastered with advertisements about items being drastically reduced. I thought for sure I would die from thirst if there wasn't a water fountain or a Coke in my immediate future. I bought the biggest soda they had at the Shrimp Pocket. After I drank my drink, I decided to do a little cruising, see if there were any new sharks circling the waters. Didn't take me long to graduate from watching men take leaks at the urinals of a local movie theatre to sucking dick in neck-twisting positions through glorious holes drilled through walls of metal and fiberglass partitions.

The bathrooms were at the ass end of a spiraled hall that was cut off from the rest of the mall. The security and management offices were the only two places that did business down that hidden, hollow corridor.

I had become a regular in the tearooms. So much so that a jerri curl–haired janitor warned me that if I wasn't careful, I would get caught. But what the hell did he know? I had *only* been cruising for damn near four years. Had my eye on my own ass before I could watch anyone else's. Was always cautious of the shit going down around me. Was never caught. That's until this racist, homophobic, piece of shit, redneck toy cop threatened to arrest me a couple of weeks before. He was onto me. It was then that I knew my ass was getting sloppy and I wasn't being as careful as I thought. Guess seeing my face four or five times in the same day, in the same toilet, planted a seed of suspicion. "Yes, sir. Sorry, sir," I kept saying. The brute manhandled my person, practically dragging me by my shirt out of the mall.

It was a Sunday when the shit hit the fan. I sat in the stall that day for a good two hours at least, watching men through the slit of my stall door washing their hands, listening to fathers scold their sons about touching the dirty urinals. Some watched from full-body mirrors as I put on a jack-off show, but were not interested in partying seriously. The only way I could catch any action was if I stood and gawked over the wall of my stall. A lot of farting mostly. Funny how those animal instincts kick into full gear when guys think they're alone. When I saw this cute blond walk past me to the vacant stall next to mine, he was a hot relief from the daddies trolling around, scavenging for college age ass. As he went in, I heard that familiar sound of a stall door being shut, a latch of metal being pushed closed. Wasted no time in attempting to take a peek, studying for the slightest movement that would give me a reason to think he was into men. Tapped my foot to let him know that I was cool. I watched religiously for his response. He slightly slid his Asics across the cold tile floor, but it wasn't the signal I was familiar with, the signal all men like me give. Due to sitting for hours, my legs were starting to fall asleep. In an attempt to get more comfortable, I mistakenly knocked over a roll of toilet paper that had been sitting on a small, metal banister screwed to the partition between us. It rolled under the trade's stall, bumping his foot. I swiftly snatched the roll off the floor and sat it back upon the place from which it had been knocked.

"Sorry," I said.

"Not a problem."

Regaining my composure after that split second of awkwardness, I tapped my Rockports once more to his attentions. This time he gave me that signal. He nudged me with the tip of his shoe. I bent and bowed my body until my muscles burned in an attempt to see if he was doing something lewd and lascivious, but to no avail: all I witnessed were shoes, white tennis shorts and legs with hairs of honey gold. I figured hell, if he tapped that foot, he was cool, right? I had a while left before my bus was due to arrive. I didn't want to miss my chance with this beefcake. He was too good to pass up. I figured it would be quite a tawdry entry for my journal. I could barely stand due to my numb lower limbs. With my jeans down around my ankles, I dropped to my knees and thrust my dick beneath the wall that separated us. I didn't hear him move, there was no shuffling of shoes, no rustling of bunched clothing.

"All right, I need you to stand up and step out of the stall," he said. His voice was stern and serious enough to startle my heart, turning it into a heavy mass of terrified muscle. I pushed myself off my knees and yanked my jeans up around my bare ass.

"Open the door and step out," he said. I didn't act dumb, didn't have to guess what was going on. I was caught. I started thinking of that jerri-curl janitor who tried to warn me; that redneck cop, and the feel of his gritty mitts around my neck. The blond was no trick, but one of the mall security guards. He took me by the arm and escorted me out of the bathroom and into the office that read SECURITY painted in black on plate glass. It was weird seeing it from the inside, experiencing its confines firsthand. He pointed to a metal chair that was pulled out from the desk and told me to have a seat. So scared, my pits were dripping with sweat. He opened one of the desk drawers and fished out a Polaroid camera. He told me to stand up against the wall behind me where I was immortalized in that horrid, green tee. He pulled a carbon-paper form out of a paper organizer to gather some personal info. After he took my name and other contact information, he offered up some of his own. "I'm Officer Sutter," he said. He explained that they were getting some complaints about men having sex in the bathrooms, men like me. I instantly thought of this one old fuck in particular who may have tipped them off just to get the tearoom to himself.

I couldn't think, could barely speak. Wondered if jail was anything like those prison movies. Perish the thought of getting butt-fucked against my will. Sutter took his walkie-talkie and spoke in that cop talk only cops use. He mentioned a name: Grisham. I could not remember at first until I forced my memory back to that day I was tossed out on my ear. It was him; the hick guard that had warned me with hot words that were still embedded in my brain like poisonous thorns. I'd never forget his fat, round face, his name branded in metal pinned to his standard issue uniform. Sutter and I sat silently as he filled out form after form. When Grisham arrived, I looked off to the wall littered with JUST SAY NO posters and pics of those who had committed crimes against the mall. Grisham walked in, big, breathing heavily like the pig he was. His gut was tight under his uniform shirt, unlike Sutter who looked cleaner and handsome in his own. Grisham's black belt glistened beneath the white office lights. Sweat poured from his face, soaking the stiff collar of his shirt. He was such the stinking brute standing over me.

"Thought I told you to stay out of here?" he said.

I noticed the wedding band on his finger and felt for his wife. This porker had to be at least 350 pounds, unlike Sutter who was built like a brick Texas shit house with feathers of golden hair, fire-blue eyes and a face strewn with freckles. His flesh looked firm where those white tennis shorts rode between the crack of his pert butt. Sutter's body was poetry in motion. I studied his hands for any signs of marriage. There was none. Then my view was obstructed by fat-ass himself. I looked at him with contempt and gave him the kiss-off.

"I told you if you came back here, I would arrest your black ass." It felt like he wanted to say something else. The slip of his true colors was showing. He jerked my mug toward his own and said, "I'm talkin' to you, boy."

"Grish, take it easy," Sutter chimed in. "Here's his ID."

"So where you live at, boy? Looks here like a Woodville address. Is that where you live, boy, out in the sticks? Didn't know they had niggers livin' out there."

"That's enough, Grish," said the golden-haired Sutter who seemed to be a bit more sympathetic to my plight.

"I tol' him what I would do to him if I caught his ass back in the shitters," said Grisham.

"We're not doing that. Remember what happened to the last guy we did that to?"

"So whatchu wanna do with 'im?" I looked to Sutter wondering just what the hell he meant. Now I was really scared shitless. Terrified they would beat me to a pulp and toss me out like so much food-court trash.

"You wanna call it in?" Grisham askd.

"No. They're just going to let him off with a summons to appear in court. I have a better idea." The two guards huddled in a corner. I couldn't hear what they were saying. Thought about making a run for it, but figured the athletic Sutter would be on my ass before I could say *cinnabon*. I hoped that whatever they were saying involved my being let go.

"Stand up and turn around," said Grisham. I asked what was going on.

"Just do it," said Sutter.

I turned and searched the blond's face for signs of mercy, but there was none.

"Now place your hands on your head and cross your fingers."

I felt like I was in some crazy fucking episode of "Cops." The steel cuffs were cold as they shut around my wrists. I started to think of who I could call to bail me out of this: Linda, Todd, Jarret. Someone who was good for the money.

"Don't move," he said.

My face kissed the cold cinders. I stared through the venetian blinds that shrouded the plate glass of the door at a woman yapping away on a pay phone. The sound of the toy cops rustling about echoed through the office. *What are they doing?* I fixed my eyes where I was able to focus on their images reflected in the glass. I was shocked to find that they were undressing each other, unfastening buttons, undoing polyester pants. The whole spectacle was freaky and gross, but I couldn't look away. Grisham's bearlike chest showed waves of dark fur spilling over the neck of his T-shirt. I felt like I was in some morbid Stanley Kubrick movie. How was it possible that a hot blond of an angel like Sutter was into this sweaty mammoth of a beast? Who were they really? Were these guys even real cops or were they imposters, lovers on the down low? It would be the perfect setup. The only way they could see one another without drawing suspicion. Jesus! Who would have guessed that these butch bastards were actually punks?

Grisham wasted no time dropping to his knees. He worked Sutter's dick out of the cotton panel of his underwear and began to stroke him. Sutter's thick uncut cock curled up like a banana. Foreskin damn near covered the blond's entire dickhead only leaving the piss slit exposed. The scene caused my own dick to harden uncontrollably in its stone-wash confines. Grisham looked like a typical porker with his wife-beater tee and white boxers. He peeled Sutter's foreskin back and began to lap at the head. Sutter stood with bent knees and a freckled, unconcealed ass, watching me as I stood there pressed to the wall. I was beginning to lose feeling in the right side of my hand, but I dared not complain out of fear that it would be the end of me. I had no other choice than to watch the plate glass scene of unadulterated fornication. Grisham was going full force on his partner. Stroke, suck, repeat. Grisham was loud. I was surprised he couldn't be heard through the walls and down the hall, the way he went on. Sutter lifted the tail end of his shirt exposing a ripped, tan torso as he continued to fuck Grisham's fat face. Grisham's balding skull bobbed and weaved in an attempt to keep up with his partner. My own dick was twitching crazy in my pants, aching for release. This was better than any cheap porn flick. Sutter pressed Grisham's head deep into his crotch until all of him disappeared into the other guard's mouth. Hard to believe the mutt was married considering the way he sucked dick.

My balls turned to brass, my guts to steel as I turned to watch Sutter and Grisham. The action was much better than when I was watching it reflected in the smudged glass. They were so into it, they didn't notice that I had moved. I couldn't keep my eyes off Grisham, the way he kept at Sutter. I noticed that the carpet matched the drapes as I studied golden wires of Sutter's pubic hair, in the process of growing back after it had obviously been shaved. I attempted to shake my bound hands awake. I would have given anything to know what Sutter's dick would be like wallowing around in my own mouth. Suddenly, Sutter turned his attention to my privates, startling me when he reached over to touch my zipper. I was glued to his doings. Afraid that I would be turned to dust if I looked into those eyes of fiery blue. Sutter smelled of cigarettes. He started to fidget with my jeans. I'm nowhere near as well-endowed as Sutter, but proud of what I do have between these knees. It tickled as he crept up and through, pulling elastic over my hard-on. I shut my eyes: darkness as I felt a dry palm around my dick. There was a tug and a jerk, and another, and another. I shut my eyes tighter till it hurt. Ass and aftershave filled my lungs. I breathed through my mouth. There was that line of sweat cascading down my back again. As Sutter took me, I thought of all those boys during my boyhood: Von Ash's lips around my dick, Daniel Stewart's buck teeth, John David referring to it as a *boner.*

And then there was a calm, sleek cool that overran me from below. I cracked my left eye to find Grisham bearing down on my dick. He had moved from Sutter's to mine in this lewd crime. Was going back and forth really. Giving them both equal attention. I opened my eyes wide. Grisham pulled me in close. The aches and pains from the cuffs would surely come in the night, whether I spent it in a jail cell or in the comfort of my own bed. As Grisham turned to Sutter, Sutter refused and forced

Grisham's face back to me. As if he'd become more interested in watching me get sucked than in being sucked himself. Sutter ran his hand over my groin as Grisham blew. Sutter pulled my jeans further down to expose my butt. I pivoted myself into Grisham's mug, taking my anger out on his tonsils. Sutter reached behind and fingered me. It hurt at first, but once he was well in, I took it like a trooper. The taste in my mouth was metallic. I was growing closer and closer to that climactic end. Grisham sucked the dickhead and that sealed the deal, forcing me to come in the brute's mouth. He didn't swallow, but spit into a coffee cup that was sitting on the desk. As Grisham then continued at Sutter's dick, Sutter pushed me aside into the wall. I slid into the chair with my spent dick hanging out over my briefs. Grisham held Sutter's ass with grubby mitts. Sutter looked boyish with innocence as Grisham kneaded fingers into his butt. Sutter's face was redder than dawn. The blond grimaced with satisfaction at his orgasm. He held me in his glare the whole time as if no one else was there. Grisham sat hawking, gagging from Sutter's cum. His eyes were red and watery.

"What do you wanna do with 'im?" Grisham said.

Sutter pulled me from the chair, tucked my dick back into my jeans and zipped me up. He turned me around and freed my hands from the steel cuffs. He told me that a trespassing warning would be issued, and that if I ever came back onto the premises I would be arrested.

I rode the bus home that evening with a sore ass to remember Sutter by and a mind that would never forget the way that country bumpkin Grisham went at Sutter.

ABOUT THE AUTHORS

The closest **STEVE BERMAN** has ever been to incarceration was back in his days with a fraternity. Any rumors about him teaching his fellow college students the true meaning of "Greek life" are vastly underestimated. When he's not being a law-abiding citizen, Steve writes. He has sold over seventy short stories and articles and his young adult gay novel, *Vintage: A Ghost Story,* released from Haworth Press in 2007.

P. A. BROWN writes: Born in Winnipeg, Canada—which probably explains my intense dislike of all things cold—I actually spent most of my early years in Ontario. At twenty-two I headed for Hollywood, where I spent eight years writing screenplays that never saw the light of day (you should all be eternally grateful for that blessing). My first novel, *L.A. Heat,* which deals with the more public side of Chris and David, was recently published by Alyson. I also sold a short story to *Men of Mystery,* an anthology from Haworth Press set to come out in 2006.

DALE CHASE has been writing gay erotica for eight years, with over one hundred stories published in various magazines and anthologies. His collection of Victorian gentlemen's erotica, *The Company He Keeps,* is due from Haworth Press in 2008. His first literary work was recently published in the *Harrington Gay Men's Fiction Quarterly.* Chase lives near San Francisco.

M. CHRISTIAN is the author of the novels *Running Dry*, *The Very Bloody Marys* and the critically acclaimed best-selling collections *Dirty Words*, *Speaking Parts*, *The Bachelor Machine* and *Filthy*. He is the editor of *The Burning Pen*, *Guilty Pleasures*, *The Best S/M Erotica* series, *The Mammoth Book of Future Cops* and *The Mammoth Book of Tales of the Road* with Maxim Jakubowski and over fourteen other anthologies. His short fiction has appeared in over 150 books including *Best American Erotica*, *Best Gay Erotica*, *Best Lesbian Erotica*, *Best Transgendered Erotica*, *Best Fetish Erotica, Best Bondage Erotica* and...well, you get the idea. He lives in San Francisco.

VINCENT DIAMOND's most recent erotica sales include Alyson's *Best Gay Love Stories 2005* and *2006*, the *Men of Mystery* anthology forthcoming from Haworth Press, and several pieces on Ruthie's Club, an online erotica site. Carnifex Press will publish "The Tale of Trapper Tommy" in *Florida Horror: Dark Tales from the Sunshine State.* In addition, Diamond was also selected for the Atlantic Center for the Arts Residency Program with author Maggie Estep this past spring. His first novel is complete, agented and being marketed to publishers, with a sequel in the works.

HANK EDWARDS is the author of the novel, *Fluffers, Inc.*, a humorous erotic mystery. His stories have been published in

Honcho, 100% Beef and *American Bear*, as well as in various anthologies. He lives in a suburb of Detroit with his partner of many years. Visit his website at www.hankedwardsbooks.com.

T. HITMAN is the nom-de-porn for a full-time professional writer who claims over three thousand publication credits to his resume. Today, he lives in an enchanted 1930s bungalow house on a large stretch of land in New England with his longtime partner Bruce and their two cats, writing short fiction, feature articles for several national magazines, a pair of monthly columns, and novels. Fifteen years previous to his work as a screenwriter on two episodes of a popular Paramount Scifi TV series, he fell head-over-heels in crush with a high school pal who entered the police academy right after graduation. That same lawman once pulled down his shorts and underwear and offered up his erect cock behind a woodpile in the small town in New Hampshire where they both grew up.

WILLIAM HOLDEN lives in Atlanta with his partner of nine years. He works full time as a librarian on LGBT issues. He has seventeen published short stories and welcomes any comments. He can be contacted at Srholdbill@aol.com.

ZEKE MANGOLD is a Las Vegas blackjack dealer. "The Rubber Room" is his first published story.

JEFF MANN grew up in Covington, Virginia, and Hinton, West Virginia, receiving degrees in English and forestry from West Virginia University. His poetry, fiction and essays have appeared in many publications, including *The Spoon River Poetry Review, Wild Sweet Notes: Fifty Years of West Virginia Poetry 1950-1999, Prairie Schooner, Shenandoah, Laurel Review, The*

Gay and Lesbian Review Worldwide, Crab Orchard Review, West Branch, Rebel Yell, Best Gay Erotica 2003 and *2004*, *Bear Lust* and *Appalachian Heritage*. He has published three award-winning poetry chapbooks—*Bliss, Mountain Fireflies,* and *Flint Shards from Sussex*—as well as a full-length book of poetry, *Bones Washed with Wine*. A memoir, *Edge,* and a novella, *Devoured,* included in *Masters of Midnight: Erotic Tales of the Vampire*, appeared in 2003. A book of poetry and memoir, *Loving Mountains, Loving Men* was published by Ohio University Press in 2005. Forthcoming are a collection of poetry, *On the Tongue*, and a book of short fiction, *A History of Barbed Wire*. He teaches creative writing at Virginia Tech in Blacksburg, Virginia.

SEAN MERIWETHER's fiction has been defined as dark realism. His work has appeared in *Best Gay Love Stories 2006, Out of Control: Erotic Wild Rides*, and *Best of Best Gay Erotica 2*. In addition to writing, he has the pleasure of editing two online magazines, Outsider Ink (outsiderink.com) and Velvet Mafia: Dangerous Queer Fiction (velvetmafia.com). Sean lives in New York with his partner, photographer Jack Slomovits, and their two dogs. If you are interested in reading more of his work, stalk him online at seanmeriwether.com.

C. B. POTTS never met a cop he didn't like—or at least imagine that he could like! However, he's far too cowardly to be behind the thin blue line and is instead resigned to life at the keyboard. You can read CB's other stories in *Huge Gay Erotica*, *Trucker Sex* and *Cowboys*. Find out more by visiting: www.cbpotts.net.

NEIL PLAKCY is the author of *Mahu,* a mystery novel featuring Honolulu police detective Kimo Kanapa'aka. A contributor to

Men Seeking Men, My First Time 2 and *Dorm Porn*, he is also the coeditor, with Sharon Sakson, of *Paws and Reflect: Exploring the Bond Between Gay Men and Their Dogs*, from Alyson. He received his MFA in creative writing from Florida International University and is a professor of English at Broward Community College.

ADAM RYDER lives in the United Kingdom but has spent time in North America, France and Poland. He is interested in the interplay between people and how they take on different roles in different settings before and after, as well as during sex. Sex consists of a relatively small vocabulary of acts that can be combined in endless permutations. Each scene brings something new and different. Good sex is about discovery, stretching boundaries, and fun. It is an adventure: sensuous, erotic, mysterious, and exciting. He aims to show this in his work.

DOMINIC SANTI is a former technical editor turned rogue whose dirty stories have appeared in many dozens of anthologies and magazines, including *Best Gay Erotica 2007*, *Best American Erotica 2004*, *Secret Slaves, His Underwear* and *Luscious*. Santi's latest solo book is the German collection *Kerle im Lustrausch—Horny Guys* (Bruno Gmunder). Forthcoming plans include a heretical novel and buying new handcuffs.

SIMON SHEPPARD is the author of the books *In Deep: Erotic Stories, Hotter than Hell and Other Stories, Kinkorama: Dispatches from the Front Lines of Perversion, Sex Parties 101* and the forthcoming *Homosex: 60 Years of Gay Erotica,* a historical anthology of gay porn. His work has also appeared in over two hundred books, including many editions of *Best Gay Erotica* and *Best American Erotica,* and he writes the syndicated column

"Sex Talk." He lives in San Francisco, is decidedly left of center, and hangs out at www.simonsheppard.com.

MARK WILDYR was born and raised an Okie, but he presently resides in New Mexico, the setting of many of his stories, which explore developing sexual awareness and intercultural relationships. Approximately thirty-five of his short stories and novellas have been published by Alyson, Arsenal Pulp, Companion Press, Southern Tier Editions of Haworth Press and STARbooks Press. He also has a story in an upcoming issue of *Men's Magazine.*

ABOUT THE EDITOR

SHANE ALLISON has been published in countless literary and online journals and anthologies such as *McSweeney's,* Velvet Mafia, *Mississippi Review, New Delta Review,* Suspect Thoughts, Outsider Ink, *Best Black Gay Erotica, Ultimate Gay Erotica 2006* and *2007, Best Gay Erotica 2007, Cowboys: Gay Erotic Tales, Truckers: True Gay Erotica, Best Gay Love Stories: New York City, Love in a Lock-up, Muscle Worshippers, Sexiest Soles: Erotic Stories about Feet and Shoes* and many others. He has authored five books of poetry, *I Want to Fuck a Redneck* being his most recent. When he's not masturbating to his own stories, he's hard at work on his collages. He lives in Tallahassee, Florida, where most of his stories are based.